Part I

Main characters

Elinor Taylor – a young girl, missing

Agnes Taylor – her mother

Tristan Jones – Agnes' partner

Albert Jones – Tristan's father, missing and presumed deceased

Esther Morton – Agnes' sister

Billy Morton – Esther's son

Joe Morton – Esther's husband and Billy's father, missing

Jessie Morton – Tristan's employer and friend, and Joe's twin

Augustus Riley – Elinor's secret grandfather

Xavier Riley – Augustus' son and Elinor's secret father

Monty Harrison – local gangster and Esther's employer

Tilly Harrison – Monty's niece

Ronan – Agnes and Esther's step-father, deceased

Papa Harold – family friend and hermit neighbour of Agnes

Jimmy and Penny – uncle and aunt to Agnes and Esther

Ethan – Jimmy and Penny's son, on the run with Elinor

Joshua – Ethan's twin, taken and still missing

Prologue – Jessie

Didn't think we'd get as far as we did.

Didn't think we'd be gone for so long.

A few days – maybe a week or so. But I didn't think we'd be leaving them all behind for as long as we did. Billy, Agnes, Esther even – they'd have been out of their minds once the first few days had gone by.

I'd think about them all the time – Tristan did, too. That sense of temporary loss came and went, though. Some days we'd sulk in it, and it slowed us down like mud around our ankles, dragging our progress. But other days we pushed through it, resolute – we just looked ahead, pushing forward with our search for the truth.

Our search for the men who'd doubtless killed Tristan's father.

Our search for Elinor, too.

And I started my own search. The further we got away from our city – the further we got to whatever, to wherever those that left our flooded town behind went – the closer we got to what we hoped was dry land. The closer we got to answers.

And I found myself looking for him.

Looking for my twin, looking for Joe.

'I can't promise you will,' Nathaniel said, like a warning, when I shared this with him. 'Not out here, but I promise you'll find the truth. You'll see what's really going on.'

Nathaniel.

Our guide? Our saviour? Our benefactor? I'm not sure exactly how to describe his role in what happened. He did help us – but he also lured us in and gave us little choice. But what he promised came true.

We found out what was really going on.

What the authorities had done to us.

The truth about the water.

The truth about the takings.

And the truth about the dogs.

And when we found the wall…

When we found the wall, we found so much more….

Asleep

I'm in a small room, with grey brick walls and grey vinyl flooring – specked with blue, yellow and red. Not sure how big it is – maybe two metres by one, maybe slightly bigger.

No window to the outside.

There's a single bed – its frame is metal, not painted and the mattress is hard, covered in a layer of plastic that crackles under my weight.

Adjacent, there's a small table, bare.

Under the bed, there's a clear, oblong box with a lid. I pull it out and it has clean clothes in it. These are intended for me, but they're not mine.

There are two other things in the room that confirm its purpose.

Above, in the centre of the ceiling, there's a spherical glass shade that glows harshly – like a large, pupil-less eye staring me out, accusing me.

Then there's the door – grey metal, no handle, opened and closed from the outside only. A small rectangular grill two-thirds of the way up would give me a view of what's beyond, but a shutter is slid across it.

So I'm in a cell, but what I don't know is how I'll get there.

I just know that I will.

Awake

1. Augustus

Everyone and everything has secrets.

Every single person – I did. People thought they knew me, but there was always something I held back. Something I hid. Because I was ashamed, or just because it was safer. Agnes knew more of me than most. She knew my name, to start with. I wondered how long that would stay under wraps. She knew, in turn, who my son was – she'd even conceived a child with him, albeit Elinor had grown up in Xavier's absence.

Absence – now there was a word that lay heavy on my mind. Easy to say, but harder to swallow.

I digress... But Agnes didn't know it all. She didn't know my history. Didn't know where I or my son, Xavier, had come from. My lost son – lost in so many unaccountable ways. Absence and its unbearable weight around my shoulders again... Agnes knew nothing of our roots. And she believed I came here looking for him. And that's not a lie – but it's not the entire truth, either. But that's the thing I found out about Agnes pretty quickly – much of what was true was unknown to her.

The truth about me.

The truth about Tristan – but then I wasn't certain Tristan knew the truth about himself, either.

And she definitely didn't know a thing about Otterley.

Otterley.

Ah, that's one I kept to myself for as long as it was possible.

But it wasn't just people who hoarded secrets – places did as well.

If you looked across the landscape of our decimated city, there were so many places to hide. It was only natural to assume secrets had been stowed away in its dark corners, or drowned in the depths of its ceaseless river road. Oh yes, I wonder just how many bad deeds had been reflected in the murky mirror of its surface, before a face, a body was plunged through its cold pane – a life extinguished, the truth of what happened washed away forever. I imagined our tragic circumstances had been a welcome accomplice for many.

And deeper down, further out, I'm sure the floods had their very own mysteries – their origins, the truth of their endurance, answers, answers and more answers.

Maybe Tristan and Jessie would find out on their foolhardy venture to the unknown?

A house can surprise you, too, with its ingenuity on the secret front.

It can present a picture, make a clear impression to one person, while shielding another one in plain sight.

To an outsider – to a visitor – it may present a backdrop of disorder. A carpet of leads and tubing, snaking in and out of each other. Red, black, white and grey wires and cables, woven haphazardly together and glued with dirt and damp dust. Room after room after room of old bits and pieces crammed together – dead machines with their rusty casings removed, their mechanical innards exposed, spilling out onto the already muddled space. All of it appearing without any order, no doubt like the crazy brain of the old man that lived amongst it all.

Yes, some would have looked at my habitat and thought they were seeing inside my head, my soul – the rust, the decay and the random insanity. The dangerous thatch of wires, tubes and cables like the addled matter just beneath my skull.

And maybe they were, just a little. You don't live in all this mess, all by yourself for so long without becoming a little bit barmy.

But it was a wonderful deception. A superb sleight of hand. See you, while the eyes were staring at the disruption, at the unorthodox living conditions, they were looking away from what was hidden in front of them. They'd walk in and they'd be drawn to look left – but not right.

Never to the right. So they missed what was staring them in the face.

Not all of them – but most.

Not Billy – no, young Billy asked all the right questions.

'Where do they go?' he asked me, looking right, pointing at two doors, one either side of the entrance to the spiral staircase that twirled up through the core of my house.

'Try them,' I suggested and he did, turning the knobs on both, giving them a short rattle. When neither door budged, I asked him his own question back: 'Where do they go then?' I posed, grinning.

'Nowhere,' he answered, smiling back, seeing the trick.

'There you go,' I said, walking away, heading out the back, 'you knew all along.'

But it wasn't the truth – just a trick with words.

He asked again – *Where do they go?* – of course he did. And I admired his depth of thought, his visionary imagination. It was never *what's in there?* Always *where do they go?* Like he knew, like he had insight – he saw not only a space, but a journey, another story up ahead.

And it goes without saying that eventually he found out. In the end, I had little choice – I had to unlock those doors and let him see for himself…

There were days when I thought the damn downpour would never cease.

I didn't worry for myself – I was one of the lucky ones with a house already risen out of the water. The worst that could possibly happen to me if it got any higher was I'd lose a floor or two – but when you already had five storeys, it hardly mattered. In the scheme of things.

But what of Agnes?

What of Billy, and his mother, Esther?

And their families and friends – Tristan and Jessie on their crazy mission into the unknown, the aunt and uncle that lived in that precarious tower block.

I worried and feared for them all.

But it wasn't safe to venture out – not until it had stopped or settled.

So where did that leave my long absent granddaughter?

I kept recalling of the state of Ronan's flat. His carcass ripped across the floor, the chaos of blood and flesh suggesting the work of a wild beast. But the way the surrounding area had been cleaned up implied only one type of animal could've done this – the evolutionarily advanced species to which I deplorably belonged: human.

'Oh, Elinor, where did you go, and what, *who* were with you?' I'd asked myself, looking out of the window, as the rain splattered onto the river road, shattering its still surface. 'Who took you?' Because it had to be that, didn't it? After what Ronan – the man she called grandfather – after what he'd done, exploiting her implicit trust in him, she'd never have gone willingly with anyone else. So surely she was taken – against her will? I kept these imaginings to myself – they were no help to any of us.

Every time I thought of Ronan's ruined body, still in that flat, I knew we had to go back. No matter how things appeared, no matter that he had been holding Elinor captive all that time, no matter that'd he'd played a part in the taking of children from their families, in the testing and the experiments. No matter, we had to go back – to clear up, to move him, to cremate him and rest him in peace.

And when the rain eventually stopped, that's what we did. Agnes and I. Esther and Billy, too.

'But only because it was Mother's place,' Esther insisted, reluctantly getting in her boat, bringing a bag of cleaning essentials with her. 'Not for him. Never for him.'

We had stopped by her house – Agnes and I – to pick her up on the way.

I'd spoken to her in advance, which had surprised Esther. *How did you get this number?* she'd barked, crossly, infuriated that a stranger was invading her privacy – her mind neglecting the fact that her child had dwindled away endless hours in this same stranger's company.

Agnes hadn't wanted to call her sister – not to explain what I'd proposed. When I'd spoken to her in the days that followed the visit to Ronan's flat, Agnes had sounded empty, withdrawn and it seemed she was reliving her grief again. Only, with Elinor slipping so easily through her fingers, it was ten-fold, and there was part of her that believed she'd never see her daughter again. That she would always be just out of reach.

And I was beginning to share that belief – but in silence.

So, with Agnes reluctant to negotiate her sister's services, I made the call to Esther, suffered her abuse and fury at what I was proposing and left my number, in case she reconsidered. To my surprise, she did.

'But I'm not doing this for him,' she kept insisting, her face a scowl.

Then who are you doing it for? I asked myself.

Esther insisted she was doing it for her mother – the flat had been hers, apparently. But I wasn't convinced – something told me Esther's sentiment for the place had died along with her mother. So my question kept on creeping back: *who are you doing it for?*

We rowed our way back to Ronan's flat ten days after the heavy rain started.

It hadn't completely stopped by then, but the deluge of translucent shards slicing through the atmosphere had reduced to a gentler pitter-patter. Feeling just a soft tapping against my protective garments reassured me we were over the worst and safe to venture out.

It was the first time I'd seen Agnes since dropping her home after we'd made the shocking discovery at the flat – and the first time I'd seen Billy since his drama at the old shop his great-aunt and -uncle owned. *A decaying, Dickensian affair,* according to Agnes.

Though it had been just a matter of days, Agnes looked older than she had. Thinner, too, as if she hadn't eaten for weeks. It was true, the rain had meant many of us had not been able to pick up our weekly food supplies, but I doubted this would have had any impact. Not yet. Her skin was coloured grey, her eyes yellow and red – this I could put down to a lack of sleep. But her whole countenance seemed overwhelmed with something – not just her grief. Her immeasurable grief. I couldn't quite put it to words, but in my head

I imagined a long, sharp needle attached to a huge syringe and saw it pushed into the back of her head, the plunger pulled back and something invisible being drawn out. Her life-blood. That was it – Agnes' life-blood had been drawn out of her.

'Dear, are you sure you want to…?' I trailed, just as we turned the corner and rowed towards her sister's house. 'I can always…'

But she shook her head. No words – just a shake of her sorrow-heavy head – and I rowed us both on.

Billy was keeping a watchful eye out for us – I hadn't realised at that point that he'd be joining us. Looking up, I saw him waving frantically through the glass of an upstairs window and I gently returned the gesture.

'Hello Merlin,' he said, minutes later, following his mother out, his protective mask still pulled up, resting on his head, like a hat.

'Hello Billy,' I answered, checking Agnes for a response – would she think it odd that he still used my pseudonym?

'Pull that thing down,' Esther hissed, turning back to her son, once she was in her own boat, her box of cleaning tricks secured in its well. 'What if someone should see?'

Both Agnes and I had ours in place – we didn't fear the atmosphere anymore, we just wanted to avoid drawing any unnecessary attention to ourselves.

'Best you do as you're told,' I advised him gently, before turning to his mother. 'Esther, are you sure…?' I asked, nodding in the boy's direction. Another unfinished question from me that morning – this time to a different sister.

'I'm not leaving him by himself, not after all that's happened,' she insisted, beckoning him to get into the boat. 'Billy, come on! We haven't got all day!'

'And Agnes told you how bad…' I trailed off again, but Esther had already pushed the boat away. I just hoped she knew exactly what it was we'd face once we got to her mother's old flat.

She didn't.

By the end of the first day of rain, many of the local houses had seen the flooding rise up to their first floors. Both Agnes and her sister had been affected. The water level had since reduced, but the damage was still to be assessed. I'd been luckier. While the murky tide had battled viciously against my doors and windows, the reinforced materials used for my relatively new home had fought back effectively.

At the flat, the water had crept up into the first floor – and dragged some of its contents back out, coating the sodden stairwell with debris, which we stepped over, as we ascended to where we'd found Ronan.

Despite warnings, Esther had stormed in, holding her domestic toolkit in one hand, hauling Billy along in her other one.

'Jesus Christ!' she gasped, entering a minute ahead of me, as I came up the rear with Agnes. 'It's alright, Billy. It's okay. Just turn away. That's it,' I heard her reassure the boy, who'd begun sobbing the minute he'd seen the body.

And then she did something that surprised me – she joined him. Threw her arms around her distraught son and began to shudder and cry in rhythm with him. She managed a few *there theres*, but her words were blurred with grief and spit.

'Esther, should you…' I began, continuing a newly formed habit of half-finished lines. 'Maybe it would be…' I directed her and Billy to the room we suspected Elinor had been held in, and she nodded, guiding their shaking frames away from Ronan's corpse.

It was worse than I'd recalled. In the ten days since we found it, Ronan's body had suffered a further attack.

'An animal has been in here, Agnes,' I told her, not looking back, but feeling her slower presence behind me. 'That's worrying.'

She said nothing, but Esther called out from the small bedroom.

'Can you manage? If you can move him, clear him up, I can help with the rest.'

'Yes,' I cried back, knowing I had to, but wondering if convincing the sisters to come back had been the right thing after all.

I couldn't leave the man unburied – then again, there was little of the man remaining. What hadn't been ripped from his broken body was beginning to decompose. The smell was just bearable, as the room was ventilated – the lower door was not secured and several windows were broken. I didn't recall the latter damage from before.

'I was wondering if we should just go,' I said, testing the feelings of the others. Maybe they were just looking for an excuse to leave.

'No, it's mother's place,' Esther responded, her composure regained. 'If you can move him, I'll be fine. I just can't deal with the…'

The half-finished lines were catching, but I understood.

'I'll deal with that, Esther.'

And so, I got to the business of removing Ronan's fragmented body from the flat. Yet, I didn't give him the respectful ending I'd intended. That old brain of mine hadn't thought the logistics through – too much going on in there, sometimes, to get a clear enough thought. I'd envisaged wrapping him up in an old blanket and taking his body to the north-east of the city. There, I'd find the authorities' buildings – the police station, the hospital, the smaller surgeries. There were several funeral directors there, too – all rumoured to come under the same government umbrella. My plan had been to take his body to one of these. There'd be questions – I had no doubts about that – but we'd done nothing wrong. And we couldn't help the fact we'd left it ten days – the rains had kept us all enclosed in our homes.

He wouldn't get a burial, though. That tradition of laying the deceased to rest had been abolished with the floods – too many old friends and relatives had risen from their graves and taken the river roads back to their loved ones. I'd heard distressing horror stories of bloated bodies floating into the living rooms of their former lives, terrifying their grieving families. Old Harold – Agnes' hermit neighbour – heard rumour of a woman who'd woken up next to her husband, even though he'd been dead some ten years. It was impossible, of course. Just myth rising out of the hysteria.

'And how would she have recognised him?' I asked Harold, on a visit one afternoon.

'I'd recognise that ribcage anywhere,' old Harold had replied, mimicking the possible response of the widow. 'Still, it makes for a good, ghoulish tale, eh?'

'There's no denying that, Harold,' I'd answered.

But we *would* be denying Ronan his right to rest.

Since the floods, all bodies had been cremated. There was just the one crematorium – north-east, like many of our public amenities. But Ronan's remains were now too ruptured to transport that far. And the more I thought about the state of him, the more I thought about the questions we'd be asked. There was no way the finger wouldn't point at us, and I didn't want that kind of attention from the authorities. They'd be round before I knew it, poking around my house, finding things I'd rather they didn't. It was clear we needed another plan.

In a cupboard in the larger of the flat's two bedrooms, I found the blanket to wrap him up in. The cupboard was white, built into an alcove and crammed with old sheets, blankets and towels. The room itself made me sadder than ever – an orange, florid bedspread covered the bed (no doubt from his years with Agnes and Esther's mother), a mahogany chest of drawers with a large oval mirror at the back, damaged with black patches at the edges, and an array of black and white family pictures displayed upon it. Was he really the family man he'd appeared to be? Was the business with Elinor good intentions gone sour? I simply couldn't fit my different perspectives of Ronan into one.

Knowing I didn't have time for these reflective distractions, I grabbed the blanket – rough and pink – and took it back into the living area. There, I set about gathering the dead man up together as best I could. Once this was done, I tried lifting him up on my own, but he was heavier than I'd estimated and I knew I needed just a little extra help.

I slipped into the smaller bedroom – the one where we'd found the single bed with the restraints attached. They were the oddest thing, the restraints – they suggested Ronan had planned to take Elinor in advance, anticipated the need to have her held in place. I shuddered, trying to focus on practical matters.

Esther and Billy were stood by the window, the mother shrouding the son in a protective embrace.

'I've a favour I need,' I said, startling both, 'and I wondered if the young man was up for the job.'

In other circumstances, I'm certain I wouldn't have made my request – and I'm even more certain Esther would never have agreed to it. But we weren't in other circumstances. I needed someone to help me carry Ronan's remains out of the flat, down the stairs and into my small boat. Agnes was in no state to help and Esther didn't suggest herself as an alternative, either – she was still adamant she wouldn't leave the smaller bedroom until *he was out of the way*. So, she agreed to let young Billy assist me, despite his age, despite his own shock reaction to the macabre display on the living room floor.

'And he's all covered up?'

'Yes.'

'In an old blanket?'

'Yes, Billy, nothing to see. Nothing for you to touch – just the ends of the blanket.'

Billy nodded, taking on board my reassurances, steeling himself for the task ahead.

'Okay, I'm ready.'

I'd managed to roll the body over twice, sealing the corpse in two layers of the woolen shroud, and then I'd secured the ends with some string I'd found in a kitchen drawer.

'No one will see us,' I continued to assure the boy, as we carefully lifted our load from the floor and carried it out of the room. 'It seems abandoned round here. Anyone who does see us will be up to no good themselves, so they won't be saying anything. They won't be reporting us.'

As we reached the stairs and reconsidered our position – how would we get it down the twelve sodden steps without slipping – I wondered if my words might have the opposite effect. *Abandoned. Reporting.* These might be scary to a ten year-old, but he didn't seem affected. In the end, I took the front end, and Billy the rear, and we got Ronan down those stairs by letting him slide, giving the blanket a gentle tug whenever it jarred against the treads.

'What now?' Billy asked, once Ronan was lying in the boat, his makeshift, crumpled coffin taking up less space than I'd imagined.

'The not-so-nice bit,' I said, thinking honesty was the best policy. 'I need to dispose of him.'

The words came out harder, colder than I'd intended, and Billy appeared to flinch at their expulsion. I wondered if his bravery might dissolve again – but I needn't have worried. He took in a hearty breath and braced himself for the job ahead.

'Okay – so where are we taking him?'

I hadn't been to the train graveyard – as Billy called it – in a long while. In recent years, I'd turned to Jessie for all my junk needs. Rare parts, clapped out motors, scrap metal and necessary bric-a-brac – nuts, bolts, wire, fuses – all of this was supplied by him. But in my early days in the city, before friends were made and my networks established, I'd made several visits myself – searching out the gems amongst the jumble.

There was a certain order to the train graveyard, particularly as you got closer to its core. The abandoned vehicles were set out in an orderly manner – cars lined up and stacked, larger vehicles single-story, but packed in tightly against one another. There was a whole section dedicated to gutted-out coaches and buses. With our boat secured, I suggested we headed towards that.

I knew we'd have to hide Ronan carefully, secure him somewhere he wouldn't be found – where children like Billy and Elinor wouldn't be able to look. I asked Billy to pick a coach that held the least appeal – he found one with the windows smashed, the exterior weeping with rust and the interior gutted – not a seat remained and the dashboard had been ripped of all its controls. We managed to board it, squeezing in the gap between it and its neighbour, and placed Ronan's body on the floor. I noticed a square panel beneath, still screwed tight. Anticipating the need, I'd brought a couple of tools with me – a pen knife, a small hammer and a screw driver – which I'd slipped in my pocket. I pulled out the last item and worked hard at loosening the rusty screws. They eventually gave and we were able to shift the rusty, metal square over to one side – revealing a space below.

'It looks like it leads into the old luggage hold,' I explained to Billy, who looked a little puzzled. 'You might have gone on a trip in one of these – a long trip, a holiday – and your bigger bags would've been stored under the vehicle.'

'Oh,' he said, nodding, probably working through the alien concepts of long distant road travel and vacations in his fledgling head.

'Come, help me get the old guy down there, will you?' I instructed, indicating our pink, woollen parcel. Despite the fact it transpired his conduct had been somewhat less than human, and in spite of his appearance, I referred to Ronan in human terms – as a person – whenever I got the chance. Billy would still be thinking of him as a grandfather, regardless.

'Of course, let me grab the other end.'

We lowered him down slowly, with relative ease. Then, we slid the panel back in place and returned the screws to their holes. Next, I used the head of the screwdriver and the hammer to obliterate the grooves in each of the screw heads, ensuring they couldn't be easily removed again.

'We're done,' I told Billy, giving his shoulder a gentle rub. 'Time to leave?'

I posed it as a question, in case he needed a moment.

'Time to go,' he affirmed, showing he didn't.

As we rowed back to the flat, I took the opportunity to catch up with my young friend. Now we'd been relieved of our burden, we were both more inclined towards conversation – our outbound journey had been characterized with anxious silence.

'Tell me, Billy, how are you bearing up?'

He shrugged, between rowing – he'd insisted he could cope on his own, so I allowed him to take control. I could easily step in, if his arms wearied.

'I feel a bit odd, I guess,' was his initial response and he pondered for a few minutes before continuing. 'I'm not sure how I feel about Ronan.' It was the first time I'd heard him use his name since the truth had been revealed – but already he'd dropped the familial *grandad* he'd been using. That revealed more about his feelings than anything else he could say. 'I can't quite fit all the pieces together. I know all this bad stuff about him – but it doesn't fit with anything I saw, anything he did or said when I was around.'

'No, that must be hard,' I replied. 'Left here,' I added, ensuring he stuck to the route.

He nodded, acknowledging the instruction and following it.

'I'm angry at him, I know that. For what he did to Elinor, for lying. She wasn't really missing – he knew that, he let us think she was dead. I can't get my head round that either.'

He paused, still rowing, but I could see him struggling to keep his composure.

'I'm sorry, Billy, you don't have to…' I said, trailing away.

Like his aunt and mother, he seemed to understand the full meaning of my unfinished lines.

'No, it's fine,' he said, blinking away tears, but remaining solid. Remaining strong. A boy turning into a man. 'I want to talk. I've not really been able to talk about some of it. Mother won't let me talk about Ronan at all. She wants to pretend it didn't happen, that he never existed. *It would've been better if that man had never entered our lives – so we'll just pretend he didn't.* She said that as soon as we got the news. It seems so cold, despite what he's done.'

'People have their own ways of coping,' I said, offering an excuse – though I noticed how Esther was coping. And, despite her emotional episode when she came across Ronan's ravaged remains, she was extraordinarily taciturn about it all.

'Then there's my cousin,' Billy added, as we turned into the river road we were destined for.

'Elinor?' I said, thinking he had more to say here.

He shook his head. 'Ethan.'

Ah yes – Ethan. The damaged cousin – one of twins, snatched from Penny and Jimmy when they were just boys. Ethan – the only one returned to them, locked away after a savage attack on Ronan. An attack now being viewed anew in light of what we'd learned.

You think Ronan was involved in whatever happened to Ethan? Do you think Ethan remembered him?

I'd asked this of Agnes, in the few calls we'd had during the days of rain. She'd not offered an opinion, though.

'He's still out there, then?' I said to Billy.

'Yes. He could be anywhere. No one is saying this, but I don't think Great-Aunt Penny will ever forgive me for letting him out. But I didn't know. I didn't-.'

This was the point it became too much – the man returned to boy. All of a sudden, his tears came easily and he slackened his grip on the oars.

'Shall I take them?' I said, and he released them fully. 'We're almost there,' I added, saying it like we'd find comfort back at the flat.

But of course, we wouldn't. We'd be returning to anything but.

Not wanting to offer any more misplaced words, I rowed us the rest of the way in silence.

I'd heard rumour of Esther's extraordinary cleaning abilities – but seeing was truly believing. And, returning to the flat, I saw living proof of her legend. Aside from blood stains already ingrained in the floorboards and the treads on the stairs, there wasn't a trace of the horror Agnes and I had stumbled across days earlier. The smell had gone, too. I sniffed the air as I looked around.

'Pine,' Esther said, announcing the word with pride.

'Where did you get…'

'Best you don't know,' she answered, so I didn't push her.

The whole place had been tidied – books, papers, ornaments and other items returned to order. There were a few broken items of furniture, but these had been moved to the small bedroom – the one where Elinor had been restrained – and the door closed. I even noticed a gleam across all the surfaces – Esther had conjured a high polish where none had existed before.

'When Tristan and Jessie get back, I think we'll get them to finish what we started,' she said, speaking to all three of us. But Agnes wasn't listening and Billy wasn't interested – so it was really only to me.

'And what will you do with the place then?'

'I don't know. We'll have to think,' she answered, including Agnes in the *we,* although her sister remained out of our conversation.

'Agnes – are you ready to go?' I asked, needing some kind of response.

'Yes, Augustus,' she said, without thinking, without realising until it was out of her mouth.

Billy looked sharply at me, and Esther's mouth curled into an amused smile.

'Not Merlin?' she said, checking.

And I nodded – there was no point retracting it.

'Yes, Augustus Riley,' I said, announcing my full name and watching her reaction. Her countenance revealed it meant little or nothing to her.

'But it's a secret,' Billy jumped in, not thinking either, instantly making it a bigger deal than maybe it needed to be – but I was past caring.

'Well, your secret is safe with me, Gus,' she said, winking, picking up her cleaning toolkit. 'Come on Billy, time to leave.'

And with that, they led the way out, and Agnes and I followed.

Later, back in my own home – struggling a little as my mind skipped over the day's events – I distracted myself with my usual tinkering. I needed a chance to breathe and think – I needed space to work out if there was anything we'd forgotten, anything else we needed to do to cover up what had happened.

I had an old radio I'd been working on for months – trying to get it to pick up a signal from the authorities. I'd almost got there on a couple of occasions, including one time Billy that had caught me. That time, I'd managed to get on the frequency the police used, but I'd not heard anything of interest, before Billy interrupted me – and I'd not successfully intercepted them since. I suspected they regularly changed their radio coordinates for security reasons.

It was a quirky old thing – oblong, with a wooden exterior and a cracked plastic dial at the front. I'd had the back off it several times – putting in new circuit boards, re-wiring it and replacing the battery on a variety of occasions. It wasn't the only radio I had, but I saw this one as a challenge. The odds were against it – and me – but I wasn't going to be beaten. It had an aerial that collapsed to just an inch – a series of tubes that slotted down into each other. I extended this, jiggled its dial, and listened as it emitted its usual crackle. Thinking elevation might be an advantage when it came to picking up a signal, I took it with me and curled up that spiral staircase to the apex of my house – the part I thought of as my personal quarters.

But it made no difference – the radio continued to hiss with dead air.

Giving up, I left it on a small table next to an old sofa and took my weary bones to the corner of the attic where my bed was.

I didn't sleep for ages – images of what I'd seen at the flat and thoughts of how my friends might be suffering, how quiet and withdrawn Agnes seemed, keeping me awake. When my thoughts eventually fell away, my slumber was deep. So deep that I almost missed it. I assumed I was dreaming when I heard the voices.

'Can you confirm you have everything in place?'

'Yes. Everything is set. My contacts have been informed. And the army is ready.'

I sat up, still sluggish, rubbed my face and then threw off my bed covers, moving to the source.

'The army?' I whispered to the empty, still night.

The voices continued, though they fazed in and out as I got closer, the radio frequency unstable.

'Good... Ready to execute tomorrow night. Twenty two hundred hours.... Operation retrieval is active...'

The transmission cut dead.

In the quiet early hours of that day, I considered what I'd heard, over and over. *The army is ready. Execute tomorrow night. Operation retrieval is active.* It had to be the authorities – and they were planning something big. But what exactly? The fragments of their plan were not enough to conclude anything so far. I needed more. So, I set a pot of coffee going on the small stove I kept in the attic, pumped my body awake with several shots of caffeine and waited patiently, hoping transmissions would resume.

At 5am, they did.

Asleep

It's different this time.

I'm on a bed, but I'm not the me I know – I'm smaller, younger – but I can't remember being this young.

There's a sheet on the bed – it's white. And I'm in a gown – nothing else, just a gown.

Above me, lights shine, huge round illuminations, blinding me with their brilliance.

And ***they*** *are all around me.*

The men.

Dressed in pale blue gowns, with paper masks over their faces, as if protecting them from infection. And their eyes are covered with clear goggles, blurring their identities. So, it looks as if the same man is repeated again and again, in the semi-circle of people that are gathered around me.

This has happened already. I'm certain. This is the past – I just don't remember it.

'This won't hurt one bit,' one of them says and there's a sharp, warm feeling in my left arm...

Awake

2. Esther

I went back to the flat that night.

Left it till very late – till Billy was fast asleep and even then I locked him in his attic bedroom. He didn't have to know I was going out. He'd only ask questions, and I needed to quell his inquisitiveness. After his misadventure at my aunt and uncle's shop, his curiosity was proving dangerous.

I'd considered asking Aunt Penny to keep an eye on him – but that might have solicited questions from another corner of my family, and I needed no questions at all.

My best option was to go out in the dead of night, unnoticed by the sleeping habitants of our drowned city. So, I took a measured risk – locked up my little treasure and slipped out into the creepy stillness of the dark, early morning.

I didn't intend to be long.

I just needed a quiet moment in that flat – now it was clean, now it was empty. Without all those keen eyes watching me.

I'd never been out in the boat that late before. As I rowed myself along the river roads to my mother's old flat, I was taken aback by the eerie beauty of our somnolent city. The moonlight gave the buildings and the water a striking midnight blue hue, and the black sky above me was free of clouds, a map of stars twinkling across this sable oblivion. Part of me just wanted to take the oars from the river, lay them in the boat and let it drift along. Let me take in the ruins of my home town, veiled in the illusion of night.

But I couldn't afford this luxury, this indulgent romanticism. I needed to get to the flat and then back to my own home quickly – I'd left Billy on his own, after all. And, though I'd secured him in his room, there was always danger afoot in our submerged world. Always something just out of sight, lurking with sinister intent.

So, I kept the wooden oars in a firm grip and maintained a proficient, rhythmic row all the way.

Once I got there, I felt a little unnerved. Although I knew it was a more or less abandoned part of town, the cold, still night gave it a different twist. I felt as if there were eyes on me, despite the lack of company. His eyes, maybe – watching me beyond the grave.

I shuddered, tried to shake the feeling off, as I lay the oars in the centre of my boat and secured it to the mooring with rope.

Back inside, I took myself to what had been mother's room, sat on the bed and wept quietly to myself.

You're probably wondering why I went back? Hadn't I seen enough that day – enough blood, enough ghosts, enough horror to last me a good while? And hadn't I hated that man – for replacing our father in Mother's life so effortlessly, for being so easily accepted by everyone else, and for what he'd obviously done to Elinor? Our lost Elinor, who was missing once again.

You'd be right to question me – but things are never that simple, only seeming so when you have just one perspective. Just one side of a story.

I'd come back to exorcise a ghost – something I'd been unable to do earlier, surrounded by my sister, my son and that strange old man who'd broken the news to me.

Sat on Mother's bed – taking in the orange flowers on the bedding, the oval mirror on the dressing table, where Mother had watched her own reflection brush out her long hair – I took myself back a few years. Took myself back to when I'd first met him…

It was eight, nine years back; Billy was around two years-old. At an evening function, hosted by Monty Harrison – a very public display by the man, an attempt to appear as the pillar of society he'd fooled himself he was. As such, only a selection of his regular cronies were present – including Joe, who was under strict instructions to *bring that lovely wife of yours* and to *wear a suit and tie.*

I can still hear Joe repeating those words back to me – *that lovely wife of yours* – mocking Monty behind his back in a way he'd never have done to his face.

As well as the elite of his employees, Monty had invited a range of other associates – people who worked openly for the authorities and those who did similar work, but in the shadows. There were representatives from the police, the health authority, the food board and other public services. All good citizens on the surface, mingling with the very best of the underworld.

Ronan was among these guests.

Monty held the occasion at his grand house, north-west of the city.

It was the first time I'd had occasion to go there – and my last, until after Joe fled and I took his place as Monty's employee. And it was simply like nothing I had seen before.

If I used words like gargantuan, ostentatious and vulgar you might think I was jealous of what this untouchable criminal had achieved – but they were words that genuinely described what I beheld, as we were driven onto the generous grounds that somehow swallowed his substantial manor.

In all, he had about four acres of land and in the very centre – elevated by a small hill and surrounded by a moat that was built to ward off the dogs – was Monty Harrison's monstrous mansion. *Like something from Jane Eyre or Wuthering Heights,* I told Agnes, reporting back a day or so later – she was the only person I told about the night I'd spent there. We didn't openly discuss Joe's association with Monty in our family.

Once across the flamboyant moat via an equally pretentious bridge – which expanded and retracted by some whizzy electronic mechanism – a long drive stretched ahead to the grand entrance. A staircase of stone steps led up to a double-doored opening, which in turn led into Monty's entrance hall.

The hall itself, like in most houses, was a simple conduit that led to other rooms, but that didn't mean we were spared Monty's grandiosity here. The floors were a pink, orange and white marble swirl; multi-jeweled chandeliers swung from the ceiling, smattering crystals of light upon us all; a grand, open staircase, laid with plush, blood-red carpet curled around two of the walls; and the doors to the various rooms that led off the hall were cleverly hidden in the wood paneling on the walls – creating an illusion that there were no doors, when they were all closed.

We were greeted by waiters and waitresses offering champagne and canapés from silver trays and then directed right, into an equally grand room where the main throng of the party was gathered. The reign of spectacular décor continued its overbearing sway in there, too – a black and white harlequin-style tiled floor; more chandeliers dazzling us with tiny diamond stars; and, around the edge of the room, clusters of chairs and tables offering more champagne, chilled in silver coolers. I noted an emblem in gold leaf on the back of all the chairs – M and H, surrounded by a simple circle.

'Hasn't he done well for himself?' I muttered to Joe, as we were led to a table and introduced to some people whose names I don't remember, but they were *important people* (Joe's words) and I recall he threw me a quick glance that meant *be careful what you say.*

And so began an evening of meeting more and more *important people.* There was an orchestra in one corner of that colossal hall, so the evening included some distraction from the business chatter, but no dancing, as I'd hoped. And, once I'd had my share of *important people,* champagne and fancy finger food, I left Joe's side, with the excuse of needing the bathroom.

He claimed our eyes met when I left the hall – I glanced back, to check who was watching me and it was then, according to Ronan, that I locked his stare.

You didn't smile or anything, but I remember. You looked right at me.

But I didn't.

It was later, when I'd lost myself in the upper quarters the house, that I first saw him – first noticed him.

Glancing back every other second, expecting to be called back, cautioned for veering away from the social gathering, I didn't make my way to the toilets at all. Instead, I took to the treads of that grand staircase, and crept my way up.

At the top of that staircase, the red carpet stopped and a deep cream one took its place, smothering the long upper hallway in a thick, warm snow of wool. The walls were white and the doors also. I tried a few – poked my head round a few. The rooms were mainly bedrooms and their theme was uniform throughout – king-sized beds adorned with plush covers and mountains of cushions, some with a canopy above them, a swoop of luxury curtains gathered in a fancy knot giving these centre pieces a majestic quality. I recall the urge to dive into one and allow its soft folds to swallow me up. Some of the rooms were bathrooms – marble and gold leaf featuring heavily in each one.

At the very end of the first floor corridor was a hidden door. Like the doors below, it was hidden in the wall, appearing as a panel. But I saw it open, and someone come through it – and quickly drew myself into one of the bedrooms, keeping the door ajar and watching as the person passed by. They wore a uniform – not black and white, like the waiting staff below, but blue and white – like a nurse. From where I spied, I could see she hadn't quite pressed the panel back in place.

Thinking of the boredom waiting for me in the grand hall full of increasingly drunk, self-important men and their *lovely wives,* I allowed my curiosity to lead me further astray. I slipped out of the room I'd hidden in, crept to the end of the corridor and slipped behind the hidden door. Once behind it, I found another staircase – smaller, curling up in a spiral. Without thinking it through, I climbed up this corkscrew of steps and entered the second floor.

What I discovered wasn't what I expected. Not at all.

At the top, there was a door. I tried it and it opened. But as I did this, I was greeted by an electronic humming that I hadn't heard on the stairs – suggesting the place was sound-proofed.

Inside, I discovered one big open room – like an attic, but expansive, covering the whole area of the house. And equipment I couldn't even begin to describe was all around – it looked medical, like the kind of machines you saw in hospitals. Scanners, x-ray machines, tubes, funnels and leads, tall white cabinets that were locked – I tried a few. I wondered if this was Monty's true business – supplying equipment of a medical nature. Maybe to his contacts in the government? Maybe his business was legitimate after all? I doubted this, but couldn't help but question. And yet, if this was a warehouse for business supplies, it wasn't a very practical one. No one of any sound business mind would've created such a warehouse at the top of their house, with very limited access via a narrow, coiled staircase. It had to be something else.

And it was – though I didn't get the answers that night. But, at the far end of the room, something drew me forward. There was something dividing the attic space up – up close, I found thick, transparent rubber curtains, hanging in long, foot-wide strips that overlapped by an inch. I pushed through these, creating a slapping sound amongst the panels of the divider. And beyond that rubber barrier I found the reason for all the medical paraphernalia. In a huge bed – equally as luxurious as those I'd spied below, but of a more practical nature, on wheels, with various levers to adjust it – was a tiny girl. Aged maybe seven or eight, she had tubes coming out of her nose, a drip in each arm and various pads attached to her small body, from which leads trailed, hooking her up to a monitor that beeped and flashed what I assumed was her heartbeat.

Attached to the end of the bed was a plastic holder, with a clipboard, a cardboard folder and several papers resting in it. I stepped a little closer and read what was written across the front of the folder – the tiny girl's name.

'You shouldn't be in here,' came his voice, the first words I ever heard him speak, which almost frightened me to death.

'Jesus!' I cried, looking round to find a stranger behind me, instantly looking back to the tiny girl, to check if I had disturbed her. I hadn't.

Turning back to the stranger who'd caught me, any fears I had that I was in trouble were instantly quashed – a wide smile beamed across his face and he held a glass of champagne in each hand. He offered one to me.

'It's a party, after all,' he said, by way of an explanation.

I took one from him and returned his smile, enjoying the fact that someone was obviously flirting with me. Someone who wasn't my husband.

I wasn't unhappy with Joe. Aside from the work he did for Monty Harrison, I was happy with every aspect of our lives together. But our two year-old son was very demanding and he did restrict the time I had to get out and spend with others. I hadn't expected an evening in the company of Monty's crooked cronies to serve up anything interesting. But this handsome stranger, arriving from nowhere, with his winning smile and offer of sparkling refreshment was pleasantly unexpected – and I found myself drawn. I wasn't doing anything wrong – and didn't *intend* to do anything wrong, either.

'We should get out of here, you know,' he added, signaling around the room – acknowledging it was all clearly out-of-bounds. Private. 'I don't think that nurse will be away for long.'

So, he'd seen the nurse leave, too – he couldn't have been far behind me.

'Have you been watching me?' I asked, still playful in my manner, still keeping it fun, but harmless.

He shrugged, still smiling.

'We really should get out of here,' he repeated, not an answer, but it would do.

With that, we left the girl and the vast array of medical equipment that surrounded her behind.

At a later point, I asked Joe what he knew of the poorly girl in Monty's care and he said he knew nothing. When I mentioned her name – the one I'd seen written on the paperwork by her bed – he shook his head. No, it meant nothing to him – and it was an unusual name, not the sort that you easily forgot. I thought that sooner or later, I'd hear something – a rumour, or suddenly Monty would start introducing this child at the soirees he held, presenting her as his daughter or ward or whatever she was. She'd be a perfect token of his human side. Even when I started working for Monty myself, there was no mention or trace of this unwell girl.

However, about year after Joe left, Monty Harrison announced the arrival of his young niece, Tilly. I wondered if maybe the child I'd seen hooked up to monitors and his young niece might be one and the same – but as she looked different and was the absolute picture of health, that it seemed so very unlikely.

Leaving the vast echo of Monty's attic behind, the man I'd soon come to know as Ronan and I made our way back down to the ground floor – but instead of returning to the grand hall, we slipped out and briefly explored the grounds.

That's when it happened – the betrayal. It was nothing more than an intertwining of fingers and brief kiss on the cheek, from which I drew away instantly. But it was enough.

'I would like to see you,' he'd said, as I'd faced away from him, looking out into the black oblivion of the night, trying to make out the shapes in the shadows.

'I'm married,' I said aloud, in case he hadn't noticed my rings or seen me arrive accompanied.

'Joe's a lucky guy,' he answered, revealing he knew more than I'd realised.

I turned back to him, startled. I couldn't think how to respond, so instead I said something that would bring an end to whatever was happening between us.

'I'm out of champagne,' I said and began to walk back to the big house.

'I'll see you again,' he replied – not quite a statement, demand or a question. Something else.

For the rest of that night, I avoided him, taking myself back to Joe's side. I kept so close to him that he became a little concerned.

'You sure you're okay – we can always go?' he offered a couple of times, but I brushed it away.

'I'm fine. Let's not stay too late, as I don't want to be too tired when Billy is returned by Agnes tomorrow. But we're fine for now.'

And, by luck, I didn't see Ronan again that evening. But his statement stayed in my head, staining my thoughts – *I'll see you again* – like it was a pledge of the sins we might commit in the future.

He was true to his word, though – I saw him just over a week later when Mother introduced him as her *new beau* at a family party. Agnes had been delighted for her – but try as I might, I couldn't show him anything but contempt. After all, this was the man who'd caused me to unwittingly cheat on both my husband and mother with one brief, stolen kiss.

'I'll never forgive you,' I hissed at him, the first opportunity I got him on his own.

And they thought it was all me: that my bitterness towards Ronan – my refusal to accept him as family – was misplaced, stubborn and childish.

'For goodness sake, he's not trying to replace Father.' Agnes.

'I just wish you could just be happy for me.' Mother.

'You need to let go of the past, Esther.' Joe.

'Maybe you should just give me a break – embrace me as a member of your family, like everyone else has done.'

Those last words – from Ronan himself – were enough to make me spit. If it weren't for how Joe might have reacted if he'd learned of my indiscreet encouragement at Monty's party, I might have told him everything. Used it to help me usurp Ronan from the comfortable position he was carving out for himself at the head of our family.

Instead, I kept quiet – but not forever. Not once Joe had gone. No, after Joe disappeared from our lives, I used what I knew to try and get shot of this fraud who'd wormed his way into my mother's heart.

What would she think about you trying to seduce her married daughter?

Who's to say you aren't like that with other women?

And what would she think about your fraternizing with a local gangster?

He'd told the family he was a retired former employee of the government – something vague to do with policy. So, the latter revelation would be news to Mother, damaging news. But two things happened that stopped me taking my threats any further.

One – Mother fell seriously ill. And two – Ronan told me he knew how to contact Joe. While he couldn't tell me where he was – it wasn't safe information for me to possess – he could pass messages back and forth.

'So, rather than see me as the man who's pulling your family apart,' he proposed, hoping to keep my silence for good, 'you could see me as the man keeping it together.'

And so we struck a deal – and it was that deal, or the end of it, that was at the heart of my sudden grief when I caught sight of Ronan's decimated remains. It was also this agreement that drew me back to the empty, sanitised flat on my own, in the middle of the night…

Resting on the bed, in the room Ronan had shared with Mother, reflecting on all that had happened – things only *I* knew now that Ronan was gone – I wondered where to start with the task I'd set myself.

Just being there and thinking over the past, had been enough to rid myself of the ghosts haunting me for long. Yes, I'd never quite forgive myself for that kiss – I hadn't instigated it, but had in my own way encouraged its approach. And the wretched mess of Ronan's remains stained my mind as much as they stained the floor. But now my tired mind could focus on the next job in hand. And I *was* tired – my sore eyes struggling to stay open, as night stretched into early morning.

I'd come back to find the one thing Ronan had kept back from me – Joe's location, held back to *keep me from danger.* I'd never been fooled by this sentiment. While such information was dangerous, Ronan held it back because it gave him control. I'd kept my eye out while cleaning the place from top to bottom – tapping for loose panels in the walls or floor, taking note of every drawer and cupboard – briefly glancing inside each – and feeling my way under furniture for slips of paper. Back there on my own, I started in their bedroom. Ransacking the chest of drawers, I tried not to be distracted as I came across the clothes, jewels and trinkets he'd kept of Mother's. I took the back off the photograph frames on display, pulled the bedding and the mattress off the bed, and even ripped away the underbelly of the frame. Nothing. In the smaller bedroom it was much the same, although I found it hard to be in there knowing what had gone on. The living room – despite the array of hiding places I'd plundered with a meticulous methodology, ensuring I didn't miss a thing – turned up very little as well. I did find a final letter addressed to me. But it wasn't Joe's handwriting on the front – handwriting that had deteriorated to a shaky scrawl over the years. It was Ronan's – Ronan had written a letter to me. Left here for me to find, his words from beyond the grave? Who knew. Deciding whatever this man had to say to me could wait, I slipped it in the back pocket of my trousers – saving it for later, when I wasn't battling against time.

There was one place remaining – the landing just beyond the entrance to the flat. I hadn't thought about there to start with. It was only once I had my protective clothing back on and was about to leave the flat, defeated, that I considered it.

The entrance was officially shared, but I couldn't see signs of any other residents remaining. I shuddered when I thought about just how isolated Elinor would've been – shut up and restrained in this uninhabited part of town. There was another flat on the first floor – its main door tucked around the corner on an L-shaped landing. Turning this corner, I saw the door and a window that looked out to the side of the building. Below that was a small, stout bookcase – packed tightly with colourful spines.

It was so out of place and immediately drew my attention.

I pushed my face mask up to get a better look, wearing it on my head like a clumsy hairband.

I suddenly recognised it as a piece of furniture that had belonged to my parents – something that had taken pride of place in my childhood home, crammed with novels my mother had loved to read and my father had loved to ignore.

Moving closer, I recognised some of the books as well – the Brontes Agnes and I had devoured during many summer and winter holidays, the Hardy books mother was alone in her admiration for, crime novels I had particularly loved, and plays and poetry that also periodically grabbed our attention. This was all ours – something once treasured and so personal. So why had Ronan seen fit to move it out of the flat and rest it so close to his neighbour's?

'There has to be something here,' I told myself, ripping the mask from my head and stripping off my outdoor gear again – its rubbery materials too restrictive and uncomfortable. I was strictly still indoors – what harm would I come to? And no one would see me, so no one could report me to the authorities for rule breaking.

I took every single book from that shelf and checked every single one – flicking the pages, shaking them out to see if a letter, a slip of paper or any clues to Joe's whereabouts could be found. There was nothing. With all the books removed and checked, I stared at the empty casing and faced defeat. Nothing. Yet – why was it here, on the landing, adjacent to a stranger's home? That didn't make sense. There had to be some reason and I held out some hope that the reason was connected to Joe. I dragged it forward, away from the window and checked behind it – nothing. I tipped it forward and carefully checked its base – still nothing.

But, as I pushed it back in place, deciding to return all the books out of respect for the memories they held, something struck me as odd.

The book case had three shelves in total – a taller one at the bottom for bigger books, and two shorter ones in the middle and top. It was made from solid pine, stained with varnish and age – apart from the backing on the middle shelf. It was pine, like the rest of the piece, but it was lighter and the grain different – the streaks of blond in the wood wider, suggesting it came from a different source. Wondering if there was something in this, I pulled out the shelves and saw that an additional oblong panel had been affixed to it – its screws hidden by the thickness of the shelves above and below it. I retrieved a knife from the flat – I hadn't seen any tools during my search – and carefully released the wood, my hand shaking, anticipating that taking it off would present a revelation.

It did – but it wasn't what I'd hoped for.

It wasn't news of Joe – it wasn't an address or even clues to where I could find him. At least, I couldn't see how it could be.

When the panel was removed, I discovered a brown envelope, folded over to make it small enough to hide behind the slim board. Written on the front in black pen were two words: 'Cadley's blueprints'. I knew the name Cadley – he'd been responsible for designing and building the house on stilts that crazy old man lived in, at the top of Agnes' road. What had my sister called him? Augustus – that was it.

The envelope wasn't sealed, so I put my left hand in and pulled out the contents. They were indeed blueprints – and they appeared to outline the structure of some kind of network, a system of tunnels.

While my body flooded with disappointment – exhausting me as the effects of hope drained away – I took a minute to study the papers I'd found. And scanning it over just once, I realised something startling.

It was a map of our city. At least, part of a map – on closer inspection, the vertical edge to the right was rough, as if folded and carefully torn.

Folding the papers back up, I returned them to the envelope and set about quickly putting the shelves and the books back in place. Then, I pulled on my protective outdoor clothing, covered my face with the mask and began my journey home.

It seemed to take forever to get back home.

I couldn't tell if the sky had got a little lighter, or if my eyes had simply adjusted to the night light. It was just after 2am when I left Ronan's flat, so it couldn't have been that morning was breaking. By the time I reached home, my bones ached with exhaustion and I had to focus to ensure I moored the boat securely.

Through the door and up the stairs, I removed my protective gear in the upper hallway and hung it from a hook on the wall there. Then, I took my somnolent self into my living room and gave that strange map of tunnels a second look with my tender eyes, over-blinking them in an attempt to focus.

And I found something.

It wasn't what I'd gone out for – but it was something personal, something very close to home.

In amongst the drawings, I found my address.

I found my house.

Asleep

It's dark, wet and cold – and I feel closed in, as if I'm in a narrow space.

I reach out to either side of me and touch the walls. They are damp and feel slimy.

'I'm in a tunnel,' I think, keeping these words inside.

I'm not alone.

Ahead, I can make out a flicker of a torch – and there's a group up front. It has a mix of voices within it – male, female, old and young.

I blink.

The torch is flickering all over the place, so I can't tell if they are coming towards me, or whether I'm following them, catching up.

The whirl of the light eventually settles on something and the group stops. The beam is illuminating a ladder attached to a wall.

One voice in the group speaks out.

'We're here,' it says.

Awake

3. Tilly

It started with a silly game. Something fun, that didn't need much thinking. Well, maybe just a little bit. It involved *getting-our-stories-straight.* And it had the potential of *getting-us-in-trouble*, if we didn't pull it off successfully. But there wasn't anything serious to think about. We still expected to go home at the end of school. We still expected to go back to being ourselves at the end of our game. That either of those things might *not* happen – well, it wasn't part of the plan. Not that we really had a plan.

It was just a silly game after all.

'Okay,' Marcie Coleman had agreed. 'I'll do it.'

And that's how it started – Marcie's lucky escape and my unexpected adventure.

Billy wasn't there that day. Not that we were in the same classes anymore. He was in the top one, Miss Cracker's, where I should've been. But Uncle Monty had intervened *for my own good,* and I'd been immediately moved down to the second-from-bottom class. Not that I could see why this was a *good* thing. I was now keeping the company of Mr Burnham – and a bunch of badly behaved *ne'er-do-wells,* as he called us all, me included. I'd told Uncle Monty all about this, but he didn't really listen. He said things like *you let me worry about those things,* but he didn't seem to think about them, let alone worry.

Mr Burnham was bulky, wore a blue suit that looked like it dated before the floods, had thick glasses, ginger hair on his head and grey hair on his face. Marcie Coleman was the second smartest in the class – next to me, even if I say so myself – so she was an obvious choice as a friend. Although, Billy was my preference. Uncle Monty's, too.

'You still hanging about with young Billy?' he'd ask and follow up with a 'good, good,' when I confirmed I was.

But on the day Marcie and I played a silly game, Billy wasn't anywhere to be seen. If he'd turned up for school at all, he must have gone home early, as he wasn't on the grass at break or lunch – and we always met on the grass, whether it was raining or not.

It wasn't raining heavy that morning. It was the fifth almost-dry day in a row. I'd been counting them down, as I'd been stuck indoors the whole time it'd been pouring down *violently* – Uncle Monty's description, said like he approved of the weather's behaviour.

I shared a house with my uncle and various other people, who came and went. They were our servants, in truth, but they were allowed to be friendly – just not too friendly. And they were never around for that long, so it didn't pay to get too close. Sooner or later, they'd be gone and I'd have to deal with my loss again.

But I was good at that – dealing with loss.

I'd been dealing with loss for as long as I could remember – and further back.

My mother died when I was just two. I didn't remember her at all, but Uncle Monty had told me about her. He said I'd come to live with him shortly afterwards – something else I didn't really recall – and I'd grown up with his family of comers and goers, in his massive big house on the north-west side of our city.

Although I didn't remember her – Mother – Uncle Monty did have a book of photographs he kept in an album in his bedroom. It was a large, square book, covered in red velvet, with a gold tassel along the spine. I found it one day in a drawer at the bottom of a wardrobe. Took it out and sat on the quilted satin cover on his bed and flicked through page after page of colourful photographs. I knew they were of her – there was something of me in her face. In some she was by herself, others she had my uncle by her side. There were none of my father, though. I'd asked more about him as I got older, but Uncle Monty said he couldn't answer my questions, as Mother had never told my uncle about him. Another loss for my list.

When Uncle Monty found me with the velvet album, he was furious. Like I'd invaded his most private moments. He almost threw himself across the room in his attempt to retrieve the photograph book. But I'd simply cradled it and withdrawn into myself and he'd had to calm himself. It's what I did whenever that temper flared – withdrew and became silent, until he calmed. It worked that time too.

'Tilly, you can't just go through-.' he began, concentrating to still his anger.

'I knew it was her straightaway,' I interrupted and that got him curious. I looked straight into his eyes and saw a glimmer of intrigue appear. 'She looks just like me.'

'Ah, I see,' he'd answered, gathering his thoughts, edging himself next to me on the bed, but making no attempt to take the photograph album away. 'She was *very* pretty, wasn't she?'

Once we'd gone through everyone – him recalling stories from some of the snaps, unable to attach specific memories to others – he let me keep it.

'In a drawer, kept away from prying eyes,' he instructed, like she was a secret, like no one should know about her or ever see her beauty. Only me and my uncle.

But I agreed. I wanted to keep her, after all.

'In a drawer,' I agreed, cradling the red velvet against me. 'Like a secret.'

'Like a secret,' he'd echoed, confirming that's exactly what she was.

Uncle Monty's house was the biggest in the city, I'm certain. At times, it felt like it had a million rooms. I wasn't allowed in all of them. There were some rooms on the first floor that were out of bounds, rooms Uncle Monty said were for business. And sometimes I'd see men going in, looking a bit secretive and there would be loud laughter and hissy whispers. And there was another whole floor above the first – but that was sealed off and no longer used.

'It was badly damaged when the floods came,' Uncle Monty explained, when I asked. 'A terrible storm. No longer safe up there, so I've had it blocked off.'

'Will you get it mended?' I'd questioned.

'One day,' he answered. 'But no rush. It'd take a lot of work to put it right – and we've already got enough rooms on the other floors. More than enough for us, eh?'

A few years ago, we had a house servant called Gemma. When I'd asked about the damaged floor, she'd given me a slightly different story.

'It's just locked up,' she'd told me, when I brought up the subject. *'Not damaged, just private. Full of secrets!'* She'd said the last line excitedly, and suddenly I wondered what exactly was up there – and if my uncle had lied, why?

I'd find myself standing outside in the vast grounds of Uncle Monty's estate, staring up at the top of the house, looking for clues. It didn't look damaged – and there *was* clearly a second floor, as there was a long row of windows, parallel with the first floor. However, it looked as if they were covered up, shutters pulled across them.

So, I'd questioned my uncle about this again, telling him what Gemma had said. But this led to a terrible row, and Uncle Monty had hit her. That'd frightened me and he'd spent a lot of that same evening apologising to me, as if I'd been the one injured, not her. I never saw Gemma again, and she was quickly replaced by a new house servant. But none of them ever stayed long – sooner or later they did something wrong and were gone.

Whenever Uncle Monty had a little too much to drink, he talked about *the glory days* – about the days when he threw magnificent parties, when everything sparkled and glittered in his big mansion.

'Just before you came,' he'd say, as if somehow I'm the reason it all came to an end.

I'm not, although I wonder if my mother's dying somehow dulled some of the shine.

But I know he means before the floods. Before the food shortages and the poverty. And when I look at the photographs of Mother, I can see that other world. A world of blue skies, golden drapes, green fields and cherry red lips.

And when I wandered around the endless succession of rooms, going into the empty ones where the doors weren't locked, I tried to re-imagine it all. Tried to obliterate the greys, the browns and the blacks that the dark skies and heavy rains had washed in, and imagined the vibrancy that sunshine could return. I'd think about those *glory days*, and I'd whirl around the ballroom on the ground floor, wishing the lights on, wishing the floor polished, wishing a band in the corner playing old favourites, wishing waiters carrying silver trays, wishing dancing, laughter and mindless chatter, wishing a swishing of beautiful gowns.

Some days, the ballroom was out-of-bounds – its grand doors locked, with private business going on behind them.

So, during the rainy days, when I couldn't go outside at all, I trawled the rooms and my imagination. I couldn't really complain. We weren't as badly affected by the floods as some. Not like Billy, whose house was half under water. The flooding was shallower where we lived and we had a moat surrounding the house, from which the water still drained – something I understand Uncle Monty sorted long before the Great Drowning. But we were still affected by other things – the restrictions on travel, the fear of what had caused the disaster in the first place and the rumours about what might be out there. Everything we owned was still discoloured by the poverty surrounding us. And while Uncle Monty got hold of luxury items – bath salts and chocolate for me, champagne and cigars for himself – his contacts and his methods were no different from anyone else. But we did have more money to spend, more *capital*, as he said, *to bargain with.*

My education was the one thing that was exactly the same as everyone else's. *In the old days,* Uncle Monty explained, *we'd have had a choice. And I'd have sent you somewhere better. Somewhere you'd be nurtured. But St Patrick's is all there is.*

So, that's where I went, every week day – albeit Uncle Monty had intervened and made me a special case, moving me out of Billy's class *for my own good.* Moving me into Marcie Coleman's class and company – not realising that this really *wouldn't* be for my own good.

Quite the opposite.

The day of our game, our teacher – Mr Burnham – wasn't in school.

Having his grey beard died ginger.

Marcie's idea of a joke.

Having his pebble glasses mended.

Having his ancient blue suit dry-cleaned.

'Dry-what?' I'd asked her, sat at the back of our class, whispering, as the fearsome Miss Cracker had just entered our class.

For one terrifying moment, I thought she was our replacement teacher for the day, but it turned out she was just there to settle-in someone else.

'Dry-cleaned,' Marcie murmured, hoping our chattering wouldn't be noticed. 'It's something my dad says. *Must get my old suit dry-cleaned.* Him and Mum think it's hilarious.'

'Right,' I answered, not really sure what to say next. Like I said before, Marcie was the next-smartest person in my class – but there was a bit of a gap between us. Still, she was good company and easily-led into doing the things I wanted – so I couldn't complain.

Miss Cracker introduced Mr Burnham's replacement as Miss Douglas – a young woman who looked like she hadn't long left school herself. And she appeared a little shocked when Miss Cracker said: *Right, I'll leave you to it.* As if she was expecting her to stay and tell her what to do next. For a moment or two, she remained at the front, startled, still figuring out what to do it. And in that moment, I made a suggestion to Marcie that would change our lives.

'What if she finds out? We'll be in trouble,' Marcie initially fretted.

'She won't, and it's just a bit of fun. Not really naughty at all. Not a crime or anything.'

Marcie mulled this over for a second or so, before finally relenting. It's how it usually went with her – a resistance and then quickly complying with whatever I'd suggested.

'Okay, I'll do it,' she agreed.

'Okay, here goes,' I said, sucking in a deep breath and shooting my hand in the air, arm straight. 'Miss, miss?'

'Yes,' Miss Douglas said, startled by my cry, but then smiling, as if my speaking up was some great kindness. 'Yes?'

'We're doing maths, Miss.'

There was a long, resentful groan around the room and daggered looks were aimed in my direction. But I wasn't bothered. I just needed an excuse to speak up, to get her attention.

'Okay, settle down and thank you…' Miss Douglas' voice trailed as she searched for something she didn't have: my name.

'It's Marcie, Miss,' I said, keeping my face straight.

'And I'm Tilly, Miss,' Marcie piped up, a little unnecessarily and I wondered if her grinning face might just give us away. Instead, Miss Douglas took her inane grin as a symptom of idiocy – which wasn't entirely wrong.

'Settle down!' our teacher repeated, raising her voice, glaring around the class. 'And thank you Marcie, Tilly. Now, let's see where you got up to and get started.'

And so our lesson began, once Miss Douglas had checked our books and found some instructions left by Mr Burnham. But so did something else. No one said anything outright – although there was the odd bit of whispering. No, it was more like we just *started* something – our silly name-swap game simply caught on.

Johnny Briggers did it first – putting his hand up, asking to be excused to the boys' room.

'Please, Miss!' he asked, exaggerating the urgency with his voice, clutching the front of his trousers.

'And you are?' she asked, a little crossly – she'd well and truly got to grips with her role by then.

'Jimmy Nichol, Miss,' he answered, causing the real Jimmy Nichol to open his mouth like a dead fish, as if he hadn't quite heard properly.

'Go on then,' she said, rolling her eyes, as *Jimmy*, also-known-as-Johnny, sped out of the class, as if his bladder might burst there and then.

The swapping trend continued, much to mine and Marcie's delight.

Shannon Burley swapped with Jenny Baker.

Jeannie Shaw with Olivia White.

Peter Hudson became Philip Williams, and Walter Simmonds took Kelvin Spaders name, although the latter pulled a reluctant frown that almost gave the game away.

'Is something wrong?' Miss Douglas asked, directing the question at Kelvin.

He shook his head.

'And who are you?' she followed up, and you sensed everyone in the room hold their breath, wondering if he'd give the game away.

There was a delay in Kelvin's response and Miss Douglas was just about to repeat her question when he said: 'Walter, my name is Walter, Miss.'

A mass sighing in the class followed, with the odd muted *phew*.

Miss Douglas paused for a moment, surveying us all, as if sensing there was something she'd missed. But, after a second or so, she moved on, picking up a text book from the desk at the front.

'Right, Trigonometry it is, then...'

It was weird – the effect of our little game. Not only because of the way it caught on, but the way it silently brought the whole class together, uniting us.

There were points where I thought we might get caught. Another teacher, Mr Jones, popped in and said he needed to *borrow two strong lads for five minutes.* He didn't say what for – and no one asked, either. Miss Douglas offered Peter and Philip, introducing them the wrong way round. Mr Jones frowned, but you could tell he just thought she'd them mixed up. The school nurse popped in later, asking for *Jenny Baker.* When the real Jenny stood up, Miss Douglas frowned and narrowed her eyes ever so slightly – scanning the class, letting us know she was suspicious. But she didn't say anything – she couldn't, it wasn't enough to go on. Besides, maybe she was just mistaken?

But there was a third incident that I was certain would blow the lid on our trivial prank. The school secretary nipped into our class and passed Miss Douglas a note. She read it, frowned to herself and then looked up at Marcie.

'Tilly?' she asked. I'm not sure if she was checking or just grabbing her attention.

After a pause – Marcie's brain was catching up with events – Marcie answered:

'Yes?'

'You need to follow Miss...' She stumbled, releasing she didn't know the secretary's name.

'Miss Jackson.'

'You need to follow Miss Jackson to the headmaster's office.'

Another pause from Marcie, as she looked to me, questioning. I gave her what I hoped was the subtlest of nods. Then she stood, took herself up to the front and left with Miss Jackson. We didn't really know the secretary and there was no reason for her to know our individual names. But I thought our cover would be blown at any second. Even after she'd gone, I kept expecting Marcie to be marched back in, our silly game discovered and for us all to face the wrath of the nurse, our teacher, the headmaster. But nothing happened.

Nothing at all.

And, as five minutes became ten, as half-an-hour become three-quarters – a whole – I began to worry about something else. I began to worry about what had happened to Marcie. Marcie Coleman who'd said she was me – Tilly Harrison. What had I been called away for – and why hadn't our trick been discovered yet? And this worry ate away at me for the rest of the day, wiping out my worries about being discovered – *where was she, and what had they taken her away for?* It didn't make sense – it must've been something important, but then again surely, *surely* they'd have worked out who she was eventually. Surely *she'd* have spoken up.

But she didn't return – and she didn't speak up, either.

Later, I wouldn't blame her. I'd given her a chance, after all – an unexpected opportunity that she hadn't known she'd be grateful of. She didn't so much as take it, but allow it to take her along. And I wouldn't have wished that she swap places back and go through what the rest of us did. I'd never have wished that upon her, even though it was me – not her – who was meant to escape.

It started with a siren. A shrieking, whirring noise that curled round and round, vibrating its way through the whole school. Miss Douglas looked a little unsure as to what to do, but Miss Cracker reappeared and shouted sharp instructions at us all – spraying the front few rows of the class with her loose spit.

'Put your outdoor clothing on and make your way to the front of the school!' she barked. 'Quickly! Put on your protective clothes and make your way to the front of the school! Then listen to further instructions!'

She spoke to Miss Douglas, as we took our outdoor suits and face masks from the back of the class. I've no idea what she said, as the alarm drowned out anything but a shout, but I didn't see Miss Douglas again – not once we were outside and she didn't come with us either.

Once dressed and protected, we filed out sensibly, uniformly, although our pace was a little faster than usual. We were fueled with a sense of terror, but restrained by the rules of discipline with which the school operated. *No running in the corridors! No running in the corridors!* Our feet and our bodies weaved through the walkways and spilled out into the grey daylight like a huge centipede, coming together in a mass, singular exodus. As we moved with one purpose – to escape from whatever had set off the alarms – the circular, whining siren followed us. Outside, it seemed just as loud and it intensified the sense of panic we were feeling.

For a few moments, we simply stood on the green, hilly lawns that surrounded our school, clustered in classes. Not everyone was with us, though. There was no Miss Douglas. And Marcie Coleman hadn't emerged with the headmaster, either. My eyes searched for

Billy – they located his class, but not him. I wondered for a second if he was still inside and felt another fever of panic flush through my blood – what if he *was* still inside, what if Billy had been at the centre of whatever had set off the alarms? What if he was hurt?

My eyes darted around, searching for the nearest teacher or adult to ask and saw Miss Cracker. But, before I had a chance to think about what I'd do or say next, the unexpected happened. Another noise alerted my senses. A noise from above. It started in the distance and I could only just hear it above the electronic cry of the ceaseless alarm. Sounding initially like the puck-puck-puck of bullets, as it got closer and louder, the sound became clearer. It was a rapid whirring sound, the sound of huge blades whipping through the air. Looking up, I saw the source of the noise. We all did. In the sky, like the greyest of clouds was a fleet of helicopters. I knew what they were – from books, from stories, from school, and from the one time I flew in one. I've no idea how many there were, but they seemed to fill the sky and looked dangerously close together.

They didn't land, but they hovered – drowning out the whir of the siren.

Miss Cracker stood in the centre of us all, like she was suddenly the leader – a loud haler in her hand, shouting out instructions that we couldn't fully hear. I read the movement of her lips though and worked out the words *'we'* and *'evacuating'*. *We are evacuating.*

And for those who couldn't work it out, in case there was any doubt, rope ladders suddenly tumbled from the airborne beasts, hitting several of us as their last few rungs unraveled.

And then we all began to climb aboard, one pupil at a time, filling one helicopter at a time. We were with our teachers and they were giving the instructions – so we had no reason to doubt they'd put our best interests first. No reason at all. But we had our questions.

'Where are we going?' someone asked, nearby.

'What's happened in the school?'

'Where have these things come from?'

'Is someone telling our parents?'

Questions not answered during the evacuation process – and not answered by anyone once we were inside the hollow metal birds and on our way to wherever. In stark contrast to the behaviours encouraged by our school, day in, day out, once we were in the sky – on our way to who knows where – being inquisitive and showing an interest was not encouraged.

On board the helicopter, we were ordered into seats that flanked the sides and told to buckle up our safety belts. Some of us struggled to get the belts over our thick, rubbery suits and someone asked if it was safe to take them off. But we were encouraged to keep them on, including our face visors.

'For your safety,' someone said, though I'm not sure who. The lighting was dim inside and the window on my mask was steaming up. But I dared not take it off. *For your safety* the stern, strange, anonymous voice had instructed and I felt compelled to do as I was told.

To my left I made out Peter Hudson. Could hear him crying and wished so much for Billy's company. Billy would say something to turn this unknown, frightening evacuation into an adventure. Billy wouldn't be whimpering – he'd be asking questions and making plans.

Where are you, Billy? I asked myself, wondering also about another missing companion. *And where are you Marcie Coleman?* Taken from class – singled out as me. What was her fate? And why had she – why had *I* – been singled out?

'Shut up, boy!' the unidentified voice told Peter, whose simmer of tears had boiled over into a bawl. 'Pull yourself together. There isn't time for your nonsense!'

'It's ok,' I said to Peter, taking his rubber-gloved hand, hoping he could hear my encouraging words through my mask. 'I've been in one of these before. We're quite safe.'

'Where are we going?' he asked me, a sob still in his voice. Then he asked another, shorter question, as if he'd only just comprehended my words: 'have you?'

'Yes, just once,' I answered. 'With my Uncle Monty. And I don't know where we're going, but they had to get us out, didn't they? You heard the alarms? Something must be wrong.'

Peter nodded, his tears finally under control.

'I guess they just needed to get us safe,' he said, padding out the story of reassurance I'd begun. 'They'll tell us what's happening when they get a chance.'

'And wherever we're going, they'll tell our parents.'

'They'll be there when we arrive,' Peter concluded, a little too hopeful, I thought.

'Yes,' I answered, going along with it, not wanting to unsettle him again. 'Yes, that sounds right.'

We were quiet for a bit, still holding gloved hands. Then he spoke up:

'You really been in one of these before?'

I remembered the day very clearly.

It wasn't the kind of day you easily forgot.

It'd been less than two years back. Not long after my tenth birthday. Uncle Monty had bought me a new dress that year – a long red evening gown, made from silky material. I'd tried it on and made my way to the empty, dusty hallway, where I'd whirled and whirled around, dancing to an imaginary band and catching imaginary suitors glancing at me, hoping for a dance, a kiss, or at least a glance returned.

The dress had been accompanied by a pair of dainty gold shoes, covered in glitter. I remember thinking they were the most beautiful thing I'd ever seen and wondered where Uncle Monty could possibly have got them from. But these weren't things you questioned.

'Best not to ask,' he would say, tapping his nose.

When I touched them, running my hand all over their sparkle, some of the glitter brushed off onto my hands. I felt a sense of shock – these shoes were fragile things and their glitter wouldn't last, unless I was careful. Still, I'd put them on my feet; I couldn't resist.

And, as I'd twirled around at my make-believe ball – my beautiful red gown swishing, admired by invisible guests – they dashed tiny stars across the unwashed floor, making it sparkle, leaving the occasional glitter star behind.

Three sounds interrupted my dreaming.

A scream, a shot and whirring noise.

I'm not sure of the order – they could even have been at the same time. My memory doesn't make that bit clear.

But the scream came from my uncle – a deep, thick cry, full of horror, bleeding with fear.

'Tilly! Tilly!' he'd cried out. 'TILLY! WHERE ARE YOU?!'

And there was a shot – a bullet cracking from a gun, splitting the air. Followed by another and another. The sound of reloading and then further shots were released.

'TILLY! TILLY!'

I remember his thick hand grabbing mine, once he'd found me in the hall, dragging me away, panting – *this way, this way, quick!* Hauling me from the grand hall, into the lobby, then down the front stone steps, pulling me up from a stumble. There was no stopping for protection – to my horror, he took me straight out into the polluted outdoors.

I gasped at the shock of it, immediately wondering if the air I'd taken in would poison my body.

'You'll be fine, just keep moving,' Uncle Monty gasped, running with me, heading to the left of our expansive house, to a clear area that had once been covered in lush, green grass. It was by then a barren plot, brown and grey with mud and dead vegetation. 'Just keep up with me!'

Then I heard the whirring noise – the batter of blades spinning at a life-threatening speed. Was that the first time I heard them, or had I heard them earlier? Had they been circling our house all the while? Whatever, it was then that it came into view. It was huge – a grey-green capsule with two sets of blades at either end.

'It's called a Chinook,' Uncle Monty explained later, once we were inside. Once we were safe. 'It's a military helicopter,' he added and I didn't ask how he'd got it.

But I did ask – much later – I did ask him why he didn't use it to get out of the city, to take us to dry land.

'And where would that be then?' he'd answered, with a question of his own – one I couldn't answer.

Before then – as we ran from the house, towards the hovering metal beast – I watched as a rope ladder spun down towards the ground, unravelling at a vicious speed.

'Grab it, Tilly! Grab it!' Uncle Monty had cried, almost throwing us both towards the flaccid ladder, as it swung back and forth.

I remember being terrified by its lack of stability, as the ladder rope was gradually extracted back into the aircraft, taking us higher. Uncle Monty's large, adult bulk added to this effect, turning us into a precarious pendulum, swinging back and forth – my terror intensifying the higher we got.

'Just hold on, Tilly! We're nearly in! Just don't let go!'

There's a few things that have stuck in my head, as I finally reached the air machine and was pulled to safety. My dress ripped, catching on the entrance, as a stranger grabbed me under my arms and hauled me in. And one of my shoes came loose, falling into the oblivion of air beneath us. Instinctively, I turned back, looked over the edge, following its tumble into cloud.

'Tilly, no!' Uncle Monty cried, fearing I'd slip from the aircraft myself, but the stranger still had me in his firm grip. 'Tilly, Jesus, you scared me! Jesus.'

Solomon – that was his name. When I started to cry, he tried to be friendly. Offered me a hard-boiled sweet from his pocket – it was dusted with fluff and bits of wrapping that had become welded to it. I took it though, and it tasted of lime. *I'm Solomon, what's your name?* He had blue eyes and very short blond hair. Uncle Monty hadn't been pleased with his familiarity and had glared at the man to show this. But it made a difference to me. It had given me comfort. It helped calm the terror I'd experienced, running from a threat I couldn't see. And it distracted me from my loss – a childish loss resulting from a ripped gown and a fallen shoe.

'I'll buy you a new pair, I promise,' Uncle Monty had said, hoping to trump Solomon.

But that friendly stranger's face had charmed me, and it stained my brain, not fading for a long time.

And Uncle Monty forgot his promise – I'm still waiting for a new pair of glittering shoes.

We circled the skies for an hour or so, and when we returned it was getting darker. Not black-dark, but a darker grey, so everything was in half-shadow. Once we'd landed, I was instructed to stay in the helicopter with Solomon, *until the coast was clear*. I could see a member of the household staff dashing to meet Uncle Monty, as he headed back to the house. There was a minute or so of discussion and then Uncle Monty signaled for me to join him. I was escorted by Solomon up to the steps of the house, where my uncle took over as chaperone and Solomon was dismissed.

I never found out what we were running from – like the worst of terrors, it remained silent, invisible. I kept thinking of the gunshots I'd heard, thinking that it must have been something living. Thinking that it had probably been killed. But, in the days that followed, as I took my imagination from room to room in our sprawling home, I saw no traces of violence. I found no traces of blood.

But it remained vivid in my memories. The fear. The noises – shots, whirring blades, cries. The temporary sickness from flying. My shoe cascading to its demise. And the kind blue eyes of Solomon the stranger…

A sudden jolt drew me from my thoughts – we were descending. Peter and I were still holding hands, and his grip abruptly tightened.

'We'll be fine,' Peter's mask-distorted voice assured me, although I think he was trying to reassure himself more than anything else.

Once landed, we were instructed to move quickly – unclip our safety belts and exit. Unlike at the other end of our evacuation, the helicopters had landed on the ground. On dry ground, I discovered as my feet touched down.

And unlike the last time I'd been in a helicopter, I wasn't returned to my starting point. While my visor was misted a little with condensation, I could see ahead, although it was a picture in fog. There was a big square building in front of us, like the corrugated iron warehouses near the Black Sea, on the industrial side of the city. To the sides I just glimpsed a bare landscape – a dirt floor, but dry, no flooding. And I saw some chain-fencing in the distance, suggesting we were in some kind of enclosure.

'Straight ahead, keep moving,' we were instructed, pushed from the rear, making us push each other, some of us stumbling. 'Keep moving!'

And so we did, heading straight into the industrial looking building, hoping someone would explain what was going on, hoping to find familiar faces and explanations inside.

Behind us, the helicopter rotors started up again, quickly spinning into a deathly frenzy, whipping up a storm of dry earth, as they tore up into the oblivion above us.

I wondered if they'd be back. If the evacuation from the school was simply the start of a larger exodus. But it wasn't. The helicopters didn't come back with more people from our city – it was just us. The children from our school.

Apart from Marcie Coleman.

Apart from Billy.

And children from other places, other cities I soon noticed.

But just children.

Asleep

I'm in a street. I'm wearing a floating white night dress and I'm bare foot. I don't recognise where I am and I'm not sure how I get there.

I say 'get there' because it's definitely the future. It has to be. It's definitely not happened to me.

It's morning – light, but the street hasn't woken up. There's a sense people haven't ventured out yet. But they should – they should step out and see what the new day has brought them. What the night has taken away.

Gradually, doors open and people step out. They gasp at what they see – gasp freely, as no one is wearing a gas mark. No one apart from me.

Something makes me touch my face – I feel the black rubber of the breathing snout and plastic across my eyes. I try to pull the mask off, but I can't. It's like it's part of me – part of my face.

All around me, more and more people come outside, gasping in disbelief, moving forward. You see, the ground is dry – bone dry. Every drop of water has drained away, as if it's a desert. As if it's been arid for years.

But while they sigh and wonder in awe, I feel nothing but panic. I struggle to rip the mask from my face – my fingers fumbling, slipping in the rush – and my anxiety rises and rises. I can no longer feel where the rubber ends and my skin begins. I feel something rise in my throat.

Awake

4. Augustus

I think we all heard the blades in the air. Wherever you were in the city, you could hear the sound of those military beasts in the sky. And that's what they were. I didn't see them, but I'd heard the words on that transmission I'd intercepted – *the army is ready.* And there was only one army I knew of – the one controlled by the increasingly omniscient authorities.

I was at the apex of my house – up in the attic. Sat at my small dining table, drinking the last of that bitter coffee Jessie had supplied me – before he and Agnes' lover, Tristan, had disappeared on their adventure of hope and discovery. We'd still not had word from them – then again, it was to be expected. I doubt there was a postal service where they'd headed. And unchartered wilderness wasn't renowned for its telephony.

Tasting the last of the grit in the bottom of my cup, and thinking of Tristan, I felt the urge to check-in on Agnes. I hadn't seen her since we'd disposed of Ronan and cleaned his house. While that was only the day before, I worried for her – after all, she had been so close to Elinor, only to suffer her loss two-fold. Her loss was three-fold if she still held any love for Ronan, which was likely, and I'd no doubt she was still adjusting to the thought of him as the enemy – still comprehending that in her muddled mind.

I missed her, too. I'd felt relief at telling her who I was and – despite what brought us together – had reveled in her company. We'd had an instant connection and our short bond had been strong. Between the time we'd found Ronan's corpse and then returned to remove it, I'd seen an expected plummet in her spirit. And she had withdrawn into herself.

'We can't have that, Agnes,' I muttered to myself, getting up from the chair, knocking the papers I'd been urgently studying off the table. I'd pick them up later. 'Can't have that at all.'

I had several telephones set up in my house. One in the entrance hall. One at the very back, in the kitchen I used as an extended workshop. In the computer room. Another in a secret, hidden room. And here, in the attic, in the homely part of my house – perched on the small cabinet to the right of my bed. I had them set up so I could ring the various rooms by pressing a single digit – not that I needed this system, but I had time and scientific understanding. So, why not? Billy had discovered their dual purpose and liked to play around, ringing around, trying to find which room I was in. I could've found this irritating. Instead, I just felt a sense of sadness, as I imagined him and Elinor playing out this game. Something told me, by the time we got her back, she'd have outgrown such silliness.

If we get you back, I thought, feeling my own hope slipping. *Stop it, Augustus. We can't have that! When we get you back. When.*

I was about to use the attic telephone – to call in on Agnes – when I'd heard the thunderous whipping in the sky. I knew it wasn't a storm – at least, not a meteorological one. And knew what it was. It was the army. *Operation retrieval.* That's what they'd called it. Only, they were early, surely? I checked the time on my watch – just after 3pm. I was certain the message I'd heard said much later – an evening time. This was still daytime. Still afternoon.

'I don't understand,' I muttered to myself, dropping the phone gently back into its cradle, almost unaware I was doing it. It must have been a false transmission, sent out to hinder any planned intervention.

Suddenly, Agnes was my secondary concern.

I went from window to window in my attic room – there was one on each on the four walls that sloped to the ceiling, so I had a fractured panorama of the city skies. Looking out, I couldn't see a thing for grey cloud, but at times it sounded like the helicopters were circling the house. And they were definitely in the plural – there was no way of being certain how many, but I guessed enough to clear a school.

Enough to clear St Patrick's.

Even though I'd listened to parts of the authorities' transmissions, I thought I'd understood clearly. They were coming for them in the evening. *Execute tomorrow night. Twenty-two hundred hours.* So, I'd thought I had time – time to tell people, time to make arrangements for those who needed help, and time to hide as many of the intended victims as I could. I had the means, after all – plenty of room and plenty of clever hiding places. The man Cadley who'd designed and built my sprawling tower-house had been a very clever man indeed – a modern-day soothsayer, you might say, as he foresaw the needs I'd have for his labyrinthine attention to detail.

'But I'm too late,' I said aloud, as the surround-sound of helicopters appeared to circle my rooftop one more time – the hectic dance of blades intensifying, before suddenly petering away. It left a stark silence in its place – a sound like dust settling.

I grabbed the telephone again and made the call I'd intended – to Agnes. But she wasn't answering. I'd have to go round, but before I did, I made a call to the only person I'd warned about the authorities' dark plans – Esther.

'Yes?'

There was strained panic in Esther's voice when she picked up and spoke.

'It's Augustus,' I answered quickly.

Since Agnes' slip up in front of her sister, I'd decided to be open to her about my name. From her reaction, I could tell two things – she had no idea who I really was, but she knew I'd kept my name secret for a reason. Some instinct told me the knowledge was safe in her hands.

'Did you hear it, Gus?' she replied, her anxiety holding, her restraint weakening. 'Did you hear that? You said tonight! You said they were coming tonight! Jesus, why is this happening? Why in God's name-.'

'Is he with you, Esther?' I said, loud enough to startle her. I needed to cut through her rightful distress and get her to focus, quickly. 'Is Billy safe?'

'Yes, he's in the room below our house. Where I put Joe years ago. The safest place-.'

'Can you take him to Agnes'? Once they realise one of them is missing, they might come looking. Might,' I stressed, hearing her gasp and struggle to breathe calmly. 'Esther, as hard as it is, I need you to keep it together. Take him to Agnes'. If they do come looking, they'll go to your house first – so, take him to your sister's. I'm on my way myself. Okay, Esther?'

'Yes, yes,' she replied, doing her utmost to control her breathing and her tears.

'And Esther – what we discussed?'

'Yes?'

'Bring it with you. Okay?'

She paused, a jittery rasping the only sound down the line. I'd triggered a spark of distrust. I knew it the minute the words left my mouth. *Bring it with you.*

'Esther, look, you can-.'

'Yes, I'll bring it, Gus. I'll bring it.'

And the line went dead.

Putting the receiver back in its cradle, I turned my attention to the papers I'd knocked to the floor. Picking them up, I returned them to the table and secured them with an old paperweight – a tiny crab captured in a pebble of glass.

'I'll come back to you later,' I told the papers, before descending and preparing to leave my house for Agnes'.

Esther's boat was already moored out the front. As I rowed closer, I saw something else, too – Agnes' front door, wide open, held back by the weight of the surrounding water. In the old days – *the days of the dogs,* as Papa Harold called them – doors were left open at your own peril and seen as a careless invitation to savagery and death. But even now, with those old threats supposedly removed, a house with an open door was enough to set a heart beating faster – and considered bad luck. And, while I wasn't of a superstitious mind, the sight of Agnes' open house raised my anxiety levels a little. *Had the authorities caught up with them already? Despite warning you early, Esther – had they taken your boy?*

But I needn't have worried about that. No, what I discovered at Agnes' house was an altogether different concern.

'We heard an awful crying,' Billy announced, meeting me at the top of Agnes' first flight of stairs. I took each step carefully. Aware of the level the waters had risen to during the heavy rains, I could feel an algae like slipperiness underfoot. 'Mother said we should be cautious, but I insisted!'

He spoke with a boyish alacrity, boasting with pride at an apparent bravery.

'Is everyone alright?' I asked, reaching him, wondering exactly what the mystery was.

Before Billy could answer, his mother appeared, coming down from the next staircase that led to the bedrooms.

'Do you know about this? Is this why we're here? We haven't time for this! I know she's had a lot to deal with, Gus – but I've got to put my son first today! We've got to get Billy safe! We've got to get him somewhere where they won't come looking!'

I'd had little to do with Esther before – heard rumour of her general disapproval of everyone, and encountered it directly on rare occasions, too. And I was aware of her pious approach to life in general. But what I'd seen over the last few days was very different. The emotions on display completely unexpected. On the previous occasion, her barely restrained grief on seeing Ronan's torn body had been more than evident; on this day, the pain and anxiety concerning Billy's safety dominated. It was in her voice, in the twist of her expression, and running red rivers of her eyes.

I went to reply, but this time round it was Billy who interrupted the flow of conversation.

'Am I not safe?' he asked, puzzled by the whirl of emotions whipping around him.

Had no one told him?

I paused – pulled between wanting to know what Esther was talking about, wanting to get the boy away from there, and wanting to explain things man to man to the little hero before me. I went for the last option.

Aware of the spectre of Esther's fear and impatience behind him, I crouched down in front of Billy, my aged knees creaking just a little, till I was level with the ten year-old's face and began to speak.

'You heard them, right?' I asked, in a hushed tone.

'The airships?' he answered, wide-eyed with pre-teenage innocence and concern.

I nodded. 'Helicopters, I'm certain, Billy. And while I haven't been out there and checked, I'm certain they took your friends from the school. They've been taken away.'

'Taken?' he echoed, his tone lending the word gravity, as if he truly understood the weight and history it carried.

'Yes, Billy. I think they've been taken. It's why I called your mother, it's why she kept you home – brought you here to meet me.'

'What's gonna happen to me?'

'You're going to come with me-.'

'What…' The interruption – a disbelieving gasp – was from Esther.

'You're going to come to my house and we're going to have an adventure,' I continued, ignoring Esther as she tried to interrupt again. 'There's something I'm going to show you – something that will keep you safe. Something that will stop them finding you.'

'And what about the others? Are you going to find them?'

There was so much hope and expectation in that young man's voice that it nearly swept me along – and I nearly caught myself making promises I couldn't keep. Nearly.

'I'm not sure, Billy. If we can – then, yes, of course. But it's not that simple, Billy. You see, I don't know where they are. I've been listening to the authorities. That's a secret between me and you,' I said, leaning in closer to him and lowering my voice further for that annex. 'I've been listening in and hearing their plans. But so far I've got a few things wrong, so there's no guarantee.' I paused, then asked another question – directed at both him and Esther: 'Are you ready?'

Billy nodded – solemn, yet there was still a small spark of keenness. Esther gave her consent in pinched silence – she had no other plan to keep her son safe, but she wasn't conceding that mine was a good one, either.

I had a one word question for Esther: 'Agnes?'

'Just a bit of fuss. Won't come out of her room.'

'We heard cries,' Billy added, wanting to join the drama.

'Just got herself in a state, I think. She's calmer now. Won't come out, but she's talking a bit. Says she's just overtired.'

I toyed with ascending the stairs to her room and checking for myself, but I sensed Esther's urgency to get Billy away from this family abode.

'Are we safe to leave her?' I asked instead and when Esther confirmed with a quiet, measured nod, I added: 'Right, let's get going,' deciding then and there, once I'd got Billy sorted, I'd come back for Agnes – my second rescue of the day.

I was so preoccupied with getting Billy inside – to a place of safety – that I didn't give any thought to the fact Esther hadn't been in my house before. That she was seeing where her son escaped to on rainy days for the first time. The place where he and his absent cousin had explored their imaginations while the rest of their family gathered a few doors down. I'd no doubt both had told stories of the treasures to be found in my multilayered house – though whether someone like Esther had paid them much attention, I wasn't so sure. Catching her face as she crossed the threshold, you could tell she was puzzled and a little in awe – if Billy *had* told her tales, they hadn't managed her expectations on what she'd find.

'I suppose you think it's a bit of a tip?' I asked, lightly though – my tone wasn't accusing. That was another thing I knew for certain about Esther Morton – she and her entire life were clean to the point of clinical. 'Could do with a bit of a spruce, eh?'

'Well,' she announced, neither agreeing nor disagreeing, but needing to voice something all the same.

'You're quite safe, Mother,' Billy offered, sensing the clutter and grime stall her.

He took off his protective mask and began to strip himself of his outdoor clothing as if to prove his point.

'Maybe I could show you around, in a while? Show you exactly where this young man's been spending all his time?' I suggested and she nodded. This proposal seemed to reassure her – at least, it got her further inside my home. She even went as far as to lift the visor from her face.

With the front door finally closed, we were a few steps closer to safety. I got straight to business.

'Do you want to see where I'm going to hide you?' I asked Billy.

In the few minutes we'd spent rowing from his aunt's house to mine, he'd been full of eager questions. Full of sudden stories about the adventure I'd promised him.

'Where are you going to hide me? Is there somewhere in the attic? Or something I've missed – somewhere behind the book cases in the library? Is there a secret room in there?'

As we rowed on, I allowed myself a small smile, despite feeling apprehensive in the open with him. There could be spies on our street – watching us, reporting us as we drifted past their window. Any second, I expected to hear blades whip through the air again, the authorities coming for the boy who'd got away.

'There's going to be no such thing!' Esther had scolded, glaring at me. *Stop filling his head,* it said.

I could've answered, I could've told her that his head was already full – too full – so there was no room left. I didn't. Instead, I'd focused on getting further down the road and inside again.

And once we were safe inside, away from prying eyes, I was able to answer Billy's questions – and quench his sense of adventure – by revealing exactly where I intended to keep him.

'In there,' I said, pointing to the left of the steel spiral staircase that twirled in the centre of my house – to a roughly hung curtain, made of dark orange sacking. Pulling it to one side, I revealed a door.

Billy's face curdled with puzzlement.

'In there?' he echoed, questioning, but not moving, making no attempt to go further.

'Yes,' I answered, unable to conceal a smile, despite our reasons for coming to my house.

'But-,' he faltered, unable to finish his words.

Tiring quickly of our obtuse exchange, Esther pushed between us both and grabbed the door handle, clumsily twisting it back and forth impatiently with her still gloved hand. When it didn't give, I reached out and gently turned it myself, releasing it from the catch.

'Oh, for G-,' Esther huffed, staring ahead, halting her intended blasphemy at the last second. 'Is this some kind of game? A stupid test?'

The door had opened to reveal a very small recess which contained the electricity meter the house ran off. If you weren't looking for anything out of the ordinary, you'd see nothing other than a collection of dials, coloured wires, fuses and red trip-switches – twenty-one in a row. The whole thing encased in a protective black surround, with a glass door that popped open to the touch – watertight, but easily accessible. But if you knew the house, top to bottom, inside out, knew of the different rooms, understood the logic that connected this small black box with the electrical map of the house – well, then you might just query the number of trip-switches.

'Is anyone going to explain it to me?' Esther asked, her impatience rapidly boiling to exasperation.

But Billy seemed to understand what to do – at least, his boyish imagination led him to make the right conclusions.

'Do I press one of the buttons?' he asked, ignoring his mother's protest, and I nodded. 'So which one do I press?'

'Third from the left,' I said, lifting my eyebrows and tipping my head to indicate he should do the honours.

He did, and as the red switch clicked, there was a simultaneous popping sound.

'What next?' he asked.

'Push the wall.'

This came from Esther – she'd finally caught up, was finally calm. We shared a brief look – *okay, you win,* her eyes conceded.

Billy looked to me and I nodded again: 'Go ahead, Billy.'

A gentle push saw the plasterboard wall swing open like a door, the electricity box still attached. We all stared in and saw only darkness, as our eyes adjusted.

'It's just inside, on the right,' I instructed Billy, whose face turned with uncertainty again.

'He means the light switch,' Esther clarified, a tone of irritation returning to her voice.

Billy reached in, and following another click, a dim light from a single bulb gradually illuminated the space, revealing a narrow staircase, twisting down in a tight corkscrew.

'Should I go in?' Billy asked, apprehensive, looking this time at his mother for approval.

'Gus?' she asked, unsure, but certain enough I could provide assurance.

'Yes, you can go in. It's quite safe down there. Watertight, too. The architect knew exactly what he was doing when he designed this place. Careful on the steps, though,' I added, as Billy finally stepped forward. 'They're steep and they get a little slippery sometimes from the cold.' I turned to Esther. 'You'll need to take that bulky gear off, if you want to join us.'

Once Esther had peeled off her protective suit and discarded the gloves and mask, she stepped inside the recess and followed Billy down into the well of my house. Then I pulled the outer door to, pushed the false plasterboard wall back in place, felt and heard it click, and followed behind.

The descent was longer than you'd expect, suggesting you were falling further than just a single floor. When we reached the bottom, both Esther and I panted a little and the thinner, damper air impeded our recovery. But Billy burst into the room with the energy of a newborn's lungs – crying out in excitement at the discovery that greeted him.

'Wow!' he shrilled, eyes wide with joy, turning slowly in a full circle to take it all in. 'Wow!'

Once composed, I think Esther was similarly impressed, although her energy remained preserved.

'It's certainly not what I expected,' she said, a small curve appearing at her lips – not a smile, but a hint she was intrigued. 'Not at all.'

'I knew there was a hidden room when I bought the place,' I answered, looking around, as Billy continued to explore the underground area with glee, forgetting why he was actually in it. 'But I didn't know what it concealed.'

'Didn't look when you came to see it?' she asked.

I shook my head. 'I bought this blind, Esther. I didn't need to see it to know I had to have it.'

'Why? What is it about the place?' she questioned, her curiosity verging on suspicion.

'Do I really get to hide in here?' Billy interrupted, and I answered his enquiry, not his mother's.

'Yes,' I said, taking a long look around, trying to see it all through his boyish, joyous eyes – and it was easy to do.

The total space was large – twenty feet by twenty feet, if I recalled the measurements correctly. No natural light, as you'd have expected, but there were five equally spaced recessed lights in the ceiling – one in the centre, the others in symmetrical orbit; flat and round. The floor was basic – hard concrete, coloured with dirt, dust and time alone. And, while I've no doubt all of these mundane, practical details would've impressed young Billy, it was the rest of what filled the space that gave it life – that made it impressive.

'It's like I'd walked into the past,' Esther would tell me later, once we'd left the boy and ascended to the exposed part of my house. *'Like the floods never happened. A life without the dogs, even. It's a world from old photographs and books.'*

And her passionate response wasn't a bad summary of it all. It *was* full of yesteryear – from the items on display to the sense of hope, the feel of colour it emanated.

It was divided into practical areas. A living and sleeping area, a separate part for cooking and a small box room near the entrance, which housed a cramped bathroom. Billy showed no interest in this last room – he was a boy, after all – but the rest drew him in whole.

The living and sleeping section was at the forefront of the space. On the left side was a small sofa – bottle green fabric given character with a pattern of squares, defined with buttons and dark wooden arms. There was a nest of teak tables and a tall sideboard, too. In its time, the latter item would've been accompanied by a display of crystal and alcohol – glasses, decanter, whiskey, rum, advocaat left over from festive occasions we no longer celebrated. Instead, it was bare – although I suspected we'd find glassware inside, if we opened up its doors. To the right of it was a tall bookcase that stretched to the ceiling

– crammed with classics from centuries past, and I knew young Billy would delight in their foreign stories.

'There's Dumas in there,' I informed him, pointing. 'Jules Verne, too,' I added, eyeing another favourite of the boy's.

To the right of this section were the sleeping quarters. There was a double bed, covered in a purple quilt, the fabric shiny, its domed headboard covered in brown corduroy. Two white pillows lay on each side. To its left was a tall pine wardrobe, with two drawers at the bottom and to its right a plastic white basket for dirty clothes.

And all of it – from the sideboard to the headboard of the bed – all of it was covered in clear plastic. Preserved, like new, never touched – sealing the materials from dust, safeguarding the books from damp and decay.

'You've not been tempted to use this place at all?' Esther asked, running a hand along the side of the bookcase, feeling for dirt.

'Hardly ever been down here,' I answered. 'Once or twice when I first moved in.'

'Once or twice?' she questioned, her disbelief evident.

'I've had no need for it,' I told her, though from her perplexed reaction you'd think I'd explained it in a different language. 'These aren't my needs, Esther – though I can see they might satisfy yours.'

'Well,' she said, rubbing fingers together, releasing dust to the floor, no doubt.

'You can clean in here, if you like,' I offered, silencing her with those few words – a silence quickly filled by Billy, as he discovered more of the place.

'What are all these things?' he asked, moving into the second half of the space – the kitchen area, discovering all manner of knick-knacks and appliances I'd no doubt he'd never seen before. Esther neither.

'Well, shall I walk you through it all?' I offered, stepping forward, feeling Esther follow behind.

The kitchen part was narrow – like a galley kitchen – with a wall of fitted cupboards, its doors light green, with aluminum trimmings at the top serving as handles. There was a clothes horse hanging from the ceiling, hauled up and held in place by a thick, wound-up rope. A collection of metal utensils hung from a row of hooks on the wall. There was a rack of plates in different sizes and an open cupboard displaying bowls, cups and saucers. In the cupboard were supplies – every possible dried or tinned food imaginable. There was a breakfast bar, with two stools tucked under it. And along the sides were a range of never used kitchen appliances – a kettle, a toaster, an electric whisk, a food blender. Esther looked intrigued, amused almost by this display, Billy mostly puzzled. And all of it was safeguarded, sealed behind translucent sheets of plastic like the rest of the room.

'It's like an oversized doll's house,' Esther said, moving in, running hands over the protected surfaces. 'Like one that someone has kept, but never played with. Never understood that, you know,' she added, looking at me, implying it was something else, someone else she didn't understand.

'Really?' I said, finding an end to the cellophane cover on the kitchen's work surface and pulling it back. 'I imagined this might be your ideal home.'

I didn't catch her reaction, as I went about unveiling the rest of the kitchen area, finally allowing it to breathe in the restricted air. Billy began to do likewise in the other part of the room, and Esther quickly followed suit.

'I still can't believe you've never used it,' she repeated, shaking her head, once we were done, a slippery pile of plastic gathered in the centre of the living and sleeping space.

'Like I said, I used to come and look at it, on rare occasions,' I answered, unveiling just a little more of my story to her. 'I was saving it for someone who might need it. Someone who I suspected might show up.'

'Was that me?' Billy asked, although I'd not realised he was listening in.

'Of course, young man – who else?' I answered, chirpily. Who else, indeed? 'Well, I think we should leave Billy to settle in, don't you?' I suggested to Esther – as if I were his ward now, not her. Which, in a sense, I was. 'Give you and me a chance to talk, too.'

It was a loaded statement and, picking up on the clues, Esther nodded and we ascended the tight curl of steps back up to the house. As I pushed the false wall back in place and shut the cupboard door, she panicked for a moment.

'Is he *really* safe?' she asked and the enormous value of what I'd imprisoned in the secret cellar was evident in each word.

'Perfectly safe,' I reassured her. 'Would you like some tea?'

I didn't usually take people to my upper quarters. Billy and Elinor had ventured up there, but not with my explicit permission. Yet, there was something up there I wanted Esther to see – something I'd unearthed, after she'd made a revelation herself.

I was quite surprised, I have to say. While she'd entrusted me with her son's care on numerous occasions – reluctantly or apathetically, I'm not sure which – she hardly knew me. And yet, when I rang to warn her of what I'd discovered – *Esther, you need to get Billy to safety, you need to hide him, keep him from school* – she almost instantly made a confession I'd never have expected: *Gus, I found something. At the flat. I went back. Went through Ronan's things and I found something.*

Gus – no one had called me Gus in an age.

What is it? I asked and when she'd explained I'd no doubt about what she'd found.

And a day later, she'd brought it with her – in a battered brown envelope with the words 'Cadley's blueprints' written on the front.

'Here, take a seat,' I offered, indicating one of two chairs around the small round table I ate meals or studied at. 'Or you can stand,' I added, watching her hesitate. 'The offer to allow you to clean still stands, you know.'

I wondered if I'd get a response of the pinched-lip variety, or whether Esther would indulge a small smile.

'Sorry,' she said, finally sitting, proffering neither. 'You must think me rude. This is all so-.'

She paused, searching for the words. Bizarre? Frightening? Dirty? I had several I could lend her. In the end, Esther's sentence remained unfinished – so, she really *didn't* have the words she needed.

'Here,' I said, offering her weak tea. 'I've nothing to go in it, I'm afraid. My supplier's done a runner.'

She accepted the age old gesture and its accompanying merriment for what they were – a small comfort in the face of unknown adversity. Didn't even flinch at the chip and crack in the cup that held the hot, pale beverage.

'I used to wonder if she'd made it up, you know. For a long time, before it all came out.' Esther looked up at me. 'Agnes,' she confirmed, as if I'd doubted who she meant or what she was talking about. I hadn't. 'Used to wonder if she'd just run away, like the school said. Attention seeking. Trying to take some of the fuss away from her younger sister.' She took a sip from the cup and looked pleasantly surprised by its flavour.

'Darjeeling,' I said, allowing myself a smile.

'Your suppler has got taste,' she said, and I saw something colour her skin – intrigue, questions. She was wondering about me. About this house. About the relative luxury in the well of it that I could simply afford to ignore. About who this strange man was, who'd moved into the strange house at the end of her sister's road.

'You can ask me anything you like, you know,' I said, feeling in the mood to satisfy her curiosity, and maybe settle some of her anxieties a little. 'I'd be worried about leaving my son here, too. With a relative stranger. Especially one who has a house of secret rooms,' I added, sipping my tea to create a break in my speaking.

'Rooms?' Esther asked and we both smiled.

I didn't respond to that particular question, though.

'I think I've got more questions than you can answer, Gus,' she continued, placing her cup on the bare wood of the table, reaching to pick it up again, as if she'd forgotten herself.

'It's okay – it won't leave a mark,' I said, gesturing she leave the cup where she'd first placed it. 'Questions?' I posed, putting her back on track.

'Questions about why they're doing this again. After everything that's happened. Why is history repeating itself? It didn't work last time – children were damaged, or lost for good. My cousins…' Her voice faded.

'Because they can, Esther. That's why they do it. Because they don't have any other answers. Maybe they think they know where their predecessors went wrong.'

'But they're children, Gus. And they took them all. Not just the smart ones. They took them all. We know why they took the smarter children, but what about the others. What are they going to do with them?'

We knew the answer to that – it hung silently in the air after Esther's word left her mouth. We knew exactly what might happen to the others.

'It might be different this time,' I said, reaching a hand out to her, thinking exactly the same as her – thinking of her cousin Joshua – still missing and lost after all these years.

They took them both, Agnes had explained to me. *Ethan for his brains and Joshua for his brawn.*

'But Billy *is* safe, and he's all you've got to worry about, okay?'

'Is he?' she asked, doubts plummeting her confidence. Maybe being at the apex of my house made it worse – accentuating their distance, as he was hidden storeys beneath us.

'You can check, you know,' I told her, standing, heading to the telephone. I picked up the receiver and turned the dial once, finger on the digit *three.*

There was a delay of twenty seconds or so, during which I imagined Billy hunting for the source of the ringing and then doubting whether he should answer once he found it. Eventually, I heard a click and smaller, faraway version of Billy spoke: 'hello?'

'Here you go,' I said, passing the handset to his mother.

Cautious, as if she didn't quite believe in the technology, she took it from me and spoke into the mouthpiece: 'Billy?'

They chatted for a few moments – he giggling with joy, as he described the different things he'd found in his secret den (the books, I've no doubt, had occupied most of his time) and she answering in one syllable sounds, to show she was listening and to mark the gradual ascent in her conviction that all was well. Then she handed it back, composing herself, nodding.

I replaced the handset, poured us another cup of tea each and then we got down to the other business we had to discuss.

'I found them hidden in an old bookcase, not even in his flat, but on the landing,' she explained, as I took the blueprints from the envelope. 'I recognised it as a piece of my mother's furniture, in case you're wondering why I-.'

'I wasn't,' I assured her, interrupting, unfolding the paperwork, scanning it eagerly.

'What do you know about this, Gus,' she asked impatiently, desiring an instant answer. 'Why were you so keen to see them? My house is on there, you know? They mention my address.'

'Mine too,' I said, by way of an answer.

Her brow creased, revealing her puzzlement.

'But I've checked and the map doesn't reach this far – you're not on it.'

'Not on your half,' I answered, producing the papers I'd been reviewing earlier – the second part of the Cadley blueprints. 'These came with my house and I've been looking for the other half ever since I got my hands on them.'

Unfolding the papers, I lay them out on the floor and gestured for Esther to bring hers over, so we could join them at their divide.

'And do you know exactly what they're for?' she asked.

My answer was simple and immediate: 'Oh yes, Esther – I know all about these designs. They're why I bought this house in the first place. Only-.'

'Half of the blueprints were missing,' she announced, finishing my sentence.

'Indeed,' I concurred, studying them as a whole – a frail paper rug spread out across my attic floor. 'Until now.'

We'd been talking around thirty minutes when the phone rang. I answered and heard three words in a hushed voice I recognised: *on their way.* Agnes. A message clear enough that I understood, yet cryptic enough that she couldn't be accused of anything. You never knew who was listening.

'How are your acting skills?' I asked Esther, quickly folding away the maps, sliding them under my bed. 'The authorities could be here any minute. I think that's what Agnes meant. I might need you to play the tearful mother who's lost their child.'

As my words hit the attic space, we were both alarmed – they sounded callous and we were instantly reminded of Agnes' constant grief.

'I think I can manage that, if needs be,' Esther answered, her tone sober, a gentle nod forgiving me for my practical, yet thoughtless suggestion.

She's my granddaughter, you know? I wanted to say, so she'd understand my own pain, realise I wasn't as flippant of thought as I'd sounded. But I couldn't – that wasn't my secret to share.

'Okay, when they knock – *if* they knock – I'll go down and face them. Find out what they want. They won't hear Billy – he's too far down, too well protected and insulated in that hidey hole. But you'd better stay here. I'll only let them up if they insist. And as far as they know, there's no connection between our families.'

'Well, there isn't,' Esther answered, truthfully from her viewpoint.

'So there isn't,' I echoed, hiding my sadness at this lie. 'Right. Brace yourself. A visit from the invisible authorities. What an honour!'

And despite the circumstances, I saw a tease of a smile curl at the corners of Esther's mouth.

But the authorities didn't come knocking.

No one came knocking.

On their way, Agnes had whispered. It had been Agnes, hadn't it?

Some of the old telephones I had downstairs – digital ones I'd fiddled about with in my workshop – they could tell you who rang last, kept a computerised record. But the ones I'd fixed up around the house were even older. More aesthetically pleasing, with their big clear dials and colours of blood red and bottle green. I even had a cream one – grubby with finger prints – hanging in the lower hallway. But I couldn't check numbers – so I had to ring Agnes to establish if it had been her. But she didn't answer – not on my first attempt, second or third.

'Something isn't right, Esther. How d'you feel about me leaving you here?' She seemed hesitant, a little nervous. *What if the authorities finally came when it was just her and Billy?* 'I won't be any longer than necessary. Do you have to be at work or anything?'

'I rang in,' she answered, no sign of protest regarding my departure.

'Okay. And if the telephone rings, leave it. If it's me, I'll cut it off after three rings and then call again. Only answer if it does that. Okay?'

'Okay,' Esther said, but as her pale face looked down after me, while I descended the steep curl of the staircase, she appeared anything but.

The river road was empty of any other traffic – almost as if we were the only people left there. As far as I knew, there weren't many other families with children down Cedar Street – although, as children no longer played out in the road, it was difficult to know for certain. Even so, I'd expected more activity. The noise of the helicopters might have been enough to scare the residents to keep indoors – no one knew for certain who they were coming for – but surely the curiosity of the silence that followed, surely the lure of communal speculation would've eventually drawn people out from the shadows.

Did you hear the noise? Have you heard what happened? It's the authorities, patrolling the area – looking for you-know-what! They've taken the children, I hear. No, no, that can't be true – they wouldn't do that. Not after last time. Would they?

But Cadley Street was still and silent, as a grey evening coloured the grey day a little darker. And not a curtain twitched, not a light flickered as I rowed my way down to number 31.

Agnes took an agonising time to answer her door.

'You've got us worried,' I told her, a scold in my tone, as I dredged my way through her waterlogged ground floor, following her up the stairs.

She said very little in return, and it wasn't until I'd finished with the stairs and taken off my face mask, that I took in her demeanour. She looked worse than I'd expected. I knew she was grieving for our lost Elinor all over again, after getting so close to finding her. And Ronan's savage demise – no matter what he'd done – well, that was enough to scar the hardest of us for a long time. But I sensed there was more – and her sorrowful yet empty eyes told me she was holding something back.

'Agnes, what is it?' I asked, discarding my protective gloves and reaching for her.

'Nothing, Augustus,' she answered, eyes lowered, hands very quickly withdrawn from mine.

At that moment, I heard a noise above – a moaning noise – and her eyes shot up to mine again, abruptly alarmed. I wasn't supposed to hear that.

'Agnes, what is that?'

'It's nothing. No one,' she added, telling me it was definitely someone.

I tried a different tact – and it worked.

'Did you call me?'

'No.'

'But you got a call, didn't you?'

Her eyes retained their startled gaze.

'*On their way*. In a hushed voice. That's what you heard.'

'Yes.' A single word of progress. 'I thought it was you.'

'And I you – so we both recognised the voice. We were both warned.'

We were silent for a second. The house, like the street, feeling abandoned, lifeless. Then I heard the moaning again – gentle, not painful, but not from pleasure, either.

'Agnes?'

Her name in a question was enough to break our deadlock.

'I'll show you,' she answered and led the way – up the stairs, to the very top of her house, into the room I knew she'd shared many a night with her absent lover, Tristan.

Once inside the room, I saw something I'd never expected to see. Someone I'd never expected to see – yes, that might be a kinder description.

'Oh, Agnes…' I said, looking at the figure sprawled over her bed, as further words were lost in my puzzled mind.

'I don't know what to do with him,' was all she said, as we both stared in.

And I didn't have an answer. All I knew was that Agnes and I were guilty of the same crime in the eyes of the authorities – we were both hiding fugitives…

Asleep

I'm back in the cell, but the lights are out – there's no light in the cell and there's nothing shining in from the corridor, through the grill in the door.

All dark – so I can't see a thing.

But I can use my others senses and they tell me something crucial – I'm not alone.

Before I can sniff out my companion or whisper to them through the shadows, I feel a hand clamp across my face. Adjusting to the blackout, my eyes make out a figure, kneeling at the edge of my bed.

'Not a word, okay?'

I nod a promise.

'If I take my hand away, you'll be quiet, yes?'

Another nod of assurance.

'Okay. I'll take it off in exchange for your silence.'

But when the hand releases my mouth, I break my oath in less than a breath.

'Who are you and what are you doing here?' I ask, though my voice is low – inaudible outside my oblong cell.

Despite breaking my promise, I don't feel my intruder's retribution. Instead, she simply answers my question.

'My name is Elinor,' she whispers, confidently, 'and I'm here to rescue you.'

Awake

5. Esther

It was less than a day since I'd gone back to Ronan's and found those hidden drawings, and I was in the same position again – alone in another man's house, left to my own devices. Free to roam, snoop and steal.

I say alone – Billy was technically with me, hidden what seemed like miles below the surface, playing out boyish fantasies in Augustus' wartime bunker.

'It's like one of those old nuclear fallout shelters,' I said to him, once we were up in his attic.

'But with all mod cons,' he added, smiling.

It was the oddest thing – being there. Odder still to be left on my own, while he checked-in with Agnes.

At first, I stayed where I was, in the attic room that was like an old man's bedsit – well, it *was* an old man's bedsit. It probably wasn't as dirty as I suspected, but I'd wondered if this was why Billy had fallen ill more often over the last year, given the amount of time he'd spent there. While it was far from squalid, I could just imagine a place like this luring all manner of disease and infection.

Stop being such a bloody snob! an invisible Agnes scolded me and I felt warmed by this imaginary company.

'I'm just careful, Agnes,' I answered out loud, surveying the attic – the bed, the curtained-off area that was a makeshift bathroom, the books, the little kitchenette. It was a mirror of the room beneath us – but a decayed reflection. My eyes settled on the blueprints, folded again and resting on the small round table I was sat at, and I thought back over what Augustus had told me.

'The man who designed and oversaw my house was called Haydn Cadley. Those with a keen interest in architecture would know of him – he designed many of the town's important buildings and oversaw many of the changes over the years. And this house is named after him.'

'The blueprints came with the keys to my house. "Some old map, apparently," the agent selling the house had told me. "Seller insists you have it." He'd said it as if it was some quirk, some folly of the previous owner. He was never that explicit, but I could just imagine the seller telling him: "make sure he gets the map, okay?" But I knew exactly what it was. I knew what secrets it held. It's one reason I bought the house. I knew about Cadley's design – I was one of just a few who did. And I knew about this secret, too – a secret that was buried along with those who helped him create it. Yet, I'd been alarmed and disappointed to find myself in possession of just half the map.'

'But not anymore,' I'd answered, feeling myself excite a little, as I was drawn to a feeling of adventure – despite the circumstances that had led me to this odd man's company that day. *'And this <u>secret</u> – what is it, Gus?'*

'It's all revealed in these plans,' he'd answered, spreading both hands over the panorama of the map, as if that was enough. Yet, he expanded. *'Your address is on here, right?'*

'Yes, it's marked <u>here</u>,' I said, pointing.

'Ah, so you're connected to this – your house, I mean.'

'Connected to what?' I questioned, still puzzled.

Augustus smiled, showing his yellowed teeth and his pleasure in one action, as he drew out my curiosity.

'Cadley's labyrinth,' he answered, grinning wider. *'You're connected, like I am, to Cadley's secret labyrinth.'*

The mystery call from Agnes had brought his explanation to a pause – *it could wait,* he'd said. We'd come back to it all once he'd checked in on my sister. Since when had this strange old man become the glue that held us all together? How had that happened? I didn't recall. I had my faith – that's what I relied on, to keep everything together in times of trouble. But there he was – this Augustus Riley, rescuing us all from whatever, luring us in with his crazy legends.

'Trusting us in his house, alone,' I said aloud, looking around that attic room, thinking about his invitation to clean it up. But I resisted the temptation. Instead, I took up his other offer – a tour of the place, although I did this in his absence.

While I hadn't absorbed every finer detail of Billy's description of the Cadley house, what I found there was no surprise. Looking closer, from its apex down, I discovered the computer room that Billy had little interest in, the music room where *sounds came out of the ceiling, out of the sky,* Billy had dramatically exclaimed. I just glanced in this latter room – I had no idea how to work the controls, so didn't linger. There were three rooms on the next floor down: a room of children's games and toys; a smaller, oblong space largely occupied by a model railway Billy had raved about; and a modest library. Wall-to-wall book spines created a rich, kaleidoscopic tapestry in this last room – and this and the comfort exuded by two plump armchairs lured me to stay a while. In a house that was otherwise cluttered and filthy, this was a small haven. A secluded delight, tucked away. I closed its door, took a seat and was able to imagine the rest of the place didn't exist. And closing my eyes, cocooned by page after page of famous lines, I imagined them silently floating across the room, dancing round each other like small birds…

'It's a favourite room of mine, too.'

The voice startled me and for a moment I wondered where I was, but the old man's eyes drilling into mine and the cup of tea proffered in the palm of a wrinkly hand soon brought it all back.

'Billy,' I said, realising I'd been asleep, but not for how long. 'I've not checked…'

'He's fine,' Augustus said, softly.

'Okay,' I managed, still coming round, taking the tea, twisting the cup to avoid the chip, as I took a sip. 'And Agnes?' I asked, remembering why Augustus left me here in the first place.

'Yes, she's fine, too. Had to stay a little longer than I'd planned – all's fine, though. Now, we need to think about getting you home. Can't have tongues wagging about the two of us.'

He said it as a joke, chuckling lightly, but sobered when he read my thoughts in my face.

'You can't stay here, Esther. I suggested bringing Billy here in the first place as it's the last place they'd look.'

'But no one was about. No one saw me arrive. And like you said, it's the last place they'd look. And even if they did,' I continued, knowing he was right, knowing I had to leave my child here, but needing to plead my case all the same, 'even if they did, they'd never find him. Not hidden down there.'

'Probably not, Esther,' he said, reaching out, taking my hands in his like an old friend, 'but we don't want to make things any easier for them, do we?'

I conceded with a slow, reluctant nod.

'Now, why don't I take you back down to that hidey hole, so you can say goodbye for today?'

I made it a brief farewell and I was glad that Augustus didn't follow me down into the secret well, glad he didn't see me peel my tearful child from my frame and leave the boy sobbing. He may well have taken my control and composure for coldness, for lack of love – but it was the opposite. I was no use to Billy as a quivering wreck – I had to lead the way, exhibit the very strength and focus he'd need himself.

Once Augustus had rowed me back to Agnes' – where I'd moored my boat – I simply got in it and rowed home as quickly as I could. I allowed the rhythm of the oars in the water – creating small waves – to keep me calm, to help me clear my mind of the many distractions yearning to blur it.

The river roads were spookily empty. Augustus had said as much, once he'd returned from seeing my sister, but he hadn't quite relayed the sense of isolation. The sense of utter abandonment. I didn't see another traveller until I turned into my street. And only a few house lights were on, lighting my way – electricity was an expensive resource, but surely it was late enough to warrant some illumination?

Too early for sleep, the quiet and the dark made me doubt the very existence of others.

But when I turned into Chapel Lane, a very different version of the world awaited me – lights from windows and open doorways sporadically lit up the night, reflecting on the ripple of the river road. It seemed like everyone was out – most dressed in full protective gear. And if they weren't chattering in doorways or leaning out of first floor windows, they were in their boats. Heading in or out? It was difficult to tell. The silence of Cedar Street was contrasted there with loud chatter – a rowdy muddle of gossiping, shouts, tears and heated exchanges. But compared to my sister's road, the most obvious difference was marked by its absence – the children. You see, unlike Cedar Street, Chapel Lane was home to many families – families with children that attended St Patrick's.

'Oh Esther, have you been out looking?' a woman called to me – a mother, shouting from an upstairs window. I could just about see a small child held in her arms.

Emily Hudson. The child was her youngest, a girl – I wasn't certain of her name. Marie, Maisie – something like that. She had a boy, too – Peter. Billy's age, but not in his class. They knew each other through our neighbour, though.

'Yes!' I lied, thinking quickly, wondering how I would deal with their grief, knowing mine was different – minimal, indulgent, even – compared to theirs.

'They've taken Peter, too, Esther! They've taken my boy!'

A figure appeared behind her, drew her inside and the window was closed, but I still heard the howling that grew louder and louder behind its thin glass.

Other neighbours acknowledged my return, nodding or waving in the sorrowful way we reserve for death, for funerals.

'You look exhausted.'

'The evil bastards. They'll pay.'

'We'll get them back, love – all of them.'

'Oh, Esther – we've been worried sick! Has he really gone? Our boy? Is he gone?'

It was Aunt Penny, her voice coming first – from a cluster of three boats – before I saw her figure. She was there with my Uncle Jimmy, who was talking to other neighbours.

'We came when we heard the noise – the helicopters,' my uncle said, breaking his conversation to talk to me. 'When we saw you weren't in, we hoped you'd escaped with him somehow.'

I read his grief instantly – tears in his eyes lit up from the luminous reflections in the water. I could so easily have relieved him of his pain – told him that Billy's fate was not that of Elinor's, Joshua's or Ethan's. That he was safe. But I couldn't risk it.

You mustn't tell a soul, Esther. You mustn't, Augustus had warned me, when I'd suggested telling my aunt. *In desperate times, people do and say desperate things. Someone might try and bargain – with the authorities. Offer them Billy's location, in exchange for their own child. Agnes and I know, but that has to be it. It's too great a risk.*

'Yes, he's gone. They took him, uncle. They took my Billy.'

And in a sense, they had. So, once we were inside – once hot, weak tea had been brewed – the tears came easily, came genuinely. While my aunt and uncle believed our loss to be greater than it was, my grief was still colossal.

You can't just come back here, Esther. You can't just pop by. We have to be careful. You mustn't call here, either. If they've registered he's not one of the taken, the authorities are bound to be onto us. I'll contact you through Agnes – keep our chain of communication fractured.

And with my son all but imprisoned in the dark, yet luxurious well of the Cadley house, this *fractured communication* simply intensified the sense he was gone. That he too had been taken, albeit I was complicit in that heartbreaking act.

'We'll stay,' Aunt Penny offered, as our tears ceased and our tea was finished. 'We won't sleep in Billy's room, that wouldn't be right, but we're not going home.'

But that wasn't what I wanted at all. It wasn't what I needed.

'I'll be fine. Go, get a better night's sleep in your own bed,' I said, yet there was an insistence in my aunt's tone and features. 'Look, you'll be no good in the morning, for searching,' I added, my guilt growing two-fold, but I needed them gone.

'Yes, the search,' Uncle Jimmy echoed, seeing sense.

The proposed search had been the main topic of conversation among my anguished neighbours, before the crowd in the street dispersed. Aaron Nichol, whose son Jimmy went to St Patrick's, was leading on this front. He'd rallied the majority of residents to commit to a thorough search of the city from dawn. And so desperate were so many to take action, to do something practical, that they failed to see the obvious – our children, *their* children were no longer in our city. The authorities, or whoever, had taken them away in the sky – making enough noise among the clouds to alert us all, to ensure we all got the message: our children were gone.

'Yes, yes, you're right – we'll be here early,' Aunt Penny agreed, coming to her feet, shushing her clothes about, needing an activity of her own to occupy her mind, her body. 'And you'll join us, Esther?'

The *yes* was out before I could stop myself. I couldn't avoid joining in – what kind of mother would they think I was? Yet, the thought of continuing my great deception in public was as crushing as being apart from my child.

'Good, we'll call in first thing,' my uncle finished and, after long, loving hugs – a surprisingly tight one from Uncle Jimmy – they were both on their way, rowing west in the darkness, back to *North Courts* and their tenth storey flat. I'd called that place a *disaster waiting to happen* on many occasions – not to them, of course – and yet, as I watched them get smaller and smaller on the river road's horizon, I wondered if that wasn't true of everything we had left. Everything on the cusp of one disaster or another.

Certain they were safely on their way, I drew back indoors.

'You're connected, like I am, to Cadley's secret labyrinth,' Augustus had said earlier, with the relish of a story teller – with almost inappropriate joy, given the circumstances that had joined us together. And yet, despite myself, I was drawn in as he unfolded this dramatic legend and wanted to know more.

With my home empty again, I set out on a related mission, with Augustus' words whirling inside my head.

'There are many stories about Haydn Cadley and buildings he designed. Houses, like mine – grand, with kooky features and hidden places, hidden rooms, even, as you've seen. And like yours, too – modest, ordinary looking homes, if you'll pardon. Stories about what he created under everyone's noses without ever telling them… '

In my kitchen, I took a stool and stepped up onto it. I felt my way along the top of the cupboards, until my fingers touched the cold metal of a key.

'The craziest of the rumours regarded what's become known as Cadley's labyrinth. You've never heard of it? Well, the blueprints you and I have possession of – they're the plans for an underground maze of tunnels... '

I put the key in the lock that secured the door to the cellar where I'd hidden Joe all those years ago – and where I'd hidden Billy earlier that day, when Augustus had first called and warned me of the planned takings. Pulling back, I stepped onto the staircase that would take me down into the well of my own house.

'Cadley had a dream to connect all of the buildings he'd designed or created by a network of underground passages. The maps indicate the houses he chose – including mine and yours. And the rumours have it that each house named on his plans has a hidden entrance to the network – a doorway to the depths of our city... '

Feeling along the wall, there was a switch that triggered a dull light, illuminating the way down. And, as I descended I found myself taking in the details in a way I hadn't before. Looking, feeling, searching for this hidden doorway, searching for a glimmer of truth in the old man's fantasy.

'Look at the detail in these plans, Esther. This man was a fine architect. He knew his stuff. And if it wasn't true, why go to such lengths to hide these blueprints – lest they get into the wrong hands... '

But there was nothing down there but empty boxes that had once held groceries. That and a cracked, plastered wall.

I've not found the way in yet – not from my house, although I'm certain it's in that hidden room. But I keep looking and one day I'll find it – you mark my words. Or it will find me. Yes, that's it – it will find me... '

'Nothing to see Augustus,' I said aloud, confirming it to the echo of the empty cellar, feeling a little sad – seeing the old man in a different light. Seeing him as exactly that – old, maybe even a little frail, hoping for the impossible. 'And what would you do with this secret maze – assuming he built it, Gus? Assuming it got any further than the drawings we possess? What would you do once you got inside?' I hadn't asked him that question though, because I feared he didn't have an answer – he just needed to chase the possibility.

A frantic banging on the door interrupted my thoughts, making my bones jump in my skin. I paused, staying where I was in the cellar, hoping it might stop. But it didn't. My first thought was the authorities – they'd finally come for Billy, for me, after realising he was missing.

Would they really come for him? I asked myself. *All this fuss for one missing child?*

Yet, the rapping was quickly accompanied by a voice crying out, calling out my name, as what sounded like a dozen fists continued to batter my front door.

Monty's voice.

Much as I wanted to ignore it, I knew the noise would be attracting the attention of my neighbours. Some of them had probably seen him, and were wondering why this feared gangster, this flamboyant criminal was at my door – literally battering it down.

So, I climbed the long staircase back up out of my secret cellar, abandoning any hope of finding the doorway to Augustus' dream, and then hurried to the front door – eager to bring the disturbance to an end.

The minute I opened the door, Monty flew in, his bulky figure carelessly knocking into me, and stormed into my home without an invitation. And he wasn't alone. He was squeezing the hand of a young girl and pulled her in with him, her body moving jerkily, as if she was resisting. While his face was red with rage, simmering with anger, hers was equally pink – but through tears. The girl – who I assumed was his niece – had been crying.

'What is it?' I asked, a mix of emotions in my voice – impatience, irritation, weariness. But not fear – not the emotion Monty's presence usually aroused. I closed the door and gestured him upstairs, away from the flood of the ground floor. 'Careful, and please take your outdoor gear off on the landing.'

If he picked up on my tone, he ignored it. Instead, once we were upstairs and he was out of his protective clothing, he let rip what was boiling up inside him.

'They've taken her, the bastards! Bloody taken her! They weren't supposed to! She was protected! Bloody idiots – they've taken her, Esther! Taken her!'

As his rage continued, I looked at the girl he'd brought with him. This was his niece, surely? Although, I hadn't seen her in a long while, so I might have been wrong. But if she *wasn't* Monty's niece, why did he have this child?

'I don't understand,' I eventually interrupted and it brought him to temporary silence. 'Who have they taken, Monty?'

And the answer he gave me struck me as odd. It wasn't what he said – it was what it *sounded* like he said.

'They've got Tilly,' he said – those were his words. But caught in his anger and the thick mucus that hung like string between his teeth, it had a different sound. *Got Tilly. Got Tilly.*

I heard an echo from the past – a name I'd read on a clipboard at the end of a bed.

Got Tilly.

Otterley.

It sounded like he'd said Otterley.

'You have to help me, Esther,' he said next, almost pleading. 'I have to have her back. You have to help me find her.'

I was so caught up with the dramatic storm he'd brought to my house – and still reeling from so many other dramas and emotions from that day – that the obvious questions didn't occur to me at the time.

Who was this girl – distressed and clearly not here out of choice?

Why hadn't she been taken like the others – had he rescued her, like Augustus had rescued Billy?

Why was Monty Harrison here, of all the places? He had money, henchmen, contacts in the authorities. So why had Monty Harrison turned to me, of all people?

And what made him think I could help him?

Even when I did think of these questions, I didn't put them to him. It was too late by then – he'd dragged me into his search for his niece and there was no way back. Instead, I did the thing that everyone did around Monty Harrison – I said what he wanted to hear.

'Monty, what do you want me to do?'

His answer left me almost speechless.

'I want you to take me to Augustus Riley,' he said.

Asleep

I don't quite understand where I am.

The place – if it is a place – has a sense of non-reality.

I'm in a space – a cloud-like, misty space. There's no sense of floor, of ceiling or walls – just a sense of openness. Yet, I'm not floating – there's no floor, but I'm not in the air or anything like that, or suspended. Just in a sense of space that I cannot describe any other way.

I can hear things, though. I can hear a sound, a voice – it's giving instructions.

'Go through the next door,' it says. 'Go through the next door.'

That's when I see it – just ahead. A plain door – white, with a metal handle. I reach out, turn the handle down, open the door and step into wherever. And I feel a strange sense of hope, of joy – as if there's a purpose to this, as if I'm expecting to find something on the other side.

But all that I see on the other side is another door.

Instructions boom from nowhere again.

'Go through the next door,' they command.

And so I do – and this is repeated over and over. One door leads to another and another and another. And, as I step over each threshold, a sense of anxiety, of fear, of loss, of grief creeps up on me. But I just keep going through door after door, unable to stop, panic rising in my chest, and whatever I'm hoping for, whatever I expected to find is always out of reach – always just behind the next door.

Awake.

6. Tilly

I knew about what they'd done years ago – the authorities. I knew about the takings. I was never sure if they were entirely true – or just a horror story from Uncle Monty, a tale to terrorise, told thoughtlessly to a little girl who couldn't sleep. Telling Billy Morton made me doubt it a bit further. There was a look of disbelief in his eyes that said it *surely* couldn't be true – who would do such a cruel thing?

But, as we were herded into that warehouse-like building – with the sound of helicopter blades withdrawing into the distance – I knew without a doubt that it *was* all true.

Every last terrifying detail.

And it had happened again – we'd been taken.

I did my best to keep calm and stay strong, and focused on Peter Hudson, whose face said he was lost in his disbelief. I did my best not to recall all those horrific bedtime tales I'd heard from Uncle Monty – his bulky, swaying figure sat at the end of my bed, a hum of alcohol about him.

And I kept hoping it was different for me, for us.

Kept hoping they'd not be so cruel this time – that they'd learned from their lessons, at least.

But it wasn't quite how Uncle Monty had described it.

In his recollections he'd talked of a big white room, with glaring lights and row after row of desks where the children were tested for their intelligence – completing papers for hours on end. He made it seem like a school – an educational facility, rather than a prison – where you were fed regularly and had your own private room at the end of the day, with soft pillows and clean sheets.

'It's not quite as bad as some of them made out,' he'd told me in the past. *'Some of the kids were better off there, were treated better than at home.'*

'But it was wrong, wasn't it? To take them from their parents.'

He'd stared at me for a few moments when I'd asked that – a long stare that stayed in my mind. Looking back, he was thinking his answer over, carefully choosing his words.

'Yes, of course,' he'd eventually answered. *'Very wrong indeed, Tilly.'*

But what I found the day I was taken, along with my classmates, was an altogether different set up. No bright lights, no comfortable private room, and no sense that any of us were in a better place than home.

Once the helicopters had ascended to the skies, we were marched forwards into the huge warehouse. Inside, it was pitch black at first, but you got the sense that it was a big space, and, when a light was eventually switched on, that was confirmed. As the doors closed behind us, I pulled off my face mask, hoping the air was breathable inside. It was.

I looked up and sensed Peter doing the same, right next to me. The ceiling was dark but seemed miles away, like the sky itself. When I looked down and around, I couldn't really tell what was surrounding us – maybe equipment, but it was covered over with some kind of plastic sheeting.

'What is it?' Peter asked, and I could hear fear and tears in his voice again. I grabbed his hand and squeezed it through my protective glove.

'I don't know,' I answered, before we were given further instructions.

'Down here,' we were commanded by a military voice and then we were on the move again.

The light illuminating the room came from the floor – a flight of steps that led under the building, well lit and a stark contrast to the black lung above it.

'Come on, down you go, move along.'

So we did as commanded, and descended a stone stairwell, blinded by its opposing brightness, and numbed by our fear of the unknown.

I felt Peter grip my hand tighter as we went down and I squeezed it back. I could see this fast growing relationship was going to help us both through whatever was ahead. I'd give him the comfort he needed, the support – and having someone else to look out for, to think of, would help me push my own worries aside. Would give me some purpose to keep going.

And it did.

At the bottom of the steps, we met darkness again, but the lights from the stairwell remained on, so we were able to adjust our eyes. Eventually, the darkness became shadowy, and the shadows became shapes and we were able to make out the map of the room. How had Uncle Monty described the place he'd been in? *A private room, Tilly, with a comfy bed all to yourself.* But in this place, once my eyes had adjusted, it was just one big dormitory – an open-plan space, as vast as the room above us. And the sleeping arrangements didn't look inviting and comfortable – what I saw was a sea of grubby mattresses lined up on the floor, with blankets and pillows, but no clean sheets. No privacy or luxury.

'Find a bed, settle down,' we were instructed and we all conformed – picked out a mattress, stripped off our outer clothing and lay down without being specifically asked. As if we knew that was the next instruction.

Once we were all in place, our protective clothing was taken away – body suits, masks, all of it.

'To stop us leaving,' Peter whispered, but it wasn't necessary. I understood what it meant. Although, I knew the truth – I'd drawn in the air that day I'd been pulled up into the chinook and lost my gold shoe in the clouds. Drawn it in and suffered no ill-effects. But I'd had to swear to Uncle Monty that I wouldn't tell anyone. And, even though I'd not entirely understood why, I'd kept that vow of silence.

It was still early – though we all appeared ready for sleep. It was only afternoon when we'd been taken from school and the flight hadn't seemed that long. So it must've been nearer teatime than bedtime. And yet, I didn't have a sense of time – just a sense of enclosure. Of being imprisoned – by the walls that surrounded me, by the orders that were being called out.

Peter whispered a question that alerted me to something I hadn't realised.

'Where are our teachers?'

He was lying on a bed next to me. Although we'd not been told, we both instinctively felt we'd be in trouble or targeted if we were heard speaking. But his question made me sit up, made me scan our dimly lit surroundings.

The voices that had been directing our movements had been male – deep voices, their confident barks military. Since we'd boarded the helicopter, I hadn't seen Miss Cracker or any of the other teachers who'd originally herded us out of the school building and into the afternoon daylight. Hadn't seen all of our fellow pupils, either – no one from my old class before I was moved, from Billy's class.

'Maybe they didn't come?' I answered with my own question.

'Do you think they escaped, have told our parents, or the authorities?'

I felt an instant need to lie – to help Peter hang onto this thin hope. But I couldn't carry every burden for us – I wasn't strong enough and sooner or later I'd collapse under the weight of it all. So, I answered truthfully.

'I don't think they needed to escape, Peter. I think they're part of this,' I said, keeping my voice low. 'The authorities, too.'

I wondered what he might say – if he'd protest or simply break down again. I reached out for his hand, felt his fingers and squeezed. He withdrew them quickly, rejecting me and my answer in silence.

We both lay quietly for a while and I noticed that other voices around us began to rise a little, and there was soon a gentle hum of conversation. I looked about and realised there were strangers amongst us. It wasn't just my school or my class – there were other children sat upon the sea of mattresses. I couldn't see any of the adults that had brought us in and ordered us to our beds, though. Had they just left us, I wondered?

My question was quickly answered, when suddenly the buzz of voices ceased and I saw a troupe of men – soldiers, I should say, because that's what they all looked like. An army of captors. I saw a troupe of them return – about eight or nine – and they seemed to be carrying large bags, from which they were handing out small parcels. One of them went past us and a package landed on my bed. It was a paper bag containing food and drink.

Peter grabbed his eagerly, tearing it open – and a bottle of something, a small apple and a roll spilled onto his mattress. His dug his teeth eagerly into the roll and only paused from eating when he saw I hadn't touched mine. Instinct had made me hesitate. I'd every reason to fear every single surrounding thing – and no reason to trust at all.

'Why aren't you eating?' he asked me, taking the half-eaten bread from his mouth, the petrifaction evident in his eyes, even through the half-light of the room.

Because it might be poisoned, I wanted to tell him. *Because they might be drugging us.*

But I didn't. Instead, I did exactly what all the other children were doing around me – I gave in to hunger and took a hearty bite out of the apple, poisoned or not.

Reassured, Peter continued with his meagre feast until every morsel was gone.

Even though the men remained in the room while we ate, no one said a thing to them. Not one of us asked a single question about where we were or what was going to happen to us next. No one dared. No one wanted to be the girl or boy who stood out and was punished. So we remained unanimous in our fear and silence.

Once everyone was finished, one of them came by with another bag and we all put our rubbish in it. While this happened, the others came round to ask if anyone needed the bathroom – bringing protective clothing for anyone who said *yes* and taking them back up that brilliantly lit stone staircase. The outdoor garments suggested the bathrooms were elsewhere, in another building.

When they came to Peter and me, we both said no – I didn't need to use it, but Peter's *no* was a lie. He confessed this almost the moment the man who'd asked us had moved on.

'Then why didn't you say *yes*?' I asked, as if I didn't know – an impatience in my voice I hadn't intended. But I could feel myself slowly becoming annoyed with my new friend – a poor substitute for Billy, I wanted him to act a little stronger. Be a little bolder, like my absent buddy would've been.

Where are you Billy? What happened to you?

Yet, Peter didn't speak up, didn't ask to use the facilities even when he saw others being carted off and returned safely, five minutes or so later. There was nothing sinister about this offer to relieve ourselves. Instead, he remained where he was and suffered silently.

Once everyone who needed to – or was brave enough – had been to the bathroom and back, we were left alone again. And the light from the stairwell was extinguished – leaving us in darkness.

It was still and silent for a while and then it began – the whimpering. Nothing out loud, no howling – just a trickle of low whimpers across the room. The pitter-patter sound of homesickness. I kept expecting Peter to join in, and I chanted over and over in my head *stay calm, be patient,* a mantra to stop myself from getting annoyed with this weaker soul – not realising that these negative feelings were distracting me from my own fears. But Peter remained dry and quiet. It wasn't until it had all died down that I heard from him.

'It can't be true,' he whispered through the blackness, a sudden bitterness in his voice that I realised had been building up inside him. 'They'll have escaped. They'll have told our parents. The authorities will save us.'

And with that he was quiet again.

I didn't reply. I just lay where I was, hoping sleep would come. Wishing the tears that I could feel streaming down my cheeks – further dampening the already clammy pillow beneath my head – would stop. Hoping the sob I could hear wasn't mine.

Eventually, sleep did come, although as my body plunged into a heavy nothingness, I twitched and woke for a second. My eyes flew open and I'm certain there was a light on the other side of the room – the opposite side from the stairwell. Only on for a second and in the shape of a doorway. I saw a figure in it – a silhouette, momentarily. A voice – a whisper, female. But it was all momentary – brief enough to make we wonder if I'd made it up. I must have drifted off to sleep again, because the next thing I remember is waking up under the glare of blinding lights…

… I'm in a bed again. It's the past, I'm certain. It's happened – but it's not something I remember. Like it wasn't me it happened to – like it was someone else.

I'm in a big room – a huge attic. I know this because the ceiling is sloped and I can see the rafters. I'm alone to start with. There are tubes attached to me – one in each arm, liquid coming in or going out? I'm not sure. And there are wires attached to my upper chest and the temples of my head. The soundtrack to this experience is the humming of the machines that surround the bed – machines I'm plugged into.

But this never happened.

It wasn't me.

I'd remember, wouldn't I? If this had happened to me, I'd remember it?

Then, something else happens.

Someone comes into view.

From the other end of the room, she steps forward – pushing her way through a barrier of rubber panels that hang from the ceiling and create a translucent wall in the middle of the room.

I pretend I'm asleep, but I can see her.

She picks up something from the end of the bed – a clipboard, with papers attached. Medical notes, I'd guess. Reads them. Utters a name.

Otterley.

Says it as if it's my name.

But it isn't.

It isn't my name at all.

Then she's gone. And next the room fills with bright lights, blinding me….

…It was bright lights that woke me – startling me from sleep, connecting my dream to my new reality. I was still caught up in it for a moment, clinging to it, as it was more familiar than my surroundings. But as I blinked and began to focus, the dream faded, and I quickly remembered where I was, what had happened to me.

With the lights on, the place seemed completely different. In the dark, it had felt dirty and, while the shadows had been disorientating, they'd given the room a sense of decay. The mattresses on the cold floor, the small meal – all added to the feeling this was an old place, somewhere that had been abandoned, was past its best.

But illuminated, the story was different – and it was closer to the tales my Uncle Monty had recalled about the takings from his time. The light came from tubes that were fixed to the ceiling at regular intervals and they made everything seem cleaner, almost clinical – although it was clear this wasn't new and our bare mattresses were stained with age. The walls were a light grey, but I could see marks on them – scratches, scrapes and small areas patched up. The floor was tiled – grey again – and I hadn't noticed this the night before. Hadn't felt how cold and hard its surface was through my school shoes. That drew me to what I was wearing – my school clothes. Trousers, shirt, cardigan – all dark blue, not a uniform as such, just the type of sensible things we all wore. I thought of the few glamorous items I had at home – the red dress I loved and the single gold dancing shoe I'd kept hold of – and felt instantly homesick.

'I wish I was-.' I began, turning in the direction of Peter's bed. But it was empty. Peter was gone.

I quickly scanned the room – searching for him, taking in even more of the details.

Half the beds were empty – the blankets folded with military corners and placed on the pillows. And half were still occupied, with children like me, sat upright, searching the room – perplexed and lost. On the wall farthest away, were several doors – I counted six – and it must've been one of these that had allowed a moment of light to enter the room in the middle of the night, when all else was dark. I'd assumed this was where the grown-ups had gone – maybe where our teachers had cowardly hidden away. But now I wondered if Peter had gone through one of these doors – maybe they led to somewhere altogether different.

A hand on my shoulder shocked my system and I physically jumped, before twisting my head to look. I checked the fingers first – thin, the nails clean and smooth looking – and then made my way up to the face. It was smiling, a little nervously. A young female, with soft skin, blue eyes and blonde hair.

'Where's P-.' I started, but she answered me quickly.

'It's okay, he's gone to the shower block. They all have. The boys.'

I looked around the room again – all the bewildered heads belonged to girls. I saw Olivia White and caught her eye. She just stared, her expression empty.

'You'll all be next,' the woman continued, giving my shoulder a pat, before she stood up and moved on.

'Why are we here?' I asked, feeling a little brave, and less afraid of this female face than I had been of the men who'd ordered us around the night before, in the darkness. 'And what's your name?'

'It's not for me to say,' she said and I heard the uneasiness I'd seen in that initial smile.

'Won't you tell me?' I tried again, sensing something in her. Sensing she might be easily won over, become an ally.

'You will find out,' was all she said though, before hastily walking away, checking on another girl – Jeannie Shaw – three mattresses down. I wasn't sure which question this applied to.

Looking around, there were four others like her. Young female adults, checking on the girls, dressed in light grey overalls. Grey, like the walls and floor. Neutral, harmless – yet that was the idea. That was the feeling they wanted you to have.

When the boys returned – walked back in military style by the men I'm sure had barked at us the night before – Peter wasn't with them. He came back separately another five minutes later and there were two distinctive changes I noticed about him. First, the uniform – like all the boys, Peter was dressed in blue overalls, with a hint of white t-shirt showing at the top. He was still wearing his own shoes. Secondly, I noticed his eyes were red, the skin surrounding them, too – a stark contrast to the rest of his face, which was pale and drained.

'Did something happen?' I asked, as he sat down, silent.

He said nothing for a while – just reached out a hand, which I took. He squeezed hard and, as he did so, squeezed tears from his eyes.

'Just do as they say,' he eventually said, not even looking up at me, somehow shamed by whatever had happened.

Shortly after, I was pulled away from Peter's grip, as all the girls were ordered out of the vast dormitory and marched up the stone stairwell. At the top, they handed out protective clothing and masks, and waited while we suited up. Then, they opened the main doors and directed us out of the warehouse-like building across to the shower block. As we exited, I glanced back, lifted my face visor, trying to see the ground floor in the light of day, but a guff bark made me quickly turn my head to the front. All I saw was a blur of plastic sheeting, covering whatever they had in store for us.

Outside, there was a short walk across a dry, earth-covered yard to the shower block – but it was a longer walk than that from the helicopter to the main building the day before. And, as we were marched towards it, I took in all I could, flitting my eyes from side to side. As I'd noticed from the day before, there was a chain fence surrounding us, keeping us in should we try to escape – not that I had seen any opportunity so far.

To my left, the fencing was close and beyond it I saw other buildings and more fencing – so ours was not the only prison. I still hadn't seen all the children from my school – including the ones from Billy's class. Maybe they were being held there? I couldn't tell how many other buildings there were, but my senses told me that there were many – prison after prison after prison. Later, I would get to see.

To my right, the fencing was further away, like we were at the end of this territory, near the border to whatever, whoever our neighbours were. There appeared to be nothing much to see between the chain links – a barren, dusty landscape, peppered with the odd abandoned item. I saw a wheel from a vehicle, a couple of crates stacked up, but nothing else. The wheel had me thinking – where had it come from, and why would it be nearby? There was something else in that view – something I could barely make out in the distorted distance. Trees. A forest, I was certain. But I only got the briefest peek that day. It gave me hope, though. Trees meant life, indicated water, too – and water might, just might be a way out. A road to home.

'Water,' I heard myself mutter, thinking it odd that the very thing that had destroyed so many lives might be the very thing that led me to safety again.

The showers were warm – I expected to be tortured with a freezing spray – but we had to strip in front of each other and our guards, some of whom were male. And it was another new and embarrassing experience.

Every single thing about the place had the feel of a prison, although it felt like there was no one I could ask what I'd done to get in there. No one to ask what my crime had been.

When one girl made a fuss about undressing, she was impatiently pushed in fully clothed by one of the male guards and soaked to the skin. A female guard intervened, gave the offender a harsh glare and helped the girl out of her wet things. But the damage had been done by then – the girl shook with cold and embarrassment, her humiliation doubled.

No one else objected, though – we took off our things and stepped under the shower heads, no hesitation.

I wondered if something like that had happened to Peter. Had he objected when it came to stripping off in front of the other boys? I could just hear him making such a fuss, angering the guards with his mummy's boy sulk and whining voice.

I pushed these thoughts quickly from my mind – and tried to think more positively about him. Peter was all I had in there – even if he wasn't quite a match for Billy.

Once we'd finished washing and were dry again, we were handed new clothes – white underwear, white t-shirt and blue overalls, similar to those Peter had come back in.

Then we were returned to the other building. On the way back, I tried to take in more of the surrounding view, but didn't risk lifting up my mask again. I didn't want to be singled out like the girl in the shower. So, I didn't even attempt to move it until we were back inside the main building. Then, with the doors closed behind us, we all automatically took them off, as if we'd rehearsed it. Handed back the mask and the bodysuit.

'Keep moving,' we were instructed, so we did – down the well-lit stone staircase, back to the dormitory.

I found my mattress and then I lay down, reaching out for Peter's hand. He responded with a hard squeeze, his nails almost cutting into my skin. I returned it with an equally fierce grip – then loosened it, but hung on.

'You did as you were told?' Peter eventually asked me, his voice uneven, thick and thin at the same time, as if he'd been crying, as if his throat was a little sore.

'Yes, but one girl didn't,' I said, looking about to see if she'd come back with us. I couldn't see her.

Peter was silent for a second, then he spoke again.

'Do you think they're all bad, these people?'

He was glancing around the grey room as he spoke, and I followed his eyes, looking at the guards who were with us. Several of the female ones had returned and were walking between the beds again, checking on people. I saw the one I'd spoken to earlier.

'I hope not,' I answered, clinging to this optimism. 'They can't all be bad, can they?'

'Then why did they take us from our families?' Peter asked, expelling it quickly, like it had been pent up, like it had to come out with speed, before it dissolved on his tongue.

'I don't know-,' I began, but a new development distracted us.

Over by the row of six doors – against the furthest wall – there appeared three men in white coats. They looked different from the other adults with us – their coats made them look like doctors or scientists. The trio had guards flanking them and they seemed to be calling something out. We quickly worked out that they were saying names, as children began to stand up and make their way over. When they had about five or six of us, one of these men disappeared and took the children through one of the doors.

Then we waited again, under the bright lights in that grey room, trying not to think about what was happening, trying to reassure ourselves that we were safe, that there was a perfectly reasonable explanation. But I only had to think of Peter's tear-stained face, or the girl pushed under shower in her clothes, and I knew there weren't.

I don't how long it was before they came back – it seemed like forever – but the man who'd disappeared rejoined his *scientist* friends and the calling out of names began again. This happened five times before they called out for Peter. I know this, because I'd been counting in my head, to kill time. Counting out the number they took, working out just how many groups of five or six they'd have to call up before the room would clear.

When he heard his name, he stood up instantly – no delay, no disobedience. Whatever had happened to Billy when he'd been taken to the showers – a harsh scolding, a smack on the back of the legs for disobedience – it was enough to guarantee he didn't put a foot out of line this time. On command, he'd simply come to his feet and almost marched towards the men. The only thing he did that wasn't part of the instructions was to turn his head back quickly and mouth me a message.

Remember your name.

I was puzzled initially, but then it quickly sunk in.

I wasn't who I'd said I was – Tilly Harrison wasn't supposed to be there.

And suddenly I wondered if I'd missed my chance – if my name – if Marcie Coleman's name had been called and I'd not been listening. I'd stopped playing the game we'd started up in our classroom – the one we'd started when we realised we had a stand-in teacher. What was her name? I'd forgotten it already, but I could see her face. Her scared face, as she'd looked into the sea of pupils, all eager to drown her in wave after wave of pranks and mischief.

'What did she have to be scared of?' I asked myself, and that's when it started – the tears. And, like the floods at home, like the endless days of rain we'd recently had, once the tears had started they wouldn't stop. I couldn't stop them. To muffle the noise, I put my face down into my pillow and suffocated them, biting my pillow as my whole body shook and writhed in distress. The whole time the words that had triggered it all – *what did she have to be scared of?* – circled in my head, like a torturous mantra, encouraging the sob of misery, every time I nearly settled. *What did she have to be scared of, what did she have to be scared of, what did she have to be scared of?*

'Marcie?'

The question and the name startled me, and it was accompanied by a touch – a hand gently rubbed my back, as if to reassure me.

'Marcie Coleman?' the voice asked again and this time I looked up, faced the person talking.

Remember your name, Peter had said and it was time to take his advice.

The voice belonged to the woman I'd spoken to earlier – the nervous one with the kind face, who'd told me I'd find out why I was there. And I felt a little safer – somehow just her face and her softer voice had that effect. But what she said next robbed me of that reassurance.

'You're not Marcie, are you?'

The woman looked into my face, into my eyes, studying them, and then back to something she had in her hand – a clipboard with a piece of paper on it. She turned it towards me, so that I could see what she was looking at, what had given the game away. We'd fooled our stand-in teacher – Miss Douglas, that was her name, Miss Douglas! – but there was no keeping the truth from this woman. This *guard,* I quickly reminded myself. See, she had the truth in black and white. And written on her paperwork were details that couldn't be refuted – one set of details in particular.

'Marcie Coleman has brown eyes,' she said, dropping her voice, looking directly into mine. 'Not blue. So,' she annexed, lowering her body down and sitting on the mattress opposite – Peter's, 'if you're not Marcie Coleman, who exactly are you?'

I was silent for a minute for two – surprised to find myself caught out, but also caught up in my thoughts about what to do next. The natural thing would've been to tell the truth, but something stopped me. Marcia Coleman had been taken out of our class and she hadn't come with us – because they thought she was *me*. And Uncle Monty would've arranged this, I was certain – just like he'd arranged for me to be put down a class, for a reason he'd kept secret.

Secrets.

There were always secrets.

It was clear he hadn't wanted me taken – hadn't wanted me to end up here. Maybe it was for the obvious reasons, but maybe there was something else, something I didn't know. And *maybe* it was best that I didn't say who I was.

But, if I wasn't me – if I wasn't Tilly Harrison *or* Marcie Coleman, who was I?

'What is your name?' the woman said, pushing me to answer, impatience growing in her voice.

I needed to think.

'I'll tell you,' I told her, trying something out to buy time, 'but first you'll need to tell me what we're doing here. Is that a deal?'

The woman paused for a while – like me, she was thinking through her answer, her face creasing with anxiety. Then, she nodded and her face relaxed again, taking on the kinder, nervous look it'd had earlier, when I'd first met her.

'It's a deal,' she answered, her voice a little shaky, less certain.

But what she told me wasn't what I'd suspected at all.

What she told me changed all the assumptions I'd made.

7. Jessie

Our adventure began with a story – a story from Tristan's guarded past, under the cavernous canopy of the church we were repairing.

'Years ago, before the floods, before I left this place the first time round and before I knew you, I worked in a tiny shop in the Atrium. *Albert's Film Emporium,'* Tristan had told me that day, unfolding his tale with evident resistance.

I remembered the place vaguely – a small specialist film shop, rumoured to have a tiny cinema out the back that played specialist, arty films.

'After hours, Albert ran a kind of film club – just people he'd invited,' Tristan had continued, mirroring my memory. 'He never confirmed what his motive was for running the shop – it didn't have a great commercial pull from what I could see and it was expensive to lease in the Atrium. Maybe he got a good rate? You never knew with Albert – in the years I'd known him, on and off, he'd always fallen on his feet. Maybe he simply had a great passion for film, and making money – if he made any – was incidental, a bonus. Who knows? Albert and his motivations had always been a mystery to me. That's where I remember him – your *Father* Neil.'

Father Neil was the man who'd hired us for the job in the church – a man to whom Tristan had shown immediate scorn, but initially denied that he even knew him. Eventually Tristan admitted the truth – this man was connected to the disappearance of Albert. That wasn't all – Albert had been reported drowned, just like Elinor. And, as with Elinor, Tristan didn't believe a word of it.

'No body has been recovered,' he told me, as I listened to his tale, and more and more secrets about Tristan's past unfolded.

He confessed he'd come back to the city looking for a terrorist – a man he wouldn't name. But he suspected this man had been protected by Father Neil – harboured in a church, just like the one we were in at that moment. And he also suspected this unnamed terrorist was responsible for Albert's death.

And it would've all seemed so farfetched, so unlikely had it not been for one single revelation.

'Albert was my father, Jessie.'

Those five words somehow made me believe it all – and helped me make up my mind. I would do something to help Tristan – I'd get back out there and search for Elinor, search for Albert and search for someone else, too. See, he wasn't the only one of us to lose someone. In the dark times we'd survived and in the dark times we still endured, there was loss all around. So much loss, we drowned in it as much as we drowned in the waters. I had a twin brother, Joe – a man who walked out on his family one day without leaving a note, without having a reason, from what I could see. And listening to Tristan, I felt a new determination to get some answers of my own.

The dogs were what finally pushed us.

Always the dogs behind everything.

Another lifeless body was found floating in the waters – another puppy, despite a long-term ban on breading. Despite the fact they were supposedly extinct. Another cover up.

'We can't just leave this, Tris,' I told him, three days before the end of our church job. 'We've seen stuff, uncovered a part of this, maybe. Can't ignore it any longer. We need to get back out there, Tris. Check out the other labs. Do what Monty asked us to do in the first place.'

Monty Harrison – a dangerous man I'd stupidly decided to do business with. Despite what I knew. Despite the fact my twin, Joe, had worked for him and I knew the ins and outs of his criminal empire, knew the lengths Monty was prepared to go to when protecting it. A man I had lied through my teeth to. I'd promised to show him an abandoned laboratory full of canine corpses, but led him on a wild goose chase to a different one instead. Later, Tristan and I had gone back and torched the lab where we'd found the mass graves of dogs – and then laid low for a few days. Of course, Monty knew. He'd not been fooled. And he'd had us followed – had video footage of us raiding the building where Tristan and I had uncovered hundreds of tiny dead creatures. Innocent looking in their infant form, yet still a chilling sight. I'd no idea what someone like Monty would do with a room full of dead dogs. But he had money, and money meant power – especially when hardly anyone else around had any. And he was a maniac – who knows what he'd do with the bodies, what he'd think to do with their DNA. It was unthinkable – and yet a possibility. Everything was a possibility with Monty Harrison.

I kept thinking of our betrayal of Monty. Kept thinking of the tape marked *security* that he'd sent us, wondering exactly what he intended to do. His message was a simple *I know.* But his retribution would be anything but simple.

Before we could leave, there were people I wanted to see: Billy, my nephew – Joe's only child – and Esther, his mother. Tristan also wanted to check on his partner, Agnes.

She had just returned to work since Elinor's disappearance, and he was concerned about her wellbeing.

Once this was done, we went back to mine and prepared for our adventure into the unknown.

Thinking back over Tristan's revelations about his father, as the speedboat cut through the waters, I thought about my own parents.

Long dead, to my knowledge – taken during the Great Drowning. They were down by the Black Sea that day, where the devastating tsunami hit the city first, and were swallowed up with so many others in its wet, merciless jaws. Their lives consumed in a cold instant. I'd never thought to look for them – never thought to hang onto the slightest hope I was wrong. And this thought, tinged with small regret, strengthened my resolve to help Tristan find his father – and to find Joe, my twin.

Once back at my house, as we worked through what we needed to take – food that would keep us full, containers of water for our hydration, clothes and blankets to keep out the cold – the video tape we were sent continued to play on my mind. It didn't feel right leaving it behind. I imagined someone breaking in, taking it out of curiosity and it ending up in the wrong hands. Although, it was probably *already* in the wrong hands. It was always a risk leaving your home for any length of time – raiders were keen-eyed and in plentiful supply. And people knew I had stuff worth stealing – my tools alone were worth the risk, the rare consumables I sourced from various suppliers also. So, as I gathered up the tools and survival essentials we might need for our trip, I picked up the video of Tristan and me and took it along for the ride.

'There'll be other copies, you know,' Tristan commented, seeing me wrap it up in one of the blankets.

But I didn't comment. I was doing all I could to keep this under wraps – but if Monty Harrison had made copies of our illicit activity, what could I do? It was out of my control. But this one copy I had wasn't – and so I took action where I could.

I dropped the last bag of supplies into the boat and then secured my house, before stepping back into its small well and starting up its engine.

'We'll go as far as half the fuel will take us,' we'd agreed. My speedboat had a full tank and I had enough containers on board to fill it twice again.

'So that's a tank and a half – and then we turn back?' Tristan had questioned, and I'd answered with a small change to our plans.

'And then we stop and think,' I said and a nod from him said he approved – we'd keep it open ended, we'd decide as we went.

To start with the territory was very familiar – we continued on the river road, north-west, speeding past a blur of fir trees on both sides, slowing up as we neared the laboratory we'd burned to the ground. Gliding through those waters, we both scanned our surroundings, checking for anything we'd missed – anything that had changed since.

'Hard to tell without stopping and getting off,' I said to Tristan, but we both agreed we'd stay on the boat. 'It was dark when we left it.'

But it was as you might have expected a charred, wooden construction to look in the early morning light. I took a pair of binoculars I kept on the boat, pulled up my protective face visor and zoomed in on the detail from our point of relative safety –

scanning the scorched remains for traces of anything but fire damage. For traces of the bodies we'd destroyed.

'Anything?' Tristan asked and I shook my head.

'Just ash,' I answered, taking the binoculars from my eyes. 'We did a thorough job, given how damp it is out here. Too good a job.'

Tristan questioned the doubt in my voice.

'What do you mean?'

'I'm not sure, Tris, but we set out to destroy, right? Burn those bodies, but we'd never have expected to cover it up. Never have expected every single one to burn to nothing. Take a look.'

I handed him my pair of magnifiers. He pushed his face mask above his forehead, just as I had, giving himself a better chance of a clear picture.

'What do you see?' I asked him after a couple of minutes.

'Like you said – ash,' he answered.

'And no bones, no teeth, no fragments of anything that would give you a clue that anything other than wood had been in that inferno?'

'Nothing, Jessie. No clues at all,' he said, dropping the binoculars, letting them swing from his neck. 'Maybe we just got lucky, eh?' He paused, letting it sink it, then added: 'Shall we move on?'

I agreed, cranked up the engine and we sliced through the waters again.

If someone had been back and finished off what we'd started, I didn't want to be around to find out who they were.

I'd travelled a little further down the river than that first laboratory and was certain there'd be more buildings of a similar nature along the way. I was right – several miles along was another one.

'Whenever I do this salvage work,' I'd explained to Tristan, 'I usually have several locations – reserve locations, with nothing in them, in case whoever I'm doing business with tries to get ahead of me and do the salvage work themselves.'

I was talking in code and Tristan knew it. By *salvage*, I meant stealing on this occasion – and stealing from the authorities. And by *whoever* I meant Monty Harrison – it was always Monty Harrison.

'Is this one you checked out?' Tristan asked, as we approached the building, slowing up again.

'No, I've been past this before, but it wasn't one of the labs I had up my sleeve, if Monty had wanted an address or a visit. It looks similar, though.'

'Government property?' Tristan questioned and I conceded with silence. 'Take a look?'

I paused, cautious. We'd come looking for answers – but we'd been filmed at the last location. What's to say we weren't being filmed again? Reading my thoughts correctly, Tristan made a fair observation:

'Or,' he said, as if posing an alternative plan, 'we could just keep going, looking over our shoulders the entire trip.'

He'd made his point, so I stilled the engine and he tied the boat to the mooring at the end of a small muddy path leading up to the laboratory. From the outside, it looked like the other labs I'd seen over the last few months. A wooden construction, built above the current water level, as if in preparation for the flooding that had taken us all by surprise. A small set of steps led to its front door. It was this door that first alerted us that something was different. The sound it made – a gentle bang-bang-bang, as the breeze knocked it against its frame.

'It's open,' Tristan said, pausing.

I'd broken into the other buildings on my first visit – installing my own locks afterwards, to keep my finds secure. But I hadn't been inside this one before and the open door – a blatant absence of security – was suspicious.

'Should we go in?' he added, looking to me for an answer.

'We've come this far, Tris.'

So, brushing all thought of caution aside, we entered the lab. Like the others, there were several rooms within the structure and most of them were set out in classroom style, with rows of parallel benches in the middle and cabinets around the edges. But, apart from these bulky items of furniture, they were largely empty. As if someone like us had already been in and raided the place, or like it had been swept clean, like a house sold onto a new owner. It was bare. Every single room emptied – but a while ago, that was clear.

'Covered in damp dust,' Tristan commented, running a hand along one the benches, clumps of grey filth sticking to his protective gloves.

'But nothing else to see,' I added, thinking.

'Apart from the unlocked door, maybe?'

I shrugged.

'There's nothing in here to take, Tris, so maybe no reason to lock up after you'd left.'

'But this is a government building, right? No doubting that. And it would be standard procedure to lock up, leave their premises secured – empty or not.'

I had to agree.

'So someone came in here, then. And they came in here for something.'

'But what?'

'Let's keep looking, Jess.'

So, that's what we did – going back through each room. Feeling for loose boards with our heavy boots, hoping we wouldn't find any. The last time we'd lifted the floor of an abandoned government building, we'd found a mass grave of canine corpses – a sickening discovery I couldn't stomach to re-encounter. We felt under the benches for anything secured there, any hidden clues. We went through the wall-to-wall cabinets again, double checking they were empty – and that's where we found it.

One of the cabinets was locked. This hadn't bothered us too much during our first search – but on our second tour of the place, it stood out as the only one with locked doors. I sent Tristan back to the boat for a hammer with a hook and we forced it open in seconds. Inside, we found an unexpected item that surprised us – a television with a built-in video player. The sort of thing old Man Merlin would've had in his cluttered house. And lying on top of it, we found another tape. Unlike all the other items in the laboratory, the cassette was clean – not a speck of dust on it, suggesting it hadn't been there long and, like the other tape, it had the word *security* written on its casing.

I felt sick with nerves, wondering exactly what kind of game we'd been drawn into.

'Shall we play it?' Tristan asked, unnecessarily – there was no way we were walking away without seeing what was on it.

I felt to the right side of the television, pushed the *on* button, watched its screen flicker to life, pushed in the tape and waited to see what we'd been filmed doing this time. It had to be Tristan and me, didn't it? Another warning from Monty, right? But it wasn't us at all.

Tristan and I watched closely as the film ran, trying to work out what we were seeing.

A panoramic shot of trees, a dense forest – blurring as the film picks up speed. Then it slows down and the view changes – a river road comes into view and remains the main focus for a while. There are trees on both sides of the river.

'That looks like the road we're taking, Jess.'

'They all look like that, Tris. Could be any number of the roads in these parts.'

Suddenly, the river road widens, the trees disappearing and the shot is of open water. The film speeds up again, suggesting a vast area is being covered in seconds. Eventually, there is something on the horizon. There is land ahead. And, as the film reaches the shore, it slows and the detail comes into focus – a man and a woman, stood at the water's edge.

We squinted and automatically moved in closer to the screen.

'Can we go back a bit, play that again,' Tristan asked, and I played about with the controls on the side of the television – found the rewind button and wound it back several frames. Pressed play, then paused it exactly where I knew Tristan wanted me to.

We shared a long look before either of us spoke.

'Where do you think that is?' Tristan asked, as we continued to stare at the juddering, frozen frame.

'I don't know,' I answered, feeling my breath shorten, my pulse quicken, 'but I can't quite believe what I'm seeing. Can you?'

Tristan shook his head in reply, then posed another question: 'Should we watch the rest of the tape?'

I took the film off *pause* and let it roll. It quickly cut out, fading to a black shot, with lines of interference giving it character. I turned away, stunned what we'd seen, numb with shock, but as I did, Tristan caught my shoulder and turned me back.

'Look,' he said.

On the screen was a static message: *keep looking.*

'What does it mean?'

'I don't know, Tris.'

'Can't be Monty, can it?'

I shrugged, displaying uncertainty, but I knew the answer. 'No, I don't think it can. Not this one.'

'And the other one – still think that's Monty?'

'Too much of a coincidence?' I suggested and Tristan nodded, adding:

'Was there anything at the end of the other video?'

'No, there wasn't, but-.'

'But?'

'Wait a minute.'

I briefly left him, returning to the boat to retrieve the film again. Then we watched ourselves again, as we raided that first laboratory. This time, when it faded away to a blank black screen, we let the film play on until eventually the same message appeared: *keep looking.*

'Think we've had this wrong all along?' Tristan said, as I ejected the first tape, and put the second back in. I had to see it again – had to see if I could actually believe what I saw.

'Well, the message at the end confirms these are both from the same source,' I said, trying to contain all my emotions, as I anticipated watching the unbelievable scene again. 'But it doesn't quite add up. The first one seemed like a threat, but this second one – it's something...'

I lost my words completely, as the film played again – reaching its end on that unknown shore. And there was the image that had silenced us both: the man and woman, standing still, looking directly at the camera, and a docile looking creature laying peacefully in front of them. A dog. Seeing it the second time, my shock was double-fold, almost paralysing me.

'It's like it's something else, another world,' Tristan said, finishing my sentence for me.

But he was only half-right. Yes, seeing the creature – calm, tame, domesticated – did give the film a sense of other-worldliness, like a picture from a long-forgotten past. But there was something else in the footage that was messing with my head – something that couldn't have affected Tristan.

'The man and the woman,' I said, finding my voice again, bringing him up to speed with what I could see. 'I know them.'

'Who are they?'

I took in a deep breath and, as I exhaled, felt the water pierce through my eyes.

'My mother and father.'

Another pause hung between us for what seemed forever, before Tristan broke it:

'What do you want to do?'

There was only one answer. We took both tapes and left the laboratory, checking our surroundings every step of the way. Whoever was behind this could be watching us – *had* to be watching us. How else could they have been certain we'd come across this second tape? Back in the boat, I hid both in the centre of a tightly folded blanket and started the engine up again.

'What do you want to do?' Tristan had asked, but the answer had already been given in that closing message on the tapes: *keep going.*

'Until we find them,' I'd annexed, speeding down the river road, flanked on both sides by forest, hoping this was the road on the film, waiting for the river to widen and for that unknown horizon to appear. 'Until we find them all…'

Asleep

It's early morning – cold, the sun still low, but light enough to see my surroundings.

I'm outside and walking – my feet feel heavy, so I look down to them.

Mud – as I draw my eyes up from my feet and look ahead, I see mud stretching for miles. The land is bleak – nothing but sodden earth and stones as far as I can see.

But there is something ahead.

Something sticking out of the endless sea of sludge.

I move towards it, although my progress is slow, the grime sucking me in, sucking me down at every step.

At first, there's more of it sticking out – I can see arms, shoulders, a neck and a head. It's wet and covered in brown slime, but I know they are alive. They are crying out, arms flailing frantically as I gradually get closer.

But the mud stops me getting there soon enough, and, at each slurp – as I pull my feet from the sucking sludge – they are dragged deeper into the sinking pool.

The arms, the shoulders, the neck and head and finally the hands – waving to alert me, a sad, slow goodbye.

But I keep going, edging my way to where they disappeared.

And when I reach the spot, desperate with tears, something happens that makes me gasp in shock – a hand reaches out of the thick, dark pool and pulls me under.

Awake.

8. Augustus

I wasn't expecting visitors. Not that late at night. And not Esther, either – I knew she understood the risks of coming back without thinking it through, of not trusting me to look after her precious boy. So why was she risking it all so soon?

I wasn't expecting her companions, either.

The girl was a stranger to me, a similar age and build to Elinor – so much so that when I glimpsed her on my security camera, for a second my heart jolted. Had she returned? No, no – it wasn't *her*. Our girl was still lost.

Then the man came into view, confirming what this late night visit might be about after all.

Him.

Monty Harrison.

'Well, well,' I muttered to myself, thinking about my next move, as Esther pounded at the door, panic and fear in her blows, 'what took you so long?'

It had been an exhausting day, and I thought I might simply crash into sleep when I got back from seeing to Agnes. My bones were dog tired – but my mind was zipping with energy. What I'd found at Agnes' had astounded me and I'd struggled to hide my shock and remain composed.

'I had to take him in,' she'd explained, as if she read disapproval in my eyes. *'If someone else had found him... If the authorities had...'*

'Yes, yes, I understand,' I'd reassured her, and I meant it. I'd have done the same. But still, she was taking a huge risk.

There was little I could do there and then – we both needed to think, really. Time to consider exactly what we could do with the wretched creature at her house.

I did have one immediate question.

'How did he get here?' I asked, perplexed.

'He came out of the flood,' she said, making her guest sound mythical, like some legend born out of the seas.

'Okay, I'll be back in the morning,' I promised, departing, *'to check on you both.'*

But Agnes' situation was only a third responsible for keeping my weary body alert that evening. Another third was taken up by the young man hidden in my bunker – Billy.

When I'd returned from his aunt's house, I'd fully secured my premises and then checked in on him. I found him on the bed, immersed in Jules Verne, but he was easily distracted by my arrival.

'Is Mother with you?' he asked, with an eager excitement that would quickly diminish when I answered.

'Gone home,' I said, adding: 'you're safer that way, Billy. How have you settled in?'

And he was a good boy – playing along with my game of questions and answers, designed to keep him brave, to keep him focused on the important things.

How have you settled in?

What food have you eaten?

What book will you read next?

What's your favourite part of this adventure so far?

All engineered to keep those tears at bay – and to keep my own emotions in check. I couldn't allow sentiment in – it would so easily overshadow what we needed to achieve.

And he gave it a fair crack, did Billy. Answered every single one of my enquiries – including my last: *Is it alright if I leave you now, for the night?* He lied with his lips – they parted to release a *yes* – but his eyes held me with their truth. He was terrified. And it had been such a difficult few days – dealing with Ronan's death, hiding his savaged remains in the train graveyard. And then this – his friends taken and his mother kept away. A lot for the young man to deal with.

'You'll be fine, I promise,' I said, patting his hand, leaving him to settle for sleep. There was little else I could say or do. 'And just call if you need anything. Okay?'

He nodded an *okay* back and then I left him, ascending all the way up to my attic, where the thrill of my find – the second half of the Cadley map that Esther had discovered at Ronan's – drew my attention. And it held onto it too, fueling my imagination with endless thoughts and questions – until the knocking on my door and the image appearing on my external cameras took precedence. Esther, a girl and a face no one wanted to see this late at night – Monty Harrison.

I had to think quickly.

That man turning up here, after all this time – and on the day so many of our children had been so unapologetically taken. It couldn't be coincidence. And it could only be bad news.

For me.

I had an instant dilemma – if I allowed the banging on my door to continue for too long, I'd attract unwanted attention from my neighbours. I couldn't afford that – not with the boy hidden in my house. What if someone called the authorities? *And* I didn't want anyone seeing who was at my door – didn't want to be associated with the man accompanying Esther.

But it wasn't simply a case of calling out that I was on my way – or releasing the locks I controlled centrally and letting them in. I needed to be in the right position before I did that.

I crept from my attic room and took myself down the corkscrew stairs that bore their way through the centre of my house, switching off the lights on my way. That was enough to stop Esther's knocking – they now knew I was here and that *something* was going to happen. Once on the ground floor, I drew back a curtain that covered the recess on the right side of the staircase – the opposite side to secret basement entrance. Behind that was another door that I unlocked. Opening that, I stepped inside and felt my way in the dark. It was in there that the house controls had been stored. The flick of one switch would cut the electricity completely – and in turn release the central locking that kept my home secure.

Cadley really had thought of everything when he created this little fortress and, on moving in, I'd made only the smallest of adjustments. As well as the central locking system, the secret doors and rooms, it had its own solar powered generator – although it took a long time to regenerate in our current climate and I used this free energy source sparingly. I'd introduced the security cameras and the internal telephone system myself. Once I pushed down the main switch, there would be a delay of ten minutes before the generator kicked in and the lights and everything would be available again.

Ten minutes to make all the right moves.

Ten minutes to outwit Monty Harrison, get Esther and the child away from him and find out exactly what was going on. At least, that's what I hoped.

Ten minutes in complete darkness.

I flicked the switch, waited and listened.

'Try that door again!' I thought I heard Monty hiss, after a minute or so – and it must have been something like that, because seconds later the door popped open at a push and they all made their way inside.

I next heard the sound of light switches being flicked on and off.

'No bloody electricity,' Monty cursed, as I counted the number of times he'd tried them – five.

That was: on-off-on-off-on. Damn – as soon as the generator started up, the hall and stairwell lights would be back on, exposing us all. I had to move swiftly.

'I know you're in here, Augustus,' Monty called out, coming further into my house, passing the curtain I was hidden behind.

Fleetingly, I considered reaching out for Esther and drawing her into the recess with me, but I couldn't risk alarming her and exposing myself. I either had to find a way to warn her what I was planning – or I needed to get to Monty, somehow disable the man. And the latter was no option – my elderly bones were no match for his younger, meaty physique.

A flash of light flickered past me, speeding along the weave of the curtain. So, Monty Harrison had a torch – an advantage my hastily constructed plan hadn't considered.

And suddenly, it seemed a little harder. But then Monty's next move looked like it might help me out.

'You know I'll find you, Augustus,' he continued, his one way conversation gaining a little echo and I heard his shoes tap the steel of the staircase. He made his way up. 'You might've thought you'd been hiding in plain sight all these years, but I knew where you were. I'm a good man at heart, you know. So, I've just left you be. Left an old man alone to grow older, despite the trouble he might make for me. But now I need you, Augustus.' His voice was fading, a sign he was closer to the apex – and I began to think it might be safe for me to come out of my hiding place. 'Yes, Augustus old pal, now you're going to help me get something of mine back. Something you've been looking for and something I've had all along.'

Despite the situation, I found myself listening. *Something you've been looking for.* Could he mean what I thought? Yet, he wasn't a man to be trusted. And I had to think of immediate, pressing concerns – such as getting Esther and the unknown child to safety. When I'd seen Esther's face on the security camera, she'd been clearly distressed. No, I had to put her first – anything else I would come back to.

Careful to make as little noise as possible, I lifted the curtain back and stepped into the hallway. The girl and Esther were lit up despite the darkness – they were further into the house, creeping towards the back room and the moon was shining through windows to the rear, revealing their silhouettes. I saw the girl's outline turn in my direction and I held my breath in an instant. Would she cry out? Would she reveal my whereabouts with a sharp, innocent cry of fear? But she did neither of these things. Instead, I saw her shape tug at Esther's sleeve. As Esther's shadow-head turned, the girl lifted an arm and silently pointed a finger in my direction. In response, I beckoned them forward, hoping they could work out my signals, even though there was no light behind me to illuminate my shadow-play.

'Augustus,' Esther breathed with instant relief, not out loud, but not in complete silence – not thinking. And the big man above us was alerted.

'What was that? Esther – was that you?'

I saw her shadow wince at her careless mistake.

'Just trying to find him,' she tried out, hoping to fool him, but my experience told me Monty Harrison wasn't that easily fooled – and the clank of his steps descending quickly told us her distraction hadn't worked.

'Quick! In here!' I whispered, beckoning them towards me, drawing them into the room on the left, where I kept an overabundance of household appliances – washing machines, and standalone spin- and tumble-driers. Moving them away from the point of safety I'd intended for them, although we could still see it – the shrouded entrance to the basement room.

The young girl was silent and compliant – suggesting her instincts had told her she was in safe hands. We crouched behind a couple of the old, rusting machines, watching as Monty clattered down the spiral stairs, his flashlight flickering light and colour.

'Esther! Esther! Where are you? Esther, I heard voices, I know he's here! ESTHER!'

His voice erupted into fury and I wondered just how deadly his mood was going to be tonight. Monty had a reputation for being as charming as he was toxic – and I'd seen with my own eyes how he let nothing stand in his way when he wanted something. I sensed the girl shake with fear, as his voice boomed around the ground floor and torchlight continued to swirl in frantic circles, determined to seek us out. Esther's arm was round her shoulder and she squeezed the girl gently and mouthed: *it's okay, just keep still.* And the child obeyed.

When he briefly came into the room – venturing in just a few feet – I felt her shake again and feared she'd whimper and reveal our hiding place. But he only stayed briefly, before disappearing again, up the stairs – right to the very top, I estimated as I counted his steps.

'What does he want with you?' Esther whispered, once she was certain he wouldn't be able to hear her.

'It's a long story – we go back,' I said, knowing it wouldn't satisfy her, but it was all I could manage in the circumstances. I had to focus on my plan – to get them safe from him and to get Monty Harrison out of my house.

'You go back?' Esther echoed, exasperation making her voice rasp. 'What else might I need to know about the man who I've left my son with?'

'Billy's here?' the child said, a little too loudly and Esther instinctively clamped a hand over her mouth – taking it away just as quickly, when the child inhaled a breath of shock.

I decided to answer her query.

'Yes, but it's a secret. You understand?'

She nodded.

'Good. Now, I have a plan to get you to safety, okay? Get you away from Mr Harrison – would you like that?'

Another nod.

'So, you'll need to do what I say and stay quiet, okay?'

'What is this plan, Gus?' Esther.

We moved as quietly and as swiftly as we could – which wasn't easy as the floor was slithering with wires, leads and tubes, peppered with nails, nuts, bolts and screws.

'Careful how you go – but we're heading for there.'

I pointed to where the entrance to the secret room was covered by the rough curtain.

'Esther – do you remember how to get in, which switches to press?'

'I think so.'

'Okay, when the lights come back on – the generator will kick in any minute now – you'll need to get yourself and the child inside, quickly. Shut yourself in as fast as you can – do all the locks. You must do all the locks, okay? Must secure yourselves in.'

'Aren't you coming with us?'

I shook my head.

'Gus, what are you going to do?'

I took in a sharp, bold breath.

'Something I should've done a long, long time ago,' I answered, although I knew I wasn't really answering her at all. 'Do you trust me, Esther?'

She took a moment to think, but then replied.

'Yes.'

'Then just do exactly as I say. Get yourself in that safe room, secure it and don't move. Understand?'

'Okay. Yes.'

'Right. Let's go.'

We left the room, Esther ahead, the girl in between us. Apart from the odd crunching sound beneath our feet, there was little noise from us. But I could hear Monty's blusteriness five floors above and I felt myself tense. What was he up to? He knew we were hiding down here, had probably guessed where we were, but he'd left us. And he'd been gone a good few minutes. What was he hoping to find?

Reaching the entrance hall, Esther and the girl took the last few steps and were behind the curtain, in front of the door to the fake cupboard in seconds.

'This is where I leave you. And remember, as soon as the lights go up and the electricity is back–.'

'Get inside and secure the door again.'

'Good. Right, this is it.'

And with that, I crept away, catching a glimpse of Esther's worried face in the moonlight coming from the rear windows. If she knew Monty as well as I did, then that fearful façade was showing just a fraction of her true distress. I could've reassured her I'd be fine, but now wasn't the time for more lies. Instead, I hurried on as silently as I could to my intended destination, hoping the rough plan in my head would come to fruition.

The generator was in a locked room on the third floor, next to my computer room. I knew the moment I stepped onto the metal staircase, I'd give away the direction of my movements, but there was nothing I could do. If I was to keep the upper hand on Monty Harrison – assuming I still had it – I had to get to that generator and cut it out almost as soon as it kicked in.

'Think I don't know what you're up to, old man?' he called out, just two or three creaks into my ascension, but I didn't hear him move towards me in response. His voice just got clearer, louder, the closer I got to him.

Stepping off the corkscrew stairs as I reached the third floor, I drew a bunch of keys from the right hand pocket of the trousers – holding them still in a fist, with just the one I needed poking out, like a weapon at the ready. I quickly unlocked the generator room, slipped inside and secured the door again. Then I waited.

Waited for Monty to finally make his way to me and do whatever he'd come to do.

Waited for the generator to kick in – just for a minute or so.

Waited till I thought Esther and the so far nameless child had got themselves to safety.

The wait seemed like forever and when the generator hummed into action, I jumped for a second. Then I began counting. Unlike the external doors, the lock on the basement door needed the electricity supply on before it opened. As I counted, I imagined Esther moving step by step and gave her the count of up to ten to get herself and the girl into the secret room beneath us all. Then, I pulled a leaver and manually switched off the generator supply – cutting the electricity once more and plunging the house into permanent darkness.

Above me, I heard Monty curse and then laugh his raucous, bellyful laugh.

'Playing games with me, Augustus? Think you'll win? No, me neither. How could you when old Monty wins every time.'

As I considered my next move in the dark – knowing the minute I stepped back onto those metal steps he'd know exactly where I was again – I let Monty's taunting tick over in my head. *How could you when old Monty wins every time.* Was that true, or just his arrogance clouding out any failures he may have encountered. I thought of my own history with the man, to test out the truth of this claim…

It was years ago. And not in this city, but further away – beyond the forests that surrounded us. In a time when the dogs were multiplying and terrorizing whole neighbourhoods – after the truth about the takings had come out, but years before the floods. I did good work back then – criminal work in the eyes of the authorities, but good work for those with a clear head and warm heart.

Many children were lost during the takings, and I embarked upon a quest to find as many of them as I could and reunite them with their families.

While the authorities had set up a registration system to keep track of all its young captives – should it ever have to account for its shady activities – the extent to which its procedures were followed varied from unit to unit. So when it came to handing the children back to their parents, the ease of this transaction also depended on where the child had been held. Where there were no records, the authorities relied upon the memory of the child itself. But many memories had been fragmented or altered from the experiments inflicted upon them, and these children often ended up in government care. This *care* amounted to packing in as many of them as possible in large dormitories, offering food, clothes and a place to sleep. No comfort, and no education – nothing to get these lost ones back on their feet.

But it wasn't these vulnerable souls that I chose to help. No, I set out to find the others – the children who didn't make their way home or into these so-called care homes. The children who seemed to vanish completely.

The ones the government denied all knowledge of – even to this day.

The ones they damaged just that little bit too much.

Like that cousin of Esther's and Agnes'. Not the one who had escaped from the shop. Ethan? Yes – not him, not Ethan. But his twin – Joshua. Yes, that was his name. Joshua – the one they hadn't been able to find.

The ones they experimented on in ways the human imagination could not conjure. To be told about it was to disbelieve it instantly – because to believe it was to know that humanity could end. That a man or woman could stop being their natural selves.

There was a group of us. Me, my older brother, a few men he'd brought together and sometimes my son, Xavier. Monty Harrison joined us just one time – recruited by my brother for a particular job. We worked with people on the inside – employees who knew what certain fractions of the government were doing. Too afraid to make a stand themselves, they eased their consciences by leaking small amounts of information – not enough to expose themselves, but enough to get us curious. Cowards, really, but they made a difference to a few of the sufferers.

Nathaniel – that was the name of our coward. Nathaniel. And he was very helpful, this Nathaniel. Full of information he was happy to leak. But he still took a wage, he still only took limited risks and still put himself first, before all those innocent children who'd been taken. But, his help did make a difference and without the likes of him, small armies like ours would've achieved a lot less.

The information we'd received gave us a location and described what we were to look for as a *camp* – a word that took me to two extremes. We'd either find a place of summertime fun – or a cruel prison. I hoped for the former, but it was the latter that greeted us when we finally arrived. And it was much bigger than our informant had suggested.

On the previous freedom raids our small group had executed, we'd found smallish establishments – house-like buildings with a floor of bedrooms and a floor of laboratories. They were nearly always hidden in the wilderness – miles from civilisation, protected from sight by dense forest. And we'd liberate a handful of children each time.

You're probably wondering what we did with those lost souls afterwards. Well, it really depended on what we found – what state they were in. Sometimes we were able to reunite them with their families – if they remembered enough about themselves, we'd check it against the authorities' register of missing children. (I had contacts willing to do this for me, too.) If not, we took them to families we knew could be trusted to keep quiet and care for them. But sometimes we made difficult choices. Sometimes the children were in such a bad way, their minds and bodies taken to extremes they wouldn't recover from. Those times, we had to be cruel to be kind, but we always made sure the end was as painless as possible. Against the law, I know, but the right thing, in the bigger scheme of things.

On this trip with Monty, however, what we faced was different. The scale of what we uncovered was unprecedented by the group. It wasn't like the smaller labs we'd come across. And when our informant had said *camp* he should have said *campus*, because we weren't just looking at one building. We were looking at around eight.

The enclosure was a couple of acres in size and surrounded by chain fencing, topped with a coiled serpent of barbed wire. Suspiciously, we had no trouble getting in. The main gates were wide open, unlocked, as if this wasn't a prison at all; as if the inmates were free to come and go when they pleased.

'They've gone, haven't they?' my brother said to me. 'The authorities knew we were coming, and haven't even hung around to face us, to fight us.'

I'd nodded. 'Looks like it, yes.'

Inside the fencing, the eight buildings we could see were uniform in their design. Warehouse-like, they appeared like huge barns on the outside. The interior, we discovered, was on two levels – a laboratory on the ground floor, with a sprawling dormitory at a lower level, underground. The equipment on the laboratory level confirmed our very worst fears about what some parts of the government had been up to. Experiments on minds and bodies – the manipulation of thoughts and DNA. Young Billy retold me many of Tristan's stories – about the torturous Chamber of Doors and the serum injected into the eye that gave you the ability to play mind tricks on the weak and feeble-brained – and what we stumbled across that day brought those horrors to life.

I only entered one of the buildings, with Monty as my back up. But my brother and Xavier entered the others, with the rest of our small gang. As we'd suspected, they didn't find a single surgeon, scientist or guard on those premises. They'd definitely been warned of our imminent arrival. And they didn't even have the guts to stand up and fight against our small rebel troupe – more cowardly than you could imagine. We did find dozens of children, however – many, many more than we'd been prepared for. And we helped them all out of those hell-hole buildings.

The children were in better shape than we'd imagined they'd be, given the environment they were held in – cuts, bruises and shellshock on the surface of things. We found no evidence of recent experimentation with any of them, suggesting they might not have been held there long.

But the building Monty and I entered was a different experience altogether.

Later, Xavier and I questioned my brother on what he knew about Monty Harrison – how he'd come to recruit him for this particular raid, who'd verified his trustworthiness. In the moment, I'd had no time for these questions – I'd had to implicitly trust that Monty's intentions were moral, selfless, like the rest of ours.

Externally, this building was like the others, and internally too – at a first glance. A lab on the ground floor and a large dormitory underground. But when we looked a bit closer something became obvious – this place was set up just for one individual.

'Must be one special child,' Monty had said, when we made this discovery, descending into the pit of the building to find the oddest arrangement.

Above us, the laboratory was set up with all manner of equipment. Glass walled rooms – clinically isolated for operations and experiments, with visual access that was undoubtedly for senior officials who'd come along for the odd freak show. Mind control units, with blinding lights and electronic equipment designed to alter the senses. Bed after bed after bed fitted with restraints – for the feet, legs, torso, arms and head, ensuring minimum bodily disruption while mental and physical torture was inflicted. A section of the building that was a long corridor leading off into individual prison cells.

I would describe all that I encountered in greater detail, but I fear it would further age my already ancient heart. Even at the time, I felt myself grow older, wearier. This complex paraphernalia suggested so much cruelty – could it really all be true?

Monty's initial comments, as we took the stairs to the dormitory basement – *Must be one special child* – should've raised my suspicions, but I was too deep in shock to register it. Instead, I'd simply agreed and set about finding this poor wretch.

According to the others, the underground rooms in the other buildings housed between thirty and forty beds. Mattresses on floors, in truth – a basic sleeping provision for the poor individuals who'd been held there. But in the unit Monty and I entered, there was only one bed below ground. We didn't see it at first, as it was hidden away in a far corner. What we did see was a lot more equipment – not like that on the floor above, nothing suggestive of experimentation. No, instead it had the feel of a hospital – yes, a large, private room in a hospital. There were machines and monitors scattered around – some dormant, some working and flashing words and graphs on small monochrome screens. I remember a bay of sinks, too – with elbow-high taps you could knock on and off with your arms. Surgical sinks, I'm certain. So, unlike what we saw elsewhere, this room looked like it was set up to preserve a life – not destroy it.

The child itself was in the far corner of the room, lying in a single hospital-style bed. The area was cordoned off with thick, rubber sheeting that had been fixed in place, creating a dull, translucent wall. There was an oblong section of this sheeting with a zip covering three sides – we unfastened this unconventional door and stepped inside, getting closer to the child we'd come to rescue.

The air felt strange inside that sterile, clinical bubble – I couldn't put my finger on it at the time, but looking back it must've been artificial and chemically pure, and our lungs took a moment to adjust.

'This doesn't look simple, Monty,' I said, once I felt I could speak, trying not to cough – that's what my bronchial reflexes wanted do to: cough. But there was something so delicate about the arrangement that I felt certain such a reaction would upset the balance of things.

The child was a girl – maybe six or seven years in age, but it was difficult to tell. She was thin and very pale – a grey, frail variety of pale. Her skin was tissue thin – bones pushing through, sharp enough to tear it – and so translucent that the colour of her veins and arteries appeared on the outside; a biological map tattooing her surface. White pads were pressed onto her in pairs – on the temples, chest, and arms – and light blue wires led off these to a monitor on the left side of her. These same wires trailed out further down, below her waist, where she was covered in a white sheet. There was a breathing mask over her face, with a long corrugated plastic tube coming out and leading to another machine, to right of the bed.

Monty picked up a clipboard that was hanging on the end of the bed, read through her medical notes. And he took a close look, not just a glance, as if he were looking for particular details – but I didn't get a chance to question this, as we were immediately interrupted. Shouts and the sounds of boots tapping concrete came from outside the plastic lung we were sealed in.

'They've come back for her,' Monty assessed quickly.

'Jesus, that's never happened before. These brutes don't normally give a sh-.'

'We need to move quickly, Augustus. No time to ruminate,' he cut me off, suddenly seized with an authoritative voice I'd not heard in him before. He touched my left arm at that point, too, and I felt something. A pinch, a prick? I didn't pay it much notice at the time – too many other things occupied us. 'You grab the girl, take as much of this…' He waved a hand at the wires and the tubes. 'Take her as carefully as you can and run. I'll deal this end.'

And I obeyed, without a flicker of concern. Why would I? He'd left me with the girl – the apparent prize her torturers had seen fit to come back for. I tore the wires way, but kept the mask on her face, although it was probably rendered useless without the white machine that appeared to provide its oxygen. And I ran, towards the back of the building, where I found several doors. Beyond one of these was a staircase, at the top of which was a fire escape. I remember her coming round so clearly, coughing herself awake with a fit that I thought might be the very end of her.

'Stay calm, try and breathe, child. I'm getting you to safety,' I chanted over and over, striding up those stairs, heading for the outside. And I reached there – just in time, it would appear. Managed to scramble clear of the building when it went up. Boom! Instantly, a cloud covered the ground – a cloud spitting shards of brick, glass and metal all around us. I threw us both down, covering the girl with my own body and then felt something come over me. A lull. And I was gone, out for the count.

When I came round, all was still. All was different. The building was grounded, flat from bombing, with mangled, metal skeletons the only remains of the laboratory of horror. I was further away from it than when I'd lost consciousness, like someone had moved me – and spared any serious injury because of this. The girl was gone – and Monty, too.

'Must've given his life with that explosion,' my brother concluded at the time. 'Trying to save you and the girl. And those men coming back to blow it up. They really didn't want us to get our hands on any of this. Brave old Monty, though, eh?'

And for years I believed that to be true. Monty Harrison had died for a good cause. Albeit in vain, as the girl's cruel perpetrators had blown their hi-tech laboratory to smithereens and seized her in the confusion. Still, we'd saved hordes of other children – and no one from the authorities had stayed around to stop us doing that.

But small details began to niggle. Whatever had happened to that tiny, pallid creature? Why was her life so precious to a group of people who clearly didn't value life at all? And something else – my losing consciousness. How did that happen so suddenly? A day later, a bruise had enveloped on my left arm – at the centre of which was a pin-prick mark. I recalled the sharp sensation I'd felt there when Monty had touched it – had he done this?

It was Monty's innate arrogance that led me to discover the truth about him. A more level-headed man would have gone undercover after such an incident, if he had something to hide – changed his name, at least. But Monty wasn't one of those.

So, when I moved back to the city, it wasn't just because I'd heard word about my son, Xavier. A lucky coincidence brought news of a certain gangster by the name of Monty Harrison living in the same region – a corrupt, feared and powerful man. And the only Monty Harrison I knew was a hero to the cause I believed in – could they be one and the same? I couldn't just leave that question hanging – I owed it to the missing girl to get an answer.

Until that day he came to my house, I hadn't come face to face with him since he'd suggested I take the girl and flee that laboratory, all those years ago. I'd asked questions about him and had learned enough that I'd have to get much closer if I was to find what he knew about the girl. If he still had her, even. But what I'd learned to date gave very little away on that front.

Esther was my way in. And now she'd brought him to my door. This wasn't in my plans, though. This wasn't how I saw it all unfolding. And, once I'd switched off the generator and plunged us into darkness again, I made a decision – I'd confront him. Esther and the two children were safe in the rooms beneath my house and Monty would have no idea how to find them. I had no need to worry about them. And me? Without a plan in place, I was truly at my uninvited guest's mercy.

So, coming out of the generator room, I stepped back onto the steel spiral that twisted its way up through my house and took those final steps up to the attic room, where Monty was pottering about.

He spoke to me the entire time, although I didn't respond.

'Well, well, at last we get to meet again... Been a long time, Augustus... You didn't really think you were hidden from my sight... Had my eye on you since you arrived a few years back... You must have so many questions... Why did I take the girl...? Oh yes, no denying that now... Old Monty took her... And the men who blew up the lab, they were *my* men... But why? I know that question's eating at you... Oh, Augustus, she was the true prize... The ultimate treasure... She was their success story, Augustus... The authorities' one true achievement... Have I still got her...? That would be telling... But I will tell you, I will... But you must help me now... Yes, I need your help... Augustus Riley knows people, people whose help I need, people who no longer trust old Monty... People who, unlike old Augustus, have kept themselves hidden from me... So, will you help me Augustus?'

He said this as I finally entered the room.

It was eerie, being face to face after all this time. Just an outline in the darkness, lit from behind by the moon through the glass. Bigger in build than before – a rich gluttony about his barrel-shaped figure – but unmistakably the same man. There was something else distinctive about the shadow figure he'd created. He was stood near the table where I'd left the maps and he held one of them open in his hands. It was too dark for him to be able to read them, but my immediate guess was he'd seen them in the light – and was holding them out for effect.

'Ah yes, I see you've made a discovery, Augustus. A much coveted one. And is there any truth in it?'

'In what?' I asked, stalling him, wanting to keep him talking. You see, I was aware of something. Not something I could quite put my finger on. A sense – a feeling. I wasn't wrong.

'Oh Augustus, don't play that game with me. The Cadley legend – is it true, old man? You've got both halves – I had a good look before all the lights went again. And you've circled this place – and Esther's house. Did that just for fun, did we? Didn't think so.'

A sound stopped him speaking – the clank of a foot on metal.

Damn, I cursed inside. *It's Esther. She's come after me. Wondering what's happening to me. Worried for an old man.*

'Sounds like we've got company. You know she works for me, don't you? Does as she's told, does Esther. Cleans up the mess I make.'

There it was again. That *something* in the room – like a shadow I couldn't see. Monty was too distracted by Esther's gradual arrival to pick up on it.

'I've got something on you, haven't I?' he called out, as the soles of her feet continued to clank against the metal treads. 'Esther did a terrible thing. Murder. Didn't you Esther, love?'

I'm certain I heard a quiet gasp in reaction to his unnecessary betrayal.

'Murdered something dear to me.'

Not *someone*, but *something* – Monty's natural words, no doubt, when thinking about another human being. I think of Esther's long lost husband and wonder if there's a connection there.

'Got that silly little bitch wrapped round my finger, haven't I, love?'

'Tell me what you want, Monty!' I demanded, suddenly wanting an end to the game he was playing. It was one thing to mess about with me – quite another to torture my new friend.

'I want you to help me get back something of mine the authorities have taken.'

'And what would that be, Monty?'

He took in a deep breath before he answered – to enhance the drama, or because it was hard to admit failure? 'My girl, Augustus – they took my girl. The authorities have taken her back – and we can't have that, can we?'

And then it all seemed to happen at once.

Esther finally stepping into the room.

Her charging forward, crying out: *you bastard, Monty!*

His cruel, belly laugh in response.

The shadow I'd sensed forming into a person, a man – just for a split second.

The blow that knocked Monty to the floor.

Esther's crying out reaction – a shriek that left me shaken.

The man disappearing back into shadow, into invisibility.

The cold, sudden shock we were left with.

'We have to act quickly,' I told Esther, forcing myself into action. A groaning noise was emitting from Monty's slumped body. 'You take the maps and head back to the children. I'll put the electric back on, secure all the doors in the house and then join you.'

She didn't react. She was still staring into the space where *he'd* been. Then she glanced down at Monty's collapsed figure.

'Esther?'

'What about him?'

'Monty?'

She nodded.

'Don't you worry about him. Leave him to me. Okay? Just get going.'

Another nod and she was slowly on her way.

Five minutes later, I joined them in the secret room under my house.

The girl who I didn't know was silent upon my arrival, but Billy had immediate questions.

'What's going on? Who was upstairs? And why is Marcie Coleman here?'

Marcie – so that was the girl's name.

'Did you see him?'

A quiet question from Esther – easily trumping ahead of Billy's.

'Yes.'

'You know who he was?'

I shook my head, but had a question of my own: 'But you know who it was, don't you?'

Esther nodded a silent *yes,* the shock of it still in her face, paling her skin.

'Who? Who are you talking about?' Billy was suddenly asking, exasperated that no one was explaining a thing to him. 'Who did you see, Mother? Who was up there with you?'

When she answered, the look on the young boy's astonished face left a cold shiver down my ancient spine.

'He came from nowhere, Billy. From thin air. And it was Joe,' she said, expelling words she didn't quite believe. 'It was your father, Billy. Your father was here.'

Asleep

I'm not sure if it's me or the other one.

I'm never quite certain.

But it's the future again – the near future. Of that I am sure.

It's dark, but we have a torch to guide us – a wide single beam that the leader of our group is in control of.

Our group – so I'm not on my own. I quickly scan them – an old man, a boy and a girl. I sense the old man is our leader, and not just because he is up ahead, in charge of the light – a torch. I sense he has knowledge and he knows where we are going. There's implicit trust from us all in this.

We're in a tunnel. Like a sewer, we're below the surface. There's a wetness on the walls that glistens when the torch-light strikes it.

'How did I get here?' I ask and the boy turns to me and says: 'You brought us. You knew the way, Otterley.'

Otterley.

He called me Otterley.

So now I know which one of us this is.

Awake

9. Tilly

'What is your name?' the woman asked.

'I'll tell you,' I answered, 'but first you'll need to tell me what we're doing here. Is that a deal?'

'It's a deal,' she'd agreed, after a pause. She was sitting on the mattress next to mine – Peter's – leaning forwards. She lowered and softened her voice. 'But you mustn't tell anyone. Okay? Just between you and me – and then you'll tell me who you are? I could get into a lot of trouble, you know – but you'll get in worse if you don't speak up. You understand?'

'Yes, I do,' I answered.

And then, to my complete surprise, she began to tell me everything.

The reason we'd been taken.

The secrecy surrounding it.

And what would happen next – what was going to happen to those we'd left behind.

'Are you okay?' she asked, once she was done telling me.

I nodded, but stayed silent – in shock, thinking of the people we'd left behind. Fearful of their fate.

'I've taken a terrible risk, telling you,' she added and I believed her, watching her eyes glance over at the guards and the men in white coats in the far corner.

'Is everything alright?' someone called out and the woman held up a hand to reassure them.

'Yes, all fine. This one's just a little homesick,' she said, for them. And then back to me: 'So, you mustn't tell a soul, okay? Not one person. Do you understand?'

It didn't occur to me at the time that she wanted me to do the very opposite. That she wanted us all to hear her story.

I had a question:

'Have they been warned – the people back home?'

But she didn't answer. Instead, she brought me back to my side of our bargain.

'So, mystery girl – I've kept my part of the deal, now it's your turn. You were going to tell me your name.'

And I'd been thinking this through the whole time she'd been talking, while I'd been taking in the horror of what we'd left behind – of what was going to happen to everyone still there.

'We couldn't save everyone,' she'd said. *'We had to choose. We'll go back once we know it's safe. We'll pick up those who've managed to find a safe place. Yes, we'll go back for the survivors.'*

'Your name?' she reminded me, breaking my distraction, her voice a little firmer. 'Come on, tell me who you are. We've a duty to look after you, but we can't do that properly if we don't know who you are.'

So I went with the name that had been appearing to me, the name in my dreams – a name that wasn't mine.

'My name is Elinor.'

'Elinor who? What's your full name?' she pushed. A single label wasn't enough.

'Morton,' I answered, stealing the second part from a good friend I'd left behind. And thinking about Billy, I felt tears and grief overcome me again.

'We'll go back for the survivors,' this woman had promised, and I just hoped Billy was one of them.

'He has to be,' I told myself, wiping tears, looking up at her.

And, in spite of everything she'd just told me – *we rescued you all from imminent danger, we're not the enemy* – she had a small smile of triumph on her face.

'Well, Elinor Morton, let's get you sorted.' She stood and held out a hand. 'Come on, this way,' she added and, putting my hand in hers, I let her lead me towards the far end of the room, where three cold-faced men in white jackets were waiting just for me.

What happened next was what I roughly expected – I went through one of the doors and found myself with a group of other children. Five girls, similar age to me; not anyone I knew, though. We were in a small, clinical room, surrounded by white walls and bright lighting.

'Sit here,' a man instructed – one of the men in white coats I'd been calling *scientists.* He'd pointed to a space on one of three beds that were covered in crisp white sheets. I sat next to a girl who introduced herself as Serena.

'Elinor,' I answered and I noticed the man who'd spoken raise a quizzical eyebrow.

'Elinor?' he repeated, in a question, as if he was doubting it. He came towards me with a black band in his hand. 'I'm just going to put this round your arm. It'll feel a bit tight. Then I'm going to test your heart rate, okay, Elinor?'

I nodded and held out my right arm for him. He covered it in the band and then pumped it full of air, and I felt it squeeze against my skin, pinching a little.

'Just a few further things from you,' the scientist said, once my heart rate had been measured and recorded. 'Now, this will prick.' And before I could object, a needle was plunged into the same arm and a small tube of my blood extracted.

After that, I was asked to go into a side room and pass water into a small, cardboard bowl and bring it back.

'That's all for now,' were his parting words, once I'd handed this over.

I was the only girl left in the room.

'What are you going to do with it?' I asked him and he looked surprised, as if this was unexpected. I guessed that no one else had questioned him.

'I'm going to check how well you are,' he answered, almost immediately and it was hard to tell if this was the truth or not. Then, he nodded at a guard who was waiting by the door and I was led out, back into the dormitory.

Back to Peter.

'What is it?' he said to me, almost as soon as I'd returned, reading something in my face, I knew.

I couldn't help it. I'd promised the woman I wouldn't tell a soul what she'd told me. But when I saw Peter again, all I could think of was the loss he'd be suffering – of the devastation facing everyone that we'd left at home. Of the horror they'd experience.

'We came to rescue you, because of what's coming. And we can't stop it. There's no stopping it, but we've helped who we can.'

'What is it? What's happening?' Peter asked, alarm in his voice.

But I still couldn't quite find the words.

'We couldn't save everyone. We had to choose. We'll go back once we know it's safe.'

I sat on my mattress, as the woman's words went round and round in my head again. I knew I had to tell him now, but where did I begin?

'We'll pick up those who've managed to find a safe place. Yes, we'll go back for the survivors.'

'Tilly, tell me,' my worried friend asked softly, so I nodded at him, confirming my intention to say something.

'Okay, I'll tell you, but you must promise not to tell anyone else?'

He nodded and I believed him – I hadn't notice him talking to anyone there but me, in any case. And even back at school, he wasn't particularly chatty or popular.

'And you must try not to react, if you can. Even if you feel upset, you must try to hide it. She mustn't know I've said anything to you,' I added, nodding subtly to my left, where the woman was talking to another child. Peter saw who I was indicating. 'She told me, in exchange for my name.'

'And you gave it?' he asked, more interested in this, it seemed, than the impending tale of terror I was about to share.

'I gave a false one.'

'A false one?' he repeated, a little too loudly.

'Shush, yes. Something stopped me saying who I really was. I'm not sure what. A feeling, maybe.'

'And they believed you?'

I shrugged.

'Seemed to, but that doesn't really matter.'

'Who did you say you were?'

I frowned – it wasn't important, after all. But I answered.

'Elinor.'

Then it was Peter's turn to frown.

'The missing girl?' he said, as if I'd done wrong – as if taking her name was somehow shameful, a sin.

'It's all I could think of,' I answered, irritation creeping into my voice, a defense against his quiet criticism. 'But that's not what I was going to tell you about.'

'What do you need to tell me, then?'

And so, I shared every detail of the terrifying truth I'd learned with Peter.

He kept his word – kept his emotions under control and kept his tears at bay, though I could almost see them behind his eyes, trying to push through. And I reached out for his hands, and felt his grip mine very tight in response.

'Are you sure?' he murmured, barely audible, once my story was over.

'Yes, I am.'

'But she could be lying, couldn't she? The woman – she could've told you all this to make you think she was okay? So that you'd do as you were told. So you'd trust her and tell her your name. But you didn't trust her, did you? And you didn't tell her your name, either – but you trust this story of hers?'

There was something else I decided to share with Peter – something that could go either way. He'd either understand why I knew I'd been told the truth – or he'd think I was mad.

'I've been having these dreams,' I began and he looked up at me with instant skepticism.

'Dreams?' he said, his tone echoing his stare.

'Vivid dreams, ones that seem real.'

'And what's that got to do with what she said to you?'

I closed my eyes for a minute – and heard the words she said, and saw the images in my dreams at the same time. One of my dreams haunted me in particular.

I'm outside and walking – my feet feel heavy, so I look down to them... I see mud stretching for miles... There is something ahead... Something sticking out of the endless sea of sludge... I can see arms, shoulders, a neck and a head... they are dragged deeper into the sinking pool... The arms, the shoulders, the neck and head and finally the hands...

'I think I've seen what's going to happen,' I eventually said, hoping he'd take me seriously, hoping that by sharing something I'd never told anyone, he wouldn't dismiss me as a freak, a liar. 'I think I've seen what's going to happen to the land, to the people we've left behind.'

'Seen the future?' Peter questioned, and I couldn't tell if he was genuine or mocking. There was too much else going on.

'I think so,' I answered, my tone lowered to a hush, not wanting to say such a thing too loud. 'I've done it before. Dreamt things, and they've happened.'

'What things?' Peter whispered, mirroring me, leaning closer to me.

'Billy – Billy Morton,' I said, quietly, finding the memory of another dream, of who it was about suddenly saddening. 'I dreamed about him in the water, being rescued – and that came true. And I dreamed about the helicopters, too. Just their sound, but it was the exact same sound when they came for us.'

'And what dream makes you certain what the woman has told you is true?' he asked, fear in his voice.

I see mud stretching for miles... arms, shoulder, a neck and a head... dragged deeper into the sinking pool...

'Because I dreamed the city was flooded again. Flooded till there was nothing but mud for miles and everyone had drowned it in. I'm sorry. But I think that's what's going to happen. I think that when they take us back, that's all we'll find is left.'

We were quiet after that. The guards came round with food in brown paper bags and we both ate ours in silence, surprisingly hungry. And shortly after that, the lights went out. Neither of us slept, though. I was too afraid – afraid of what my dreams would bring me. Terrified I was right about my strange ability. And I knew Peter was awake – I could hear his sobbing, muffled by his pillow.

As I lay there, thinking over my dreams, thinking over what the woman had told me, questions I could've asked starting filling my head.

Where had they come from?

Where were they all living?

And how did they know what was going to happen – that the land was expecting another disaster?

And the helicopters, too – where had they come from? When resources were so scarce, where had the money, the materials, the fuel come from for these flying machines?

But it was one thing in particular that came back to me. Something that hadn't sounded quite right, but I'd dismissed it when she'd said it. Something I regretted later.

'We're not the bad guys, you must believe me,' she'd said, a desperation to be believed in her voice. *'That's why we came for you, that's why we took you from the enclosure.'*

I'd been too caught up in the horror that unfolded with her words to question it at the time. But later, unable to sleep, hearing Peter's stifled anguish, the strangeness haunted me.

That's why we took you from the enclosure.

What did this mean?

What enclosure?

Did she mean our school, our drowned city?

I told myself I'd ask her the next time I saw her, with all the other questions I had – ask her exactly what she meant.

My thoughts were quickly torn from this puzzle, as I heard a sound of swishing through the darkness, like material rubbing against itself. And I wondered who was approaching. Suddenly, a fat, warm hand clamped across my mouth and chin, and sharp words were hissed in my ear:

'You're not who you said you were, little girl.'

And then I'm certain I felt something sharp in my arm, like a needle. But I couldn't be certain as, very quickly, I fell into blackness…

When I woke up, I was on my own, in what looked like a prison cell – just like one that'd been appearing in my dreams. A small oblong room, with a bed along one wall and a small table next to it, with a jug of water and a clear plastic beaker on its surface. The door had a small grill in it.

Above me, the bright glow of a circular light seemed to burn into me, the glare blinding me when I looked into it. And I felt a little woozy, a little lightheaded from whatever had been done to me. So, I closed my eyes and tried to focus. Tried to listen for nearby sounds, too.

It was quiet to start with – there were muffled sounds suggesting something was going on nearby, behind the walls that surrounded me. But nothing definite. Nothing clear – at least, not to start with. Then I heard them coming – whoever had taken me, the guards, I guessed. Heard their footsteps, their chatter, the clank of keys and the unlocking of a door.

Then, she was at my side – the woman from before, who'd nervously told me everything about our capture. She sat on the bed.

'You didn't tell me the truth,' she said, not looking cross with me, but rather disappointed. As if my small lie had been personal. 'We know you're not called Elinor Morton. There's no one of that name on our records – we've done a thorough check now. We're only missing two people from our lists that haven't been located. One is Marcie Coleman, and we've already established that you can't be her. So, that only leaves us with one other option.' She paused, taking in a breath and I sensed she was a little uneasy, as if she was uncomfortable with the task she'd been given. 'The only other name I've got from the list we got from your school is one Billy Morton – whose surname you've used, but as

Billy is a boy, this can't be you either. So, you need to tell me who you are.' She took a breath in, leaned closer and lowered voice. 'Please, you've got everybody nervous here. And you've got me nervous, too. What I told you – I did it to get your trust, but you've lied to me. And you *can* trust me, I promise you. So tell me – what's your name?'

As she'd spoken, her eyes had flitted to another part of the small cell, and I'd followed this flicker to the doorway. There, one of the scientists in white coats was standing. He was cruel looking in comparison to her; there was a hardness in his stare. And, while I might have admitted the truth if the woman had been on her own, the sight of him made me even more determined to keep my identity secret.

'Please, you must,' the woman pleaded. 'They think you're a spy, a plant. They think you're one of them…'

Before I could ask her what she meant – *they think you're one of them* – the man in the doorway impatiently approached the bed, pushing her to one side. He came right up to my face.

'Tell her who you are!' he demanded, but I kept my mouth closed.

Looked square into his steely eyes and said nothing.

'I can always make you, you know?' he then said to me – calmly, his flare of anger quickly diminished.

'No!' the woman abruptly cried, as if something terrible were coming my way.

'Would you like me to do that?' he added, remaining calm, although I sensed my refusal to speak was annoying him. 'Well,' he said, leaning in closer and speaking into my left ear, 'you leave me no other option…'

Asleep

It's just me and a girl.

The girl.

The one who put her hand over my mouth and said she'd come to rescue me.

Rescue me – or rescue the other one? What does it matter – in a sense we are one and the same.

And her name? My mind rumbles through its vast library till it finds it – Elinor. Yes, she said her name was Elinor.

And we're further on in our story – our future story, I believe.

In a large storage unit – with bay after bay of ceiling-high shelving, set out like narrow corridors. And we're running – she's ahead, leading, looking for something specific. Each shelf is labelled with a code – a numerical and alphabetical combination. She reads these aloud as she goes.

'XY123HE1, XY124HE2, XY125HE3.'

'What are you looking for?' I ask eventually.

She doesn't answer – instead, she stops. She's found it.

'XY136HF1,' she announces, pulling a tray out from one of the shelves, tipping it towards me so that I can see the contents – a selection of upright vials holding a light yellow liquid. Each one is labelled – XY136HF1.

'This one's yours,' she says, holding a glass tube out to me.

Awake

10. Esther

Get yourself in that safe room, secure it and don't move.

Augustus' exact words – his clear instructions, and I'd agreed. But only on the outside. Was he mad? Did he really think I'd leave him – an old man, albeit a surprisingly mobile one – to his fate with Monty? I knew that gangster well and hadn't known anyone get one over on Monty Harrison.

What made Augustus Riley think he was any different?

So, once the girl – Marcie – was safe and I'd given Billy an uncharacteristic hug – long and hard, receiving a physical response of equal urgency – I made my way back out of that luxury bunker and went in search of the men.

I felt it pass me on that spiral staircase.

It? Him? I wasn't sure – I'm still not sure.

Like someone had opened the front door and let in a draft. That's how it felt, only something more solid. And it had brushed past me on those steel steps.

But what I saw in that attic… I couldn't comprehend it.

Coming out of nowhere, like someone walking through a wall; not in the room, then suddenly there. And he'd lifted something of Augustus' – a telescope I'd not noticed before. (I guess Augustus was just the sort of man to own such a thing; it wouldn't have seemed out of the ordinary amongst his things.) Then struck that monster on the back of the head and vanished.

What had Billy told me he believed had happened to Joe?

'He vanished, Mother,' he'd said. *'He disappeared into the night.'*

Had Billy been right? No, no, that wasn't what happened. Billy had got it wrong, hadn't known the truth. But as my mind considered what I'd seen in Augustus' attic, I began to think of all sorts of impossibilities – and reality and my imaginary thoughts began to blur.

But I'd seen him – it was Joe's face, clear as day in that darkened room. It was definitely him – I just didn't understand how. And when I saw Billy again, when Augustus finally joined us in that secured room under his house, I couldn't help myself. When the old man asked me: *you know who it was, don't you?* I answered without thinking.

It was Joe. It was your father, Billy. Your father was here.

Billy looked astonished, but somehow Augustus moved him on very quickly.

'I have something you need to help with, young Billy,' he asked, as if I hadn't just made the announcement. As if the old man's own agenda had to take priority over mine, no question. 'I need you to help us get out of here. But not up those stairs. It's not safe that way. The authorities could be looking for you and your friend here. So, I need you to help us find another way out – a secret way, under the house.'

Suddenly I understood – Augustus was playing up to the little boy, the one who liked to have adventures with his cousin at the train graveyard, thinking I didn't know about it.

Thinking of Elinor made me shiver for a moment. When had I last thought of her? Not for hours, I realised. Had I even thought of her that day at all? I couldn't be sure. But how quickly we moved from one crisis to another.

'Esther?'

Augustus' voice drew me away from my lamenting.

'I need your help, too,' he said, his eyes tired, but still beaming a certain energy. 'You too, Marcie?' He announced her name as a question, just checking he'd got it right.

'What is it you need us to do?' Billy asked, finding focus and strength – it was obvious he admired our elderly friend, was eager to please and obey.

It was Marcie who found the way out – the entrance to the secret, underground passage.

Marcie – the innocent bystander who'd been accidentally caught up in Monty's drama.

When Monty had brought her to my door earlier that evening, she'd been as quiet as she was then, but there had been terror in her eyes.

'They brought this little idiot back to me! Took my Tilly and left me this idiot, Esther! She was supposed to be protected! That's what they promised me – put her down a few classes and keep her away from the chosen ones! Bastards took the wrong bloody girl! Idiots!'

I later found out that Tilly Harrison and Marcie Coleman had played out a silly game – swapped names with each other to fool a stand-in teacher – a game that had convinced just a few too many people. And now Tilly was off somewhere with the rest of the children, while Marcie had been spared. It was obvious Monty had inside information that something was going to happen – and instead of warning us all, he'd cut a deal with whoever he knew on the inside to save his most prized possession. And he was so self-absorbed that he didn't think twice about how confused and upset the girl was. Didn't think about getting her back to her parents. Didn't think or care about the loss the rest of us might be experiencing – albeit mine was of a different nature.

Instead, he allowed himself to be all-consumed by his own fears and fury, ablaze with it all as he stormed into my house and demanded I take him to Augustus Riley.

'*Who?*' I asked, claiming innocence, but Monty was having none of that.

'*You know exactly who I mean – the man that little boy of yours spends all his time with. Now, you're to take me there. He wouldn't let me over his threshold, but he'll let you in. And he knows people. He'll be able to help me get my Tilly back.*'

'*And what of this poor thing?*' I'd nodded at Marcie, hopefully giving her a reassuring look with my eyes.

'*They wouldn't just hand my Tilly back. If that old man can get us anywhere near where they've taken those children, I'll need something to exchange her for.*'

So, she was currency. But I couldn't understand what good Augustus would be. Even as we sped to his house in Monty's boat – a speedboat, but smaller than Jessie's – I couldn't see how calling in on the old man would help Monty achieve his goal.

'*He knows people,*' was the only explanation Monty would give me, hissed impatiently into the wind, as we'd sped to the Cadley House, with a frightened little girl huddled against me.

But it was fortunate that Marcie was with us – she found the way out after all. With more than just a bit of help from Billy.

'I heard a noise,' Billy told us all, after Augustus had given his plea for help. 'When the lights went out in here.'

'Ah – that was me. So, these lights went out too? That must mean this part of the house doesn't have its own electricity source. I did wonder.'

'The noise came from this part of the room,' Billy continued, looking a little annoyed by Augustus' interruption. 'A dropping noise.'

'Like something opening?' I asked.

Billy grinned – despite what was happening, he sensed adventure and the boy in him hid the man he was becoming.

'Like a door opening,' Augustus said, moving to where Billy pointed – the kitchen area – looking more serious than my son. 'Did you look?'

'Yes,' Billy answered, as if the question didn't need asking. 'Once the lights came back on, but I couldn't see anything. I checked in the cupboards. Thought maybe something had fallen down.'

Augustus ruminated for a moment or two, then shared a quickly formulated plan with us all.

'Right. Billy, Marcie – there's a drawer in that kitchen, second drawer down. Two torches in there. When the lights go out again, check those cupboards and push at their panels, their bottoms. Push hard. See if anything gives. Okay?'

The children nodded, a little perplexed, but not enough to ask questions. It didn't stop me though.

'Augustus?'

'I'm going back up. Turn off the electric, just for a minute. It'll be fine.'

'What about Monty?'

'He's immobilized for now.'

'What does that mean?'

'Just watch the children, Esther. And help them. My guess is there's a door somewhere – centrally locked, like the rest of this house. And when the electric goes off, it's released, like the others. But it's hidden. I'll be back in a minute or so.'

With that, he turned and pulled himself up out of the bunker.

'It's here!' Marcie cried out – I'm certain these were the first words I'd heard from her. Maybe it was the shock of the discovery, or just the hope of escape that brought her to life. God knows what must have been going through the poor wretch's mind. 'I heard it just behind this panel here. I heard it opening. But I can't shift it. Nothing is moving. It's solid.'

She was under the sink, pushing hard on the wall panel at the back, behind the plumbing.

'Move back,' Billy said, and we did instinctively. Then, he kicked at it, holding himself steady on the floor, his left foot striking it with surprising force. I heard a splitting sound. He kicked again – another crack. 'Marcie, join in,' he encouraged, and she did, and they kicked at the panel until it detached itself from the back of the cupboard, falling away with an echoing clatter. Falling away – it sounded to me – into oblivion.

'We've got it!' I called out to Augustus, as the two children stared into the hole they had created. And he must have heard me, because the lights came up almost instantly.

'Oh no!' Billy cried, and appeared to push himself forward, into the gap.

'Billy! What are you doing?'

'The door's trying to shut again, and it's too heavy! I can't hold it!'

All the external doors locked centrally, Augustus had said. And with the lights back on, it seemed this one was closing up automatically.

'Gus – turn them off!' I cried, hoping my alarm would make him obey without question. 'Turn them off!!'

He heard and obeyed, and Billy shouted triumphantly as the door at the back of the cupboard opened again. But, as we were plunged into darkness again, Marcie dropped her torch and it fell into the hole, tumbling into the endless dark of wherever it led.

'In ten minutes the generator will kick-in and the all the doors will lock again,' Augustus said, making me gasp as he silently crept up on me. 'So, if we're going to move at all, we need to do it now.'

'We only have my torch,' Billy warned, trying to hide the accusation in his voice, but it was there.

'Sorry,' Marcie muttered, a barely audible whisper.

'Well, we might find the other one when we get down there. But we only need one torch, Billy, as we're all going down together,' Augustus answered, making everything alright for the girl.

'Down?' This came from Marcie.

'Yes, down, my dear – but only a few steps. You'll be perfectly safe, I promise you. And I'll go first, just to show you.'

He looked to me and then Billy – for our approval, I guessed. Not that we had any alternatives.

'Show us the way then, Gus,' I said, answering for everyone, and so began our descent into the well of our city.

Augustus seemed to disappear into the hole at the back of the kitchen cupboard very quickly, despite the fact it was a small gap.

'There's a small ladder, just through the hole, on the right. It's got a rail. Grab it and ease yourself on it. Who's got the torch?'

'I have.'

'Thank you, Billy. Pass it to your mother – you're coming next. Careful now.'

The torch was handed over and in went Billy, disappearing just as quickly.

'I'm fine,' he let me know, becoming just a voice in that deep void beyond.

Augustus' disembodied voice continued to give instructions.

'You next, Marcie. That's it. Don't be afraid. We're not far down, it just sounds it. You can't see us, but we're just below you.'

'Shall I light the way?' I called out.

'She'll need to get through and on the ladder first – there's not enough room. Wouldn't want to risk you getting in each other's way – an accident, or losing the torch. Found the other one down here, but it's not working now. Right. That's it. Through you come. Esther – can you light the way now? Let her see the last few steps down.'

Marcie was safely settled – then it was my turn.

Unable to pass the torch onto anyone, I wedged it in the top of my waistband and then set about following the others in descent.

The drop in temperature was the first thing I noticed. Once I was through that hole and on the ladder, I felt a chill around me – at my ankles and my neck, and in my palms that gripped the ladder's rail. And a sudden horror struck.

'We're not wearing protection!' I cried, out loud, frozen to the spot. I couldn't help it – the panic took over, not allowing sense a voice. 'We're exposed, Gus! Like Billy in the water! Remember, he nearly died! We have to go back! We have to go back!'

'Mother!' Billy cried out in that small boy's voice he'll always have, in my head. I could hear his fear – for me, not for himself. But I ignored it and continued, unable to stop the verbal outpouring.

'And he was there, Gus! He was there! In the room! I saw him, and then he was gone! It can't be true, can it? A man can't appear and disappear like that?'

'Esther-.' Augustus – calm, but I still wasn't listening.

'We need to go back! We need to get suited up! Get our masks! I need to go back! I need to go back for him! Gus, I need to go back for Joe! I need to see him again!'

'Esther, listen to me-.'

'It's not enough, the letters he wrote, the glimpse I just had – it's not enough! It's not fair! I need to go back, Gus! I need to go and find him!'

'Esther, you're in shock. You need to focus.'

'We'll suffocate, down here – without the masks. God, I can feel it in my throat, Gus. I can feel it in my lungs.'

'ESTHER!'

The rise in Augustus' voice – suddenly full of anger and impatience – was enough to silence me. And the next unexpected act of care was enough to get me moving.

'Come on, it's not so bad. And it really isn't far down.'

The voice was Marcie's and, as soon as she'd spoken, I felt the metal wall ladder creak with her weight. She'd stepped back on it.

'We'll go down together, Mrs Morton,' she continued, talking in a sweet calm voice. And it was her calmness – and a little shame – that got me down off that ladder and onto the gritty, damp floor of the tunnel under Augustus Riley's house.

Under our city, I reminded myself, as I took stock for a moment – trying to ignore what couldn't be true and focus on what was.

'We need to get somewhere,' Augustus informed the children, as I pulled myself together. He took the torch from me and shone it on a part of the blueprints. *The blueprints* – we were in *Cadley's labyrinth.* So it was true, after all. 'We're here,' he said, pointing to a spot on the map. 'And I want to get *here,'* he continued, turning the papers over and unfolding them to find his destination. 'Yes, *here*,' he emphasised, finally finding it.

'Is it far?' Billy asked, concern in his voice – there was a lot of map.

'I don't even know if we'll actually get there, let alone how long it'll take us,' Augustus explained and then he was talking and looking at me. It was time to listen and be one of the adults again. 'I've never been down here until now and before this, I thought these tunnels were just a story. A crazy old architect's fantasy. I figure if something like this really existed, the authorities would have got their hands on it by now. Used it to their advantage in some way. Used it to control us just that little bit more. But they haven't – and here it is and here we are. So, my plan is to get to *here*, if we can,' he said, pointing to the map for me this time, shining the torch on the spot he'd identified.

I knew it, but I simply nodded. It seemed a dangerous place to go, but I found myself trusting him implicitly.

'It'll be clear when we get there,' he added, giving me reassurance I didn't feel I needed. 'He's got something I've been looking for, Esther. Someone, I believe. Someone I've been searching for a long time. And we might find some answers.'

'Answers?' I managed.

'To those questions you now have in your head, Esther. The questions you have about what you saw and how it can't possibly be true.'

His words I took as a promise – although, he'd promised nothing – but they were enough to keep me going, to help me find light in the cold, dark dungeon we'd descended into.

'Okay, lead the way, Gus,' I said, sounding as solid and brave as I could. 'Are you ready for an adventure?' I asked the children and, whether they were ready or not, both managed a forced smile of courage and we began our underground journey across the city…

I'm not sure how many hours we were down in those cold, narrow tunnels. Time was lengthened by our hunger – there'd been no time to think about provisions. And emotionally we were slowed by our fear – above us were tons of water that had seeped through every crack of our town and flooded everything below the surface. No matter how many times Augustus reassured us – *these tunnels are air- and water-tight, the authorities probably don't even know about them* – there was no escaping the feeling that the ceiling would crack and we'd be flushed away at any moment.

But, whatever we were thinking, we obeyed Augustus' every word as we followed him on along those shadowy tunnels, trusting his eyes to read the map correctly, and trusting his judgment in the final destination he'd suggested.

'Are you sure, Gus? After what we've just-.'

'Believe me, this is the right thing. And I need to do this.'

Hours later, we eventually arrived – Augustus announcing it with a simple: 'Ah, here we are.'

Like it was just any old destination.

But it wasn't – and minutes later I found myself back in a place I hadn't been for years.

'This is where the real adventure begins,' Augustus said, exciting the children and himself, as we cautiously stepped our way through Monty Harrison's mansion…

11. Jessie

'My parents were scientists,' I told Tristan, sharing information about my family that I'd previously put to one side – unable to talk about them after they'd gone.

What my parents had done when they were alive had never had an influence on my own life – I was a practical man, working with my hands first, my brain second. And once I believed they were dead, what they'd done for work was irrelevant. But now I'd seen that videotape and knew their lives must've continued after the Great Drowning – suddenly what they were took on a new significance. Suddenly, it was a tale worth sharing.

'The day they were down by the Black Sea and supposedly swept away, they would've been collecting samples,' I continued. 'Their specialist area was something to do with water.'

'Water?' Tristan questioned, a small mocking in his voice.

We'd travelled a night and a day since we'd discovered the second videotape, and we'd stopped to rest and get some sleep. The landscape hadn't changed in that time – the river road was endless, as were the dense forests on each of its banks – but we were still hopeful the horizon would break. That we'd discover something akin to what we'd glimpsed on celluloid.

'Yes, *water,'* I echoed, understanding his tone. 'It sounds so very unscientific, so everyday, but it's what I remember them saying. I'm sure it had some fancy, intellectual name, but they always told Joe and me that they were *water scientists*. Studying what was in it. *Predicting what it might do,* is how they described their work. I thought this was ironic when they were killed by it. But.'

I paused, wondering whether I could go on, but Tristan encouraged me.

'But now they're not?'

'Now I know that it didn't kill them,' I corrected, able to continue, sensing it would be good therapy, 'now I know that, I'm wondering just how they got on with their predictions. How much did they know? Did they know that the floods were likely, were coming? And why didn't they warn others? And if they were planning on getting out while they could, why did they leave Joe and me? And Billy – they left Billy, too. Jesus, Tristan.'

I stopped again – could feel my composure going. Tristan and I didn't talk about our feelings. An unspoken agreement between us. We talked things through practically and kept our emotions cool. No matter what I'd discovered in those first days of our trip, there was no need for that to change. At least, I didn't feel the need for it to.

In the short silence I created, Tristan picked up on this and diverted me back onto a practical route.

'So, what do you want to do about it?'

The obvious answer was simply to keep going – to find out what was out there. And, if we got word of what had happened to my parents, keep asking and searching until we found the truth.

So that's what we did – but with a different goal in mind. With that shoreline where my parents had stood in mind, the tame beast at their feet. And we found ourselves looking for more clues – for evidence that places had been recently disturbed. I was convinced that whoever had started this trail of information would be with us all the way. I didn't know why they were doing it. But now I was convinced it had nothing to do with Monty Harrison, I wanted to follow.

'Well, we've nothing else guiding us,' was all Tristan had to say.

And we'd found all these clues or signs – I wasn't sure what to think of them as – left out so visibly that there was no denying the intention. We came across another lab – door ajar, like the last one – and in one of its rooms there was a blackboard with *keep going* chalked on it.

Back in the speed boat, we went another mile and came to a fork in the river-road.

'Our man didn't leave us a clue about this decision,' Tristan joked, scanning the horizon, like me, for the signs we were becoming accustomed to receiving. 'Any ideas?'

'I've not been this far before,' I answered, trying to make out anything different, out of place, along the wall of trees. I couldn't see a thing. 'We'll go left,' I said in the end, switching the engine back on. The petrol gage caught my eye. 'Hope it's the right decision, Tris – we've half a tank left before we're halfway through our fuel rations. Then we'll have to make a decision.'

'Whether to keeping going or not?' He said it with a smile.

We both already knew that decision – how *could* there be any turning back after what we'd seen so far?

Turning left turned out to be the wrong decision – but our invisible guide was there to point this out. We'd sailed only minutes along the river-road when we hit a barrier – several trees had fallen into the stream, blocking our way.

I laughed in reaction – whoever was steering our journey was determined we wouldn't steer away from their intended path.

'Just move in a bit closer,' Tristan requested, as I slowed down the boat.

Moving slowly, we got close enough to see clean, intended cuts at the base of the trunks.

'Back we go then?' Tristan asked, but it wasn't really a question – just a verbal confirmation of what had already been decided by someone else.

'But who?' This was my question.

Tristan shrugged. 'If we keep going, we'll find out.'

So, we turned back on ourselves and ventured along the other road. Like the rest of our journey so far, our road was flanked on each side by dense forestry. And for several miles, we saw nothing but the blur of green, flickering with the odd glimpse of sky. There were no government buildings on the banks that we could see, and no reason to stop the flow of our progress along the river, so we simply kept going.

And I didn't slow the engine until we hit a crucial milestone.

'That's half of the fuel used up,' I said to Tristan, allowing the speed boat to almost drift, looking for a safe place to stop and moor it.

Just up ahead, a couple of trees with thick trunks were closer to the river than the others. I nodded at them and Tristan read my thoughts. I steered us up close and Tristan secured us.

'Okay,' he said, unzipping one of the bags we'd packed. 'We eat first – and decide later.'

I didn't protest. A week before, I'd managed to get my hands on some chicken, which I'd roasted. And, when Tristan opened the plastic box that contained the meat, filling my belly with its succulent flesh was all I desired. I finished off with an apple that had seen better days and a few glugs of water. Despite my thirst equaling my hunger, I knew I had to ration that last item – if we ran out of everything else, I'd cope. But if we hit trouble – with the boat, or with anything else – the water would buy us time. Would keep us alive. So, two glugs it was; Tristan showed the same restraint.

We sat in silence for a bit – digesting food and thoughts, I guess. And, in that silence, I thought of all the questions I had. The ones I'd had before – about Elinor, about Joe, the dogs and the takings. And the new ones, too – the questions I had about my parents. Questions I couldn't have imagined I'd need to ask.

'Want to talk about it?' Tristan inquired, breaking our quiet.

I paused a while longer, before answering: 'Yes. It might help.'

'Okay,' was my friend's response, and I realised he was expecting me to speak. Yet I needed him to do the talking. I only had my questions, whereas he had answers – squirreled away in a dark, closed place he rarely ventured. For once, I needed him to tell me everything that he already knew.

'Tell me,' I asked, knowing I was pushing it. Knowing it was likely he'd refuse. 'Joe never spoke of it, so I've no idea what he went through.'

And for a minute, I thought he wouldn't. Watched his face harden, his eyes empty, as if he'd switched out their lights.

'The takings?'

Two words – a slow start. But two words that rang out like an invitation.

I nodded my head – *yes, the takings,* it confirmed. *Tell me what it was like to be taken.*

'People had different experiences. So, it depends where they took you. What they did to you. What they saw in you. If you were special or not.'

'Special?'

Tristan shrugged.

'We were all together to start with – one big classroom, completing written test after test. Day after day. Separated during the night – kept in tiny clinical rooms, doors locked. They felt like containers – those rooms. Like we were lab rats, Jessie, safely popped back in our cages at the end of each day.'

Another pause, and my doubts crept back in – this was it, this was all I was getting. But I was wrong – Tristan was just steeling himself for what was to come.

'We arrived in a big group – strangers from all parts of the land – and were kept in that testing facility for ten days. I counted. But after that, we were split up. They had a list of all of us that were taken, and some of us were pulled out and taken somewhere else. That included me. From the few I've spoken to, if you stayed behind, your experience was relatively benign. A few more tests, and your worst torture was prolonged homesickness. Me? It was a lot worse, Jessie. A lot worse.'

'How worse? Can you tell me, Tris?'

He sighed, heavily and so deeply I could sense the weight of it sinking in him, but he nodded. And after a lengthy pause, he continued.

'It's where I met the man I'm looking for, the terrorist. Xavier, that's his name.'

He stopped again at this point, and I wondered if it was just too much – whether I'd pushed it too far. But he was simply staring at me – holding my gaze. It was the name, I realised later. He was checking for recognition, seeing whether I knew it, and whether his revealing it would cause a problem. It was unusual, though – a name I'd have remembered if I'd heard it before. But I hadn't.

'He wasn't at the first place I was taken to, but we both ended up at the same unit after that. Had both been on the list of special children. And they paired us up a lot of the time, putting us through new tests together. Sometimes giving a pill or injection to one of us, but not the other. Checking our bodies' responses. Kept us apart when they weren't doing their experiments, but always together in their labs. Was it just Joe who was taken?'

And suddenly, the questions were his, not mine. He was telling me he'd said enough – and it was my turn to contribute something personal. As alien as this was for us, it did feel right, and it gave me the chance to air some thoughts that I'd been having. To voice something about my family history that had started to re-write itself.

'Just Joe, and for a long period. And he came back damaged. It didn't show that obviously – not like that cousin of Esther's. You know that story?'

Tristan nodded. 'Ethan and Joshua – but only Ethan came home, right?'

'His shadow came home, nothing else. Well, Joe was altered, but in a different way. He was angry. Determined not to be beaten by anyone again, but then he just became a bad boy. Ended up as Monty Harrison's lackey.' I acknowledged the irony of this statement as soon as I spoke it. 'But it's not what happened to Joe that's bothering me.'

'No?' Tristan sounded surprised.

'Well, yes it is – I know he suffered and I want to find him. Find out why he left,' I corrected, reaching for the water bottle. I needed a little more – opening my head and heart to my old pal was thirsty work. 'It's what happened to me that I'm starting to question.'

'To you – but you said you weren't-.'

'No, I wasn't taken – I stayed at home. With my parents,' I said, twisting the lid back on the water bottle. 'The scientists.'

Tristan paused, thinking on my words for a while – unsure where I was going.

'Jessie, what are you saying?'

I took a moment to think through all the thoughts that were mixed up in my head. My memories had become fragmented, like several puzzles – broken up, the pieces all jumbled. And, since I'd seen that footage of my parents on the shoreline with the dog, it was like extra pieces had been added. Pieces that didn't quite fit, but gradually my head was finding a place for them. Yes, my mind was separating out the puzzles and finding gaps for the new pieces to slot in.

'Joe went missing when we were ten. Disappeared in the night. Taken from his bed. I remember being very confused and distraught, Tristan. Very upset. Crying for nights. Being consoled, but.'

I stopped, not wanting to say what I was now recalling – but Tristan was a few words ahead of me.

'But your parents?' he said, finishing my sentence as a question.

I nodded, and found the strength to continue.

'I don't remember their tears. Their attention – yes. And I always thought they were simply putting me first, putting on a brave face. Keeping their upset for when I wasn't looking or listening. But I'd remember *something*, wouldn't I? Crying late at night, or catching them unawares, my mother drying her tears up hastily. There's nothing in here, Tris.' I tapped my head as I said this, and felt tears spill from my eyes, as if the action had knocked them out. I instantly turned my head away, wiping them with an arm – although the rubber sleeve on my protective suit simply smeared them.

'Keep talking,' Tristan encouraged, his voice level, not judging my emotional release.

'They were cool and calm, Tris. The whole time. And when Joe came back and went off the rails, they remained that way. Cold, uncaring – I see it now. They weren't hiding their feelings, as I'd believed, sparing us their upset – their true feelings were on display. And they used to give me injections, Tris. To keep me calm. In the morning and in the evening. In here.'

I touched the crook in my right arm, feeling for a vein, the action bringing the memory more alive. Drawing it out from the archives in my head.

'And I remember being on a drip for a while. Hooked up overnight. *This'll put you right.* Those were father's words. But I can't remember what was wrong with me. I've never questioned it before. They were scientists, they were doctors. People calling Mother *Dr Morton* was always strange, but I trusted them implicitly.'

'They were your parents, of course you did. Could you be wrong?'

I shrugged.

'Jessie, that video. It doesn't tell us much. There could be any number of explanations.'

But I shook my head at this suggestion – too many memories were coming back to me. Memories that strengthened the doubts I had about them.

'There's something I've never quite been able to make sense of,' I said, remembering an incident that happened one night when I was fifteen.

It had just been my mother and me at home. I was in my room, doing homework. I had text books and note pads sprawled cross my bed. Couldn't tell you what I was studying, but I think Agnes had been over earlier to help. So, it was probably maths – it was where I struggled and she excelled.

My father was out – still working. He wouldn't have been collecting water samples that late in the evening – but he was probably running some kind of test in the government laboratory he and my mother were in charge of.

Joe wasn't living with us at the time – he'd been sent away to a juvenile correction centre.

And Mother was sorting out our dinner in the kitchen, as far as I can remember.

'There was a violent knocking at our front door. Loud enough to alert me, and I heard Mother rushing to it, calling out to whoever it was to be patient. When she got there, Mother went quiet, but I heard the voice of another woman. She was crying and demanding something, so I made my way downstairs. Thought my help might be needed. When they both saw me arrive, Mother immediately tried to shut the door, but the other woman was forceful and tried to push her way in. *Go back upstairs!* Mother shouted, but I didn't want to leave her. The other woman looked like trouble.'

I was trying to piece it all together as I spoke, fitting in those extra details I'd previously ignored and stored away as insignificant or simply unexplainable. What did the woman say? What was she asking? *I want to see them! I know you've got them! I know this is where they are!* And Mother – what did she say back? She had her back to me, so it was harder to tell, even harder to remember clearly. Her face in my memory would've helped. *I don't know what you're taking about! You're talking complete nonsense!* Something like that. Her voice was sharp, scolding, that I could clearly recall. But was it anxious, unsettled by this strange intrusion? I couldn't remember.

'What happened next?'

'When the woman saw me appear behind mother, she became less angry and more upset and she called out a couple of names.'

'What do you mean?'

'She said *Daniel, James.* Looking at me, pleading almost.'

Said those names – *Daniel, James* – like one of them belonged to me.

'And then what?'

'My father was there. Behind her, and he took her away.'

I paused – the return of this memory was so sudden, so clear, I wondered why I'd ever remembered it differently. I remembered Father turning up, but I had a vision of him simply coming home, closing the door on the woman, shutting out the fuss and noise.

'You okay, Jess?'

'Father was there and he took her way. Mother closed the door and encouraged me back to my room. When I asked who the intruder was and what she wanted, she just said she was mad. *A crazy woman, knocking at doors. Father will make sure she gets back to where she came from.* But I'm only just remembering it all, Tris. How is that? I was fifteen at the time, not a young child. How could I have forgotten?'

Tristan shrugged.

'I don't know. Maybe you didn't want to remember.'

'You think they knew her?'

Another shrug, arms wide.

'I can't guess at that, Jessie. But maybe. And maybe your father did take her back to where she came from, somewhere safe. And maybe your mother just didn't want to get into the detail.'

But I just kept seeing the woman's face again, staring into mine, calling out – *Daniel, James. I know you've got them! I know this is where they are!* Who did she mean by them? Daniel and James – who were these boys? And yet, she was looking at me. My head was a whirl of unthinkable possibilities.

'What if they weren't our parents at all?' I said aloud, shocked by my own expulsion.

'What?'

I tried to stay calm as I spoke, so that Tristan would still think mine was the voice of a sane man.

'The way she looked at me, Tris. When he said those names – like one of them belonged to me. And the other… Maybe the other one was for Joe-.'

'Jessie, you're making huge leaps here-.'

'But it's all making sense. All of it, Tris. How they were towards us. And all those memories coming back to me. And why they took their chance to get out when they could – leaving Joe and me behind. If we'd been their own sons, they'd have taken us too. You'd never leave your own child behind, would you?'

Neither of us could that answer that from direct experience, as we had no children of our own – but Elinor was close and I knew it would strike a chord with him.

'You're in shock. Seeing that tape and-.'

'I'm not. It's more than that.'

Tristan sighed, deeply. Betraying a little impatience. In fairness, this unguarded talk was new territory for us – I couldn't expect all his responses to be perfect.

'And this woman – who do you think she is in all this?' he asked, trying to humour me, and knowing exactly what I'd say in return, I'm certain.

'My mother,' I answered, calmly. 'Joe's and mine. Our real mother.'

We were done with talking after that – there was nowhere further I could take it, no one there to give me the truth I sought. We'd eaten enough to refuel ourselves and it was time to make that crucial decision.

'So, we've enough fuel to get us back the way we came, or to go the same distance forward – and hope we get ourselves the answers we're looking for.'

'Or at least a supply of fuel to get us home, Tris.'

'What's it to be, then?'

There was only one answer.

While I started the engine up again, Tristan untied the boat and we carried on along the river-road, wondering what lay ahead, hoping there was a little of what we were searching for.

We'd been speeding along for a couple of hours when we saw something ahead.

Someone.

In a boat, like ours – still, in the middle of the water, blocking the way. I slowed our boat, my heart speeding up immediately. There was only one other person I knew who had a vehicle like this. Not someone I wanted to see anytime soon. And from a distance, I saw him – stood on the deck, bold and smug. We'd been drawn in by Monty Harrison, after all. The tapes, the messages – *keep going.* All part of some elaborate game to lure us out here and-. And what? Jesus, what was Monty Harrison going to do to the two of us? And suddenly, all my re-imaginings about my parents, about what had happened to Joe and I began to fall apart. This was all Monty. This was *all* Monty…

'Jessie? What do you think he wants?'

Tristan brought me back from my thoughts and I looked head with fresh eyes. It wasn't Monty Harrison at all. Nothing like him. But there was a man standing up in the boat, looking in our direction. This sudden change in perspective left me a little dizzy, but I had to focus quickly, be decisive.

'Don't know, Tris, but let's find out.'

We steered the boat slowly towards him, cautiously drawing up close to his vehicle. And, as we did, he began to address us.

'Good to meet you finally,' he said, a nervousness in his voice. And I immediately knew he was on his own. Whatever was going on, this was a one-man-band, a solo effort. 'Sorry I couldn't meet up with you both sooner.'

'Who are you?' Tristan asked, picking up on the man's edginess, using a hard tone to show who had the power here. 'And why have you brought us out here?'

'My name is Nathaniel,' he answered, quickly, still anxious. 'And I'm going to show you what you've been looking for all along.'

Asleep

I'm in a house.

In a room.

In a corner.

I'm near a window and can see out onto the street. And I realise I'm several storeys up.

The road is flooded. A river road, they call it round here.

There are people out there in boats, worried people with worried voices. Shouting, crying out. I can't hear what they're saying, but I feel their panic. I know that disaster has struck. That tragedy is nearby.

I turn away, back into the room and that's when I see him. It.

Him.

It.

He goes from one to the other in my head – a man and then a beast, a beast and then a man.

Unafraid, I ask him a question.

'What's my name?'

He answers as I hear the shot ring out.

Awake.

12. Augustus

When we reached our destination point on the map, I stopped and took in a deep, heavy breath.

'How do you know this is it?' Esther asked, when I told her.

'Well, I've been following the map precisely, and this gave me direction,' I answered, shining the torch on the compass I held in my left hand. Plus this clue,' I added, swinging the torch to a marking on the wall. It had faded, but you could make out NW15. 'North West, point 15,' I expanded, and tapped the map. 'Same reference is on here.'

'And how can you be certain it's the right place?'

'Because,' I answered, prodding the map again, 'there's an asterisk in blue ink on here.'

'And?'

'And I didn't put it there – and neither did you?' Esther shook her head to confirm. 'So, someone else must've done it to mark their territory.'

She nodded, understanding: *Monty.*

We'd been travelling in near blackness for hours. Most of the way was narrow and the walls were damp, slimy in places, leaving residue on our garments. The floor was uneven, so our pace couldn't be too fast. The torch light had helped us see ahead, but towards the end of our journey had started to fade out, as its battery weakened. The children had been quiet throughout, but there was a solemnness in their voices when they answered our questions – *are you alright? need to stop? can you see where you're going?* – voices that spoke of hunger and tiredness, although their words were limited.

So, when we reached the destination I'd chosen for us, I couldn't help but question my own decision.

Was this really the right thing to do – the right place to come?

Esther had been questioning me all the way – maybe she had a point?

What if he's there when we arrive?

What if Monty has got ahead of us?

And what are we looking for, Gus?

What's Monty got that you're so determined to take back?

'Gus, are you okay?'

That was Esther, snapping me out of my thoughts.

'Yes, just distracted there for a moment,' I said, injecting my voice with what I hoped was reassurance. 'You know us old folk, we have a tendency to drift off.'

But even in the dark, I knew she wasn't buying that.

'And you, Esther?'

In answer, she exhaled a sharp sigh and shrugged. She was much calmer that she'd been earlier, but what she'd seen was alarming, confusing and a whole lot of other things at once.

'I don't know what to think, Gus. There's so much going on in my head. So much has gone on these last few days. Seeing Ronan's body in Mother's old flat. Hiding Billy in your house. And then earlier. Was it really Joe in there with us? I mean, I saw him, but.' She took a second to inhale again, using the pause to make sense of the thoughts in her head. 'He just disappeared, Gus. Did you see him?'

'I saw someone, Esther,' I answered, knowing something I just couldn't confirm to her – that it wasn't her Joe. It *couldn't* be her Joe. You see, I knew where he was. Had seen Joe with my own eyes. But it wasn't something I could share. Not yet. 'Whoever it was,' I continued, 'they moved quickly. I might have an explanation, but not here.'

I glanced quickly at the children and, even in the relative darkness, I could read Esther's perplexed frown.

'Later then?'

I nodded, and then decided it was time to deal with our immediate situation.

'Looks like we've arrived,' I announced, addressing everyone, moving swiftly from other distractions.

I flashed the beam of our single torch around and the dim light revealed a ladder fixed to the wall on our right. Guiding the weak ray upwards, I could see a way in.

'But where have we arrived?' Billy asked – a fair question, that his mother answered.

'Monty Harrison's big house,' she said, flatly, adding: 'Augustus has brought us to Monty Harrison's house.' Her last words had the hint of accusation about them.

'Why?'

This last question from Marcie – and I knew there was no more putting off the inevitable.

'A long time ago, Monty Harrison took something he shouldn't have. A girl.'

'Tilly?'

'Who's Tilly?' I asked.

'My friend, his niece,' Billy answered. 'In my class. She's been taken.'

For a moment, my thoughts were jolted. Had I got something wrong? Had I not been listening properly? What had Monty said to me? *My girl, Augustus – they took my girl. The authorities have taken her back – and we can't have that, can we?* I thought he'd meant the girl I was after – thought he'd meant Otterley. Not that I'd believed him – I'd instantly assumed he was lying, to put me off somehow. But it seemed he was on about this niece of his, this Tilly. So, he'd wanted me to help him get his niece back – and his visit wasn't about Otterley after all.

Still, it didn't matter what Monty Harrison wanted.

'No, not her,' I eventually answered. 'Like I said, a long time ago – and this Tilly would be too young. No, he took a girl I was trying to protect. But Monty took her for some reason and I think he probably still has her. So, we're here to find out.'

'Isn't this dangerous?'

'We'll need to be careful, but Mr Harrison isn't here. He's still at my house.'

'You can't be sure-.'

'Oh, I'm certain he's not moved yet. So, he won't be home. His staff will be, but this is a big house, isn't it Esther?'

'Yes.'

'And you know it well?'

'Reasonably.'

'So, we're going to climb that ladder and take a look around. That's all. What's the worst thing that can happen? And,' I added, before someone thought to answer my rhetorical question, 'Mr Harrison will have a full larder – and I'm sure I'm not the only who's a bit peckish?'

Billy gave me his very best boyish grin, given the circumstances, and Esther put a reassuring arm around Marcie's shoulder and gave her a gentle squeeze.

'Let's get ourselves above ground again,' Esther said and we prepared to ascend.

Billy had a last minute question before we did.

'Should we have kept our face masks with us – because of the pollution?' he asked.

We'd left all our protective gear behind – its clumsy bulk would only have served to slow us down. But I looked to Esther for guidance, before simply answering him.

It was a provocative question, coming from the lad – see, he knew the answer.

He'd been exposed to the elements some weeks back – nearly caught his death in the cold and wet. And he'd been left without protection, breathing in our so-called poisonous air for hours. It wasn't his first time, either. So, Billy knew the true answer without doubt. But that didn't necessarily give me the right to voice it.

'No, we don't need them,' Esther answered for me, revealing she was losing some of the caution I'd noticed about her before. 'Not really. They were just a precaution,' she added – for Marcie, I think, in case she suddenly raised a whole host of inquiries.

Billy nodded and, even in the shadows, I saw the understanding in his eyes. The boy already knew so much about our world – the wrongs, the rights and, most importantly, the rules of the game we were all playing.

'Up we go then?' he said, in a question, and answered with a nod, before taking the first few steps.

'Let me get up to the top and see how we can get in first. Might not be the same set-up as my house, so no point in us all getting to the top, just to…' I let my words fade, as I realised, too late, how they might have ended.

Just to find out there's no way in.

I caught Esther's face and saw she understood.

'Want me to go up first, Gus?' she asked, but I shook my head.

'I'm more sprightly than you think.'

'No, you're more sprightly than you *look,*' she corrected and I smiled at her small compliment.

'I'll be fine, Esther, and I'll be as quick as I can.'

As I suspected, the way in was different – but I was relieved that there *was* a way in. We'd not have to turn back, or worse, travel further – which had been at the back of my mind, throughout our journey under the city. And it looked undisturbed, which suggested Monty didn't know it was there. At least, he *hadn't* – before he saw those maps. But he did now – the mark on the map showed he'd definitely had time to read them, to find his house.

'Any joy up there?' Esther cried out, her voice echoing upwards.

'There's a hatch,' I explained. 'And a wheel to unlock it. Give me a minute. It's a bit stiff. Rusted.' It was slippery, too – wet with damp and an algae-like film. I gripped the metal wheel and twisted it hard. I felt it give a little, but not enough to unlock it. I had to be careful. I was up quite high – twenty, thirty feet, it was hard to know the exact measurements in the blue-black of the darkness. And with my left hand on the hatch's wheel-lock, I had just my right hand to hold onto the top of the ladder – there was no other way to secure myself. I gave the wheel another tug, praying it would continue to budge, if only inch by inch.

'Gus? You okay up here?'

'Yes!' I said, expelling enthusiasm, as I reassured her and felt the wheel-lock finally give. 'Yes, I'm fine – and we're in. I think,' I added. But I immediately met with doubt – and an obstacle.

'Gus, what is it?' Esther called up.

'Something in the way, Esther,' I shouted down, running my free hand over the surface of whatever was blocking our way.

It felt rough – like wood, untreated. I withdrew my hand and took the torch from a pocket of my outdoor suit. Running its weakening beam over the hatch's entrance, I revealed something that delighted my heart.

'Gus? What can you see?'

'Floorboards,' I answered, the joy in my voice clear. 'Floorboards in a square, with hinges.'

'What's he saying?' I heard Marcie's smaller voice ask.

'A hatch!' I cried back. 'An easy way in, I hope.'

Putting the torch away, I felt my way through the dark and pushed at the door, hoping it would give, praying there was nothing securing it on the other side. There was a little resistance, but it quickly gave. While I held on tight to the ladder, it took three or four attempts with my free hand to push the door open, but eventually it swung back – and a square of light flooded the tunnel, brightening the way for my friends to follow.

'Up you come,' I instructed, and watched as Billy was first to take this offer. 'And if we come across anyone, just leave the talking to me.'

But that wasn't something we needed to worry about.

Not at first.

You see, Monty Harrison's grand mansion was all but abandoned.

'This isn't a room I've been in before,' Esther said, the last make to it up the ladder and out of the tunnel. 'It's been a while since he called me to the house. Monty. Sometimes I'd have to clean something up here.' She shared a quick look with Billy. 'But I've not been down here.'

We came up to the surface into what appeared to be a cellar. There didn't seem to be anything stored in it – although there was a long, tall rack against one wall that suggested it had been a place to store wine in the past. And, like the maze of tunnels we'd just climbed out of, it felt cold and damp.

I shone the torch at the hole in the floor and noticed that the vinyl floor covering was rotten in places. Where I'd pushed back that hatch door, it had torn through the linoleum like wet paper. The room had clearly endured flood damage, and I felt a small sense of victory that Monty Harrison had suffered a little bit, along with the rest of us. It was clear, too, that the entrance hadn't been disturbed before. So Monty wouldn't have known his house was linked to Cadley's labyrinth. Might not have even been aware of the trapdoor.

'Until now,' I mumbled to myself, running the fading torch beam around the room, looking for a light or a way out.

'What?' Esther asked, but I didn't answer.

'Let's find a way out, but quietly,' I said instead, addressing them all.

Another quick run of the torch along the walls revealed the room to be L-shaped and when we turned a corner, an oblong of natural light framed our way out – a door. I twisted its handle.

'Locked,' I announced, immediately thinking how much noise we'd make – and how much attention we'd attract – once we attempted to break it down.

'Hopefully not for long,' Esther countered, pulling something out of a pocket – a collection of keys on the metal ring.

I raised my eyebrows at her, surprised she kept such a thing about her person. She eyed me back. *You just never know with Monty Harrison,* her look said.

'I've a few of Monty's keys on here – for his house and head office,' she explained, fingering through them. 'There's a couple of odd ones I've never used. This one and that one,' she added, handing over the bunch, with two keys prominent. 'Worth a try.'

The second one fitted perfectly and within seconds we were through the door and facing our next test.

'I know where we are now,' Esther said, much to my relief, although doubt clouded her face.

'Esther?'

'It's not quite how I remember it. Something's changed.'

Beyond the door, there were a set of steps, leading up, and then another locked door at the top – the same key unlocked the way there too. And then we were in a large, industrial style kitchen – all aluminum appliances and surfaces and a black and white checkered floor.

'What is it? What's changed?'

'I don't know,' she answered, stepping further into the room, getting a better feel for whatever had unnerved her. 'It was always gleaming and it smelled fresh – smelled recently cleaned. And now it's a little stale, unused.' She ran a hand along one of the metal surfaces and her fingers left greasy marks. I saw her shudder at this filth.

'Not your handy work then?' I posed, remembering her comment before about cleaning at this house.

'I've not been called here for a while,' she answered, and her phrasing made me curious about what exactly Esther did for Monty Harrison. Although given what she'd said so far – adding in her reputation for cleaning things within an inch of their existence and the fact she had her own keys to what appeared to be every door – it wasn't hard to guess. 'I have a question,' she asked, changing our line of conversation.

'Yes?'

'What is it you're hoping to find? I asked you in the tunnels, but you didn't give a straight answer. And you've not said much since – just that there's a girl you think Monty has? Someone he took from you? Now we're here, I need to know a bit more. I'm not prepared to just wander round this big old house in the dark. We don't know who else is in here and I don't want to hang around too long to find out. So, you said he took a girl?'

I nodded, conceding her point. Yes, I'd been reluctant to give her the details, but part of me worried she'd refuse to help once she knew *exactly* what I'd come for – and what I intended to do afterwards.

'And this girl? It's definitely not Tilly?' she asked. 'Because they've got her, Gus. They took her already. The authorities took her. And left Marcie – that's why Monty came to you.'

'Another girl,' I explained. 'Definitely another girl. One he took a long time ago. The niece – no, it couldn't be her. Too healthy and too young. No, I'm looking for a girl in decline and much older now. I know he has her. He said as much. So he's probably got her hidden here, in one of the rooms, away from prying eyes. What is it, Esther? Why are you looking at me like that?'

'I saw something here once,' she answered. 'A sickly looking thing. All wired up to machines, like she was in a hospital. Like she was fighting for her life.'

'My god – you've seen her?'

'Yes. Maybe I have. Here. A few years ago. I assumed… I assumed she was Tilly. But she'd had a different name. An unusual name, but I'd been drinking and other things distracted me that time. Anyway, I just assumed I'd been a bit confused.'

'Otterley,' I said aloud and I saw the conformation sparkle in Esther's eyes.

'The sickliest child I've ever seen, Gus.'

'Where did you see her?' I asked, ignoring her last comment. Otterley would be older now, much older – there'd have been no mistaking her for a child, even a few years back. But I let it go – it didn't seem that important. 'Upstairs. There's a place in the attic. A medical room.'

'Show me, Esther!'

'What about the children?'

In my excitement, I'd all but ignored the smaller people we had with us.

'I think we need to find them somewhere safe and leave them,' I answered.

'No!' Billy immediately protested, but Esther was in agreement.

'Gus is right. We don't know who else is in this place, or what we're going to find,' she explained, her voice quite stern with the boy. 'I've dealt with Monty's employees before and his house staff are very loyal. They have to be. And, even though they know my face, I don't know what they'll say or do if they find me wandering around this place with two children. So, it's best you and Marcie keep hidden away.'

'I think they'll all have gone.'

The voice was Marcie's.

'Sorry?' Esther questioned.

'He was angry. In a rage. He told them all to leave. Every single one of them. After the school secretary brought me here. Sorry, I should've said before.'

There was a flicker of annoyance in Esther's face, but she hid it quickly. We had to remember that this poor child had been abandoned with strangers – and had initially been hurled head first into the wrathful force that was Monty Harrison. And Esther knew, as a mother of a child, that allowances had to be made.

'You've told us now,' she answered, softening her features to confirm no harm had been done.

'We were the last to leave here,' Marcie concluded. 'Mr Harrison and me.'

'So there won't be anyone to be frightened of,' Billy added, but Esther was still cautious.

'We don't know that for sure, but,' she said – adding that final word to give her thinking time. After a minute, she gave her final judgment on the matter. 'You can come with us so far, but we'll find a safe place to leave you along the way. Deal?'

The way Billy's face lit up suggested Esther rarely made such treaties with the boy.

'Deal,' he answered, jubilant and satisfied.

'Will you lead the way then?' I asked.

Before we left the kitchen, Esther sought out some of the food she'd promised the children – some bread from a container on the side and some fruit in a bowl.

'That'll have to do you both for now,' she said, handing it over to them, keeping back an apple for each of us.

From the kitchen, Esther led us into a narrow hallway, with doors leading off it – she later explained that these led to storage rooms, stocking anything from table linen to dining chairs. At the end of the hallway, another door led out into what had clearly once been the grand entrance to the house.

'Left – through there – is the ballroom,' Esther explained, as we came into the space.

She pointed towards two large, closed doors – almost hidden, as they blended into the paneled walls. Many portraits hung around us in gilt-edged frames. The floor beneath was laid with marble, swirling in pink, orange and white, and several ostentatious chandeliers swung from the ceiling above. But there was something faded, something dirty about the whole place.

'I came here for a party,' Esther said, distracted for a moment, as the memory caught her. Then she appeared to pull herself up. 'We need to go right, up there.'

A grand staircase curled impressively around the wall to our right – smothered in a rich, dark red carpet that was faded with dust and wear. With Esther leading, we followed. Both she and I remained cautious at each step – wondering if Monty's staff had returned after all. But we encountered no one and nothing – at first.

At the top of these stairs, there was another long hallway, with doors leading off.

'She's right at the end,' Esther said, pointing ahead, as if her words weren't clear enough. 'But we'll leave the children in one of these rooms,' she added, trying a few doors as we advanced. I noticed Esther check her still gloved hands as she drew them way, checking the fingers for dirt.

The first couple of doors led to a cupboard and a bathroom, but the third was a bedroom.

'In there,' she told the two youngsters – Marcie entered without a pause, Billy shuffled with a little resistance. 'Billy, don't be difficult. We need you to take care of Marcie,' she added and the boy perked, slightly. 'Stay here, okay? Both of you. Until we return. You got that?'

She waited until we'd had a nod of confirmation from them both.

'Good, because we're trusting you.'

I thought maybe Esther was a little heavy with them, but then I'd not experienced her recent worry – when the boy had truanted from school and been lost in our drowned city.

'Right at the end, you said?' I questioned, once Esther had closed them in.

'Yes, there's another staircase, leads up into one huge room,' she answered, moving ahead, looking back a few times at the door she'd just closed.

'They'll be fine.' I was keen reassure to her, but equally keen to move forward swiftly. The house seemed empty, yes, but I couldn't believe Monty's loyal servants would stay away for long. And, surely, one of his henchmen had gone in search of him by now.

'Yes, I'm sure. The girl. Otterley. This way.'

I couldn't see where she meant – she was pointing ahead, as if there was something right in front of us, but all I could see was another paneled wall.

'In here,' she said, pushing against the wall and a panel popped open, revealing a hidden recess.

'Mine isn't the only house with secrets,' I smiled to myself, as we stepped inside and began climbing a twisting set of stairs, leading to the floor above us.

It was all as Esther had described.

'This is where I saw her, Gus. But it was years ago. A sickly child, wired up to all sorts of machines,' she said, almost rambling, as we climbed.

I felt my heart pounding faster and faster. Was I finally going to able to rescue this girl – now a grown woman, surely – as I'd intended to all those years ago? Or would she be long gone by now? As I reached the very precipice of this discovery, I had last minute doubts. What had made me so sure Monty still had her? What had made me even think she'd still be alive? It was a frail thing that Monty and I had discovered, many years ago in that government building. What made me think she'd even survived a few days, hours even, after Monty had taken her – given her delicate state? And yet... And yet, Esther had seen her, hadn't she? Just a few years back. And here – in this house, at the top of the spiral staircase she'd correctly remembered.

'I came to a party, Gus. Just before the floods came. Wandered up here, when I shouldn't have. And he followed...' she continued, but then her voice faded.

'How many years ago, Esther?'

'Sorry?'

'The party. How many...'

'Oh, I don't know,' she answered, slightly thrown by my question. 'Billy was very little. About eight years ago or so. Why, Gus?'

'And you saw a little girl in here?' I asked.

As we reached the top, my doubts intensified, and the comments she'd made earlier about finding a sick child – ones I'd swept aside, not really thought about – began to plague me with hesitations.

'Yes.'

'How little, how old?'

'Eight, maybe nine. But it was a long time ago, and I only saw her briefly before I was interrupted. I wasn't supposed to be in here.'

We were at top – mere footsteps away from our destination.

'But she couldn't have been,' I muttered, wondering, in all earnestness, if I'd made one big mistake. Wondering if the Otterley I'd tried to rescue and the one Esther had found here could really be the same person. But it was too much of a coincidence not to be true.

'She couldn't have been *what,* Gus?' Esther asked me.

'Couldn't have still been a child,' I answered, as we reached a door, finally voicing my uncertainty.

'It's locked,' Esther said, after trying the handle. She pulled out the ring of keys that had come in handy earlier. 'It wasn't the time I came here before. Let's see if one of these blighters unlocks this, too. In all the years I've had his keys, it's never occurred to me use them without Monty's permission. Let's give this one a go.'

Luck was on our side – the first key she tried released the lock and we were finally inside.

I simply stared ahead, taking in a landscape that was eerily familiar.

It was like an extension of what Monty and I had stumbled across all those years ago, when we'd raided those child camps and set so many other children free.

There was equipment everywhere, cluttering the place – in the same way those old domestic machines filled the lower rooms of my own house. Crammed in, no clear order or reason.

It was as if Monty too was hoarding.

There was a scanner of some kind, an x-ray machine and a dentist-style chair surrounded by a cluster of monitors and mechanical arms on stands. Who knew what procedure they were used for. There were several tall blocks of metal cabinets. As I moved further in – my eyes searching for her – Esther tried opening a few of the drawers and they slid open easily.

'They're empty,' she commented. 'I remember they were locked last time. And it's dirty in here. It felt clinically clean last time.'

But it was dirty everywhere – Monty's plush world had decayed alongside ours. His ill-gotten wealth hadn't been enough to preserve it, after all.

About half-way along, the room was divided in two – by thick, transparent rubber curtains, hanging in long, wide panels that overlapped. The rubber screen blurred my view of what was behind it, but I knew what was there. The girl, Otterley. A woman now, surely – whatever Esther thought she'd seen, Otterley would've been an older girl when Esther spied her here, and she'd be a woman when I finally reached beyond that see-through curtain and saw her with my own eyes.

But as I pushed through those panels and advanced towards the poor creature in the corner – finding her like I had last time, in a hospital bed, wired up to machines, the whole area sealed up again in a thin tent of clear gauze, offering further protection – I discovered that Esther wasn't mistaken. Not at all.

'I don't understand,' I muttered, almost stumbling as I approached her, my disbelief physically stuttering my movements. 'It doesn't make any sense.'

The closer I got to the girl in the fabric lung, the closer I came to accepting the truth. Otterley had not become a woman – she had remained a child.

'Gus, are you alright?' Esther asked softly.

'Is it really you?' I asked, pushing my face up close to the thin tent that enclosed her. 'And will you remember me?'

And then two things happened at once – two things that made both Esther and I jump out of our skins.

A movement and a noise – simultaneously.

Otterley opened her eyes.

But it wasn't in reaction to my voice, to my question – it was a response to another noise.

And that noise came from somewhere else in the house.

'Did you hear that?' Esther – immediate fear in her voice.

I nodded – it wasn't a sound you ever doubted, if you were unfortunate enough to hear it. I waited, listening out for it again. It was unlikely that we'd all imagined it, but for a second I clung to this unlikely hope. Then it came again – a single cry.

A single, gruff bark.

Asleep

It's a dream I've had before.

A variation on a theme.

It's daylight and we're in a street. A residential street, with houses either side. And there's about twenty of us, standing, looking ahead.

The ground is dry – bone dry, not a drop of water darkening the grey surface of the road. And no one is wearing a mask – apart from me.

'Take it off, it's perfectly safe,' a woman to my left says, so I remove it, cautiously.

Unlike in previous dreams, the mask comes away with ease. But, as I pull it free of my head, I hear a gasp from the crowd of people. Up ahead, something is coming towards us. A wave of something, and the crowd breaks up, people running away in terror.

'Water,' I mouth, unable to move.

But it isn't water – this isn't another flood come to drown our city.

The waves are made up of something else and a far greater horror is rolling towards us to drown us out…

Awake

13. Tilly

After the scientist made his threat – *I can always make you, you know?* – I felt something go into my arm again. This time, I didn't fall unconscious, but I still felt the fight go in me. And, when two guards joined us and led me out of the cell, I didn't put up any resistance.

'I'm sorry,' the woman said, almost a whisper.

But I didn't react in any way – I just let them take me from the cell without any fuss.

It turned out we were in a maze of cells. We turned a corner every four or five units along and I was quickly dizzy, unable to draw a map of any sense in my head. It was terrifyingly confusing and I felt nauseous with claustrophobia.

The scientist with the cold eyes was up ahead, leading the way, and the woman was just behind. As if reading my mind, she began describing where we were.

'These cells are down another floor, under the dormitory,' she said, explaining the geography, as we made progress up a flight of steps. 'The beds are through there,' she added, as we reached a landing, pointing to a door. 'But we're going further up.'

And the man in the white coat led the way up another set of tight, concrete steps. These took us to the ground level and I swear the air got lighter, my breathing easier. But I still felt numb, as if my mind and my body were somehow separate – one half of me obeying automatically, the other half wondering why, but helpless to act.

At the very top of the steps, there were heavy, metal doors blocking our way. Pushing through these, we were greeted by another set of doors, but these were made of thick transparent rubber and were not so hefty. The scientist pushed these aside and the guards led me into what I can only describe as a vast, open-spaced laboratory.

'This way,' the man said – to the guards, not me. 'We're taking her through the laboratory.'

The laboratory was a huge room – as big as the dormitory we'd been sleeping in, maybe even bigger. I'd only glimpsed it briefly before – when we'd been led in and out of the dormitory that was a floor beneath it.

It was largely divided up into small cubicles, defined by transparent rubber sheeting – made from the same material of the doors we'd entered by. In the cubicles themselves were what looked like hospital beds and various pieces of equipment – monitors, drips, tubes and leads, small trolleys holding trays of surgical instruments, vials of liquid and other medical paraphernalia. I know this, because the woman quietly explained everything to me, as she trailed behind our small party.

It all appeared untouched – as if it had all been prepared for something, but never used. I noticed many things were covered-up – in see-through covers or wrapped in tight, thin plastic, as if brand new. And there was a smell about it all – clean, but not pleasant. Like the bleach they used in the lavatories at school.

'What's all this for?' I asked, repeating it several times. 'Why are you showing me this?'

But no one answered my questions – not even the anxious woman who stayed at the rear.

At one point, I stalled. I'm not sure why. We'd reached the furthest part of the room, passing all the rubber-walled cubicles, and found a bigger area that was cordoned off in a similar way. It took up about the space of four units. I could just about see inside – there was a bed and several machines surrounding it. And like everything else I'd seen, every item was covered in transparent material of some kind or another. As if preserved.

Instantly, there was something in my mind – a sense of being there before. A blink of an image. Men coming in. Me, attached to a machine. Someone telling me I was safe, that they'd come to rescue me. And then I mind went blank again. I had no idea where these thoughts had come from – maybe one of my strange dreams?

'No time to stop,' the scientist barked, realising I'd stalled his group. 'Keep moving! We're almost there.' This last line was not addressed to me – it was for the others.

And then it was my turn.

No more sight-seeing.

No more delaying what they had planned for me.

We went up a level, in an industrial lift – taking us up into the roof space.

When the doors opened, there wasn't much to see. There was just a dark empty room. A big black shadow that was a little disorientating. We stood still for a few moments and I tried to adjust to the darkness, but nothing changed. Nothing came out of the shadows – no shapes, no gradual lightening to grey.

The woman, who'd been quiet for a while, stepped up close to me and spoke.

'Look, just tell them your name – your *real* name this time and this doesn't have to happen.'

But I was still numb with whatever they'd given me and couldn't find it in myself to answer. I had an idea of what would happen to me if I stayed silent – *I can always make you, you know?* the man in the white coat had threatened. Yet somehow I still knew I had to keep my secret. And, from what I could see, all they'd done was take me to a dark, bare room.

When I didn't answer, there was silence for a few seconds – but eventually, I was given a new instruction to follow.

'Take three steps forward.'

I paused and sensed the words about to be repeated, so I followed the order – took three cautious steps into the oblivious space. Behind me, I heard the lift door opening and the guards, the man and the woman retreated.

'It's called the *Chamber of Doors*,' the man said, and that was the last I heard, before the lift door closed again and I heard the electronic hum as they descended.

I turned back into the room – but all I saw was more blackness.

I had the eerie sense I was surrounded by nothing. The endless dark seemed to take everything with it – the walls, the floor, the ceiling. It was like being trapped in space, trapped in chains, in ropes, in restraints you couldn't see or feel.

Then something appeared in the black.

A door.

And I could feel things again – could feel the floor beneath me, the air surrounding me. Maybe whatever they'd given me was wearing off, or its effects were changing?

Then I moved forward.

Touched the door's handle.

Pushed it down.

Opened the door.

And stepped inside.

But all I found was another door.

And behind that another door.

And another.

And another.

And another….

14. Jessie

'Who are you?' Tristan asked, of the man whose boat was blocking our way. A man who we both knew had to be behind the breadcrumb trail we'd been following. 'And why have you led us to here?' he added, revealing there was no doubt about his assumptions.

'My name is Nathaniel,' the stranger answered, quickly, no denial of the charge made against him. 'And I'm going to show you what you've been looking for all along.'

I maintained my role as observer – watching the nervous stranger in the boat, and keeping an eye on Tristan, whose almost fierce distrust of the man gave him an edge that left me uneasy.

We'd glided so close that our boats were all but touching – and Tristan could easily have reached out to the man himself, brought him down physically. There was something in my old friend's posture that suggested he might just do something like that.

'Get off your boat,' Tristan instructed, holding his position, keeping his voice steady, a little hard. 'Get onto ours – then we'll talk. And bring your keys.'

'You want me to-.'

'You've been sneaking around, Nathaniel. Taking footage of us over the last few months, from what I can tell. And now you've lured us on this trip out into the middle of nowhere. Not exactly the actions of a man who wants to build up trust. So, there is no trust. And now we've come to you, you need to play things our way. Or we turn around and go back the way we came. We've still enough gas, you see.'

That wasn't strictly true – and I wasn't sure I *could* go back. We'd set out to find answers to Tristan's questions, but now I had too many of my own – and I wasn't prepared to just walk away. I let Tristan continue, though, without interrupting.

'And what happens when I step on your boat? How do I know you won't just attack me – take my boat and sell it on to your boss?'

Our *boss* – of course, he'd been watching us. He knew all about Monty.

'You don't. But we've followed you and you've not harmed us, so far. We've no motive to hurt you either – we just don't trust you. If you want us to come any further with you, hand your keys over, step off your boat onto ours and we'll talk. If we like what you have to say, we'll stick with whatever this is. And if we don't, we'll give you back your keys and we'll go our separate ways. That's the deal.'

Nathaniel hesitated for a minute or two – weighing up the risks. Thinking, I'm sure – like I had – how easily Tristan could overpower him and haul him on board, whether he agreed to our terms or not. But he must've also been thinking how far we'd already come – and would we really be prepared to turn away and go back, just because he refused to hand over his keys and step aboard our vehicle.

'Start the engine, Jessie,' Tristan instructed, the command surprising me with its tone of sharp impatience. 'This man who calls himself *Nathaniel* has wasted our time,' he added, spitting his name, as if he doubted its authenticity.

And for a second, when it looked as if Nathaniel wouldn't react, I thought I might have to follow Tristan's instructions – start the engine and begin to back away, abandoning our quest for the truth.

'Okay, take the keys,' Nathaniel said, holding them out, a sigh of defeat in his voice. 'I guess you've not given me much choice.'

Tristan took the keys and let a triumphant grin slit his face. He held out a hand, steadying our guest as he climbed aboard.

'I think it's you that hasn't given us much choice,' I answered, holding out my own hand to him – a gesture to reassure him that he was safe, amongst friends, although we were still strangers then. 'But now I think it's time you gave us an explanation.'

He nodded at me, slightly gravely, as if what he had to say wouldn't be easy – wouldn't necessarily put him in a good light.

'I'm not sure where to begin,' he said, sighing deeply and I felt the heaviness about his shoulders in that single, weighty breath.

'At the start,' Tristan suggested, his voice softening, as if he too had picked up on our new companion's emotional load.

'And what if you don't like what I have to say? What if you don't believe it?'

But we let his questions hang in the air – until we heard his story, we couldn't answer them anyway.

'Okay,' he eventually conceded, taking a seat that I offered with a hand gesture. 'From the start it is...'

'My name is Nathaniel Jacobs – and it's my real name. Don't think I didn't hear the tone in your voice, Tristan. And I don't blame you for doubting whether I'd give my real name, I really don't. You'll soon find there are a lot of reasons why you shouldn't trust me. Some you're aware of already. I've been sneaking around, as you know – secretly watching you, filming you and, yes, I laid down some clues to get you out this far. I needed to be certain you'd take the risks – trust in them – before I took any more myself. Before I took my biggest risk.

'What you don't know is that I work for the authorities. Quite high up now – been on the inside for some years and been promoted for my hard work and loyalty.'

He paused, watched our reactions, waiting for us to break our silence. But we didn't, so he continued.

'Don't worry, I'm not here in any official capacity. I'm not here to hand you over to my colleagues because of your theft and destruction of government property. I took that footage to get your attention – and so that I'd have something to keep me safe, once I'd ventured out to the middle of nowhere to meet you both. So, if anything happens to me-.'

'Copies of those tapes fall into the wrong hands?' Tristan.

Nathaniel nodded.

'I know it won't come to that, though. From watching you two, I know you're good people. Hard working. And I'm certain I'm not in danger. Still, I'm taking a huge risk coming this far and those tapes are just a bit of back up. But that's not what I came all this way to tell you. See, I want to put things right. I've always wanted to put things right, but I've been a coward, on the whole. I've helped in my own way, along the years – here and there. But I want to bring the authorities down. I want to expose the truth. Want everyone to know what's really been going on all these years. Want to bring the government down, before it gets any worse…' He faltered, momentarily. 'And I want you to help me.'

Tristan scoffed.

'What makes you think you can do that?'

'Because I've worked my way up to a position of power, Tristan.'

'And what does that mean?'

'It means I'm in the Circle.'

I had no idea what this *circle* was, but Tristan's face revealed he did, and it was significant.

'Keep talking,' was all Tristan said in response, his tone noticeably cooling – I'd have to wait for an explanation.

Nathaniel nodded and continued.

'I know a lot of what has happened over the years, because I've worked in the right places and seen all the wrong doings. When the takings began, I was there – in the laboratories. Not significantly older than the children they brought in, I was an assistant. You were taken, weren't you, Tristan? And Jessie – your brother was, I know. I can tell you all I know about what they did.'

He paused and took our silence as permission to continue.

'They were hard times for the government – I say that not as an excuse, but as a way to explain why they started down the route they did. And the better people amongst them were so easily persuaded by those who had different goals. But things were getting desperate – natural resources running out. Fuel so very limited – homes running without electricity for days, weeks at a time in some places. Food, too. The change in the environment had a catastrophic effect for farming. And not forgetting the years of wars among countries – destroying so much, but costing so much in the process, too.'

'So much loss,' Tristan commented, breaking our silence.

'Yes, loss,' Nathaniel answered, but I doubted Tristan's meaning of loss was the same as his. 'Difficult times, indeed,' he said, finding his way to his story. 'I'm sure you remember. But whatever the cause, something had to be done and the government had run out of so many rational ideas.'

'So, they had to try out some irrational ones?' Tristan interrupted again.

'Yes, you could put it like that,' Nathaniel answered, not quite conceding the point.

And, for all the earnestness so far, I saw before me a cautious servant of the government. A yes man, a politician. I imagined as his tale unfolded further, he'd be excusing the authorities' actions in some way or other, no matter how shocking and cruel they were. For the first time since we'd invited him on our boat, I found him a little unpleasant.

'The fact is, they had to do something – find some new answers – and they looked to their scientists. And their starting point was good. Their intentions were to create new fuel and power sources. Solar and wind energies. Create new hot houses for growing vegetation. They reintroduced factory farming, despite the claims of animal cruelty. And for a while it looked like things were looking up for humanity. Normality was sustained. And even when they took the children.'

He looked up at Tristan at this point.

'Even when they took you, the intention was supposed to be a moral one. They should've been honest – they should've let people know what was happening. But they didn't think parents would give permission and it wasn't considered there was time for all that. All the bureaucracy.'

'Surely every parent would've happily agreed to have had their child tortured in the name of progress?' The bitterness in Tristan's voice was unmistakable.

'That wasn't what was intended, you must believe that.'

'Must I? It's not what happened.'

'It *wasn't* the intention – it wasn't the order that was given.'

'The *order?*' Tristan reacted, his voice and fury rising.

'Let him speak, Tris,' I intervened. 'He's already said we won't like everything he'll say. But let's hear him out.'

He conceded with a begrudging nod.

'Go on. Get it all out.'

Nathaniel took in a deep breath, steadied himself and continued.

'The order was to take the most intelligent children from schools, test them further, and put the brightest to work with our scientists. Nurture their talents as quickly as possible – use our brains of the future to solve our problems and come up with the answers. The adult leaders, after all, could not – their aim was to put all our hopes into the future, as it grew up.

'But not everyone followed that order to the word. There were factions within government that had other ideas from the outset. Certain things did follow that original plan – the smart ones were taken, were tested and the very smart did work for some years in secret laboratories. And that went on until someone started to leak the truth and it all came to an end.'

'You?' I questioned, and his eyes flicked to my face. 'You were the government leak?'

He nodded, but there was no sense of pride in that movement – he'd been involved, after all. What had he said? *I'm in the Circle.* He'd said it like it was something of importance and Tristan's reaction had backed that up. And he could've done more – spreading a few stories was a small contribution in the huge task of making things right.

'But all that did was uncover the official version of events – the palatable version. The version I'd seen in the laboratories that I'd worked in. But darker things had gone on – darker things I know you experienced, Tristan. You see, many of those that didn't pass the tests were returned to their families, but many were not. Many were sent to the laboratories all the same, but not as scientists or assistants.'

'As subjects.'

'Yes, as subjects,' Nathaniel echoed, with more than just a hint of shame in his voice. 'I did what I could over the years, once I knew.'

A daggered look from Tristan made him pause, retreat slightly.

'I did, but without risking my own life. I did say I'd been a coward. And I've been biding my time – waiting until I was in a position where I really could make a difference. But yes, other children were kept and subjected to all manner of experiments. At the time, when I found out what had happened, I thought it was just a few rotten apples. You get them in any barrel, but now I know the truth.'

'The truth?' Tristan repeated, as if he somehow doubted there was such a thing.

'Yes, the truth, Tristan. You see, those rotten apples had been there all along – way before the takings took place. They'd planted seeds generations before with an earlier experiment that many people are still ignorant of. Experiments that happened to a whole generation without anyone knowing or anyone questioning the results. And then there are the dogs.'

He followed that last line with a breathy sigh – and then we were silent for a while.

I'd long considered that there was more to the evolution of that particular species from man's best friend to his worst enemy. But I'd never heard anything concrete – not from an official source.

'What can you tell us about those vile vermin?' I asked, as Tristan waited in silence for an explanation.

'Like so many things are that wrong with our society, it started in a laboratory, with the scientists. With good intentions, maybe, only they didn't last.'

Here, he paused a minute, as if what he had to say next was even less palatable than before.

'Can I have some water? This is thirsty work,' he said, the last comment somehow crude, somehow suggesting that what he was doing was an arduous task that should be praised, rewarded. 'I've got supplies on the boat. I can pay you back, several fold. I've got fuel, too. Enough to take you further,' he continued, when neither of us answered – giving us a sneak of his intentions. *Enough to take you further.*

'Here, but go easy,' Tristan offered, holding out one of our bottles – his warning suggesting he didn't quite trust Nathaniel to share his own store. 'Who knows how long we'll be out here.'

'Thank you,' he answered, and took a couple of cautious glugs. Then, he handed it back and continued. 'The dogs. Ah – where to begin?'

'In the labs, you said?'

He nodded, following the way in I'd given him.

'Military labs.'

'Military?' The question was from Tristan – from all the tales he knew and passed on, this clearly hadn't featured.

'Cruel experiments, Tristan. Started many years ago. Of all the things that brought us to where we are today, war played a major part. It cost money, lives and sapped our natural resources like nothing else. But this was sanctioned by governments and always a high priority. And, as the traditional resources dwindled, the authorities had to find new ways of battling against the enemy. And this is where the dogs came in.'

'How?' Tristan asked, his face perplexed, a little anguish in his voice, as he feared the explanation and the cruelty it would reveal.

'They took dogs and turned them into killing machines. Played with their DNA and created a superior, larger, stronger, more vicious species. I don't know how they planned to deploy this particular weapon – set them free in enemy territory and watch as they savaged the population? I don't know.'

'But that is what they did, isn't it?' Tristan again.

Nathaniel nodded.

'Yes, but not intentionally. Not at first. But a whole pack got free from one of the bigger farms. Someone playing god, or a protest group, thinking they were liberating innocent creatures. Who knows? For all my digging, I haven't been able to find out. But a whole pack was set free and, well – you know the rest. The government's secret weapon turned rogue. There was an order to shut down all the farms at this point and, officially, they all did.'

'But they didn't, we've seen for ourselves,' I claimed.

Nathaniel shook his head.

'No, they didn't. The farming continued in secret. Armies of dogs continued to be bred, with a very different motive. One crueler than you can imagine. You see, some saw the escape of those creatures as answer to another problem – our population. As the reports of the killings grew, some saw this as the answer – a way to reduce the numbers.'

'Jesus...'

'Resources couldn't be created, Tristan, so better to limit the number of people who needed them. Not my view – but one I found documented, when I had a chance to go through the government archives. So, a small army was created for this purpose – thousands of poor creatures bred and confined. The other part of the plan was to protect some of the population, so they built a safe haven for selected survivors – a place the dogs couldn't get into. And the lack of resources meant they could do this in secret – access to media of any kind was so very limited, that only word of mouth would get news of this to the public. But there was always this threat. And the authorities got nervous. Very nervous. Nervous enough for these plans to be completely abandoned this time, even by the cruelest of men. And the bodies were destroyed – injected lethally and buried. But you know this – you found some of the perfectly preserved evidence at the laboratory you destroyed.'

'But the authorities didn't just abandon their plans entirely, did they?' Tristan asked, passing Nathaniel the water again. We could hear his voice breaking a little, but we needed him to finish his tale.

'No. They had a back-up plan. A plan that relied on natural resources after all. The government had been studying water behavior for years. Predicting its behavior. Your parents were part of this, Jessie.'

He said *your parents* – not shedding doubt on how genuine this familial connection was, as I had. Maybe I'd been wrong – maybe they *were* my parents after all and would be able to explain all their actions when I eventually found them.

'So, they built a safe haven for the selected survivors, got them out in time and watched as the floods came.'

We were silent again for a while – the enormity of what Nathaniel had revealed in so few words washing over us. Drowning our thoughts, our senses, just as the tsunami had all those years ago – killing people, destroying homes and our city forever.

'They did that?' Tristan eventually asked.

'Yes,' our new companion answered.

'*You* did that?'

'I didn't stop it – so, yes, I did.'

Another pause, and then I had a question to break the stillness.

'But why keep us fed, why let us survive, when their intention had been to cull us? That doesn't add up.'

'Because they couldn't help themselves, Jessie. They'd stopped seeing you as people, as human – you were all just subjects to experiment on. Scientists love an experiment. And that is what this became – another experiment and the enclosure they'd built around you became just another laboratory. Remember I said there'd been an earlier experiment – one they'd carried out on a whole generation, without anyone realising?'

We both nodded, wondering what was coming next.

'Well, they wanted to see out the results of that. Wanted to see if their invisible manipulation of the little people would come to anything. Whether it would teach them anything, help them survive into the future.'

'What was this other experiment they carried out?' Tristan. 'And how come, as you say, no one knew about it at all?'

'Look at your families,' Nathaniel replied. 'The generation your parents produced. What do you see that's unusual? A strange phenomenon running through whole families, whole communities.'

We both allowed his question to roll around in our heads for a few minutes. Yet, neither of us came up with an answer. And when Nathaniel gave it to us, it seemed so obvious that we hadn't considered it strange before.

'Twins,' he said simply.

'Twins?' I echoed, thinking of Joe, of Agnes' dead twin, of Joshua and Ethan.

'Yes, a whole generation of twins occurring in families. Further manipulation of DNA, but not one single complaint or eyebrow raised. People just assumed it was a natural change, some kind of evolution in fertility. Or something in the water.'

'But then it stopped?' I said, thinking of Billy, of Elinor – of the generation that followed mine.

'Yes, it did, and no one questioned it then, either. Maybe they all thought it just skipped a generation.'

'Something in the water. Skipping a generation. What some would call old wives' tales,' Tristan offered, and I instantly sensed the skepticism in his voice. Was he buying any of this?

'Yes, some would,' Nathaniel answered, suddenly cautious, as he heard the doubt too.

'So why should I believe any of this? Why should I take your word on what you've told us? I was there for the takings – and witnessed much of what you've said here. More in fact. But the rest. The dogs, the flooding, the enclosure – and this last business. Why should we believe a single word of it, when you've no proof?'

'You shouldn't,' Nathaniel answered, sounding more confident than he had before – as if he'd finally settled on a certainty. 'But you won't have to just believe me. I'll show you. It's why I set this up, after all.'

'And what will you show us?' Tristan asked, his distrust still evident.

'The wall,' he answered. 'I'll take you to the wall where the enclosure ends. And then I'll take you beyond it, too…'

15. Esther

When I heard that single bark, I couldn't quite believe the enormity of the fear that flooded through me.

'Gus! The children!' was my instant cry, but he was already focused elsewhere – on the strange girl he'd come here to find. The girl I'd glimpsed all those years ago. The girl who hadn't aged, but didn't look any healthier, either.

'Augustus! We've got to get back to the children! You heard that, didn't you?!' I yelled at him, not doubting for a second that he had, but wondering why it wasn't appearing to bother him.

'I have to get you out of here, Otterley,' he said to her, acting like he hadn't heard me at all. 'There's no need to be frightened of me. My name is Augustus and I tried to save you from all this many years ago.'

Then he began to unleash her from the tangle of wires and tubes that connected her to the many machines surrounding her bed. All the while she was silent, but compliant too, as if she was conditioned to simply follow whoever gave her orders.

'Augustus! We have to go to the children!'

'You go!' he finally answered me. 'We'll catch you up.'

'And where are you going to take this poor thing? You've just wrenched her from her life support. How on earth are you…'

'I don't think it's what's keeping her alive – I don't think that's what this is at all. But I've no time to explain now. You go to the children. Otterley and I will catch you up.'

Otterley. Said almost with affection.

I gave the child a look and she met my eyes with her pale, tired ones.

'Be gentle with her, Gus,' I said to him, while still holding her gaze. 'I'll get the children and what? Go where?'

'Back the way we came,' he answered, and I agreed without thinking it through. I simply had to get back to Billy and Marcie, check they were safe. Check the distance between them and the noise I could still hear so clearly.

A crazy thought entered my head, as I scuttled my way back down the tight spiral staircase, listening out for the next animal cry – the authorities had tracked us down. They'd worked out where we'd fled, knew we had Billy and the girl, and had come to get us. Come to take the children from us, with an army of dogs to help them.

You can only hear one of them, Esther, I told myself – scolding myself for such stupid thoughts. *It's just a single bark.*

But, as I dashed along that endless hallway of doors on the first floor of Monty's mansion, I realised that it was no longer just one yelp. It was now a succession of them. A crude arrangement of barks, growls and howls.

'Jesus!' I cried, hurtling along the hall, almost battering the door open when I reached the room where I'd left the children. 'Can you hear that?' I asked, entering, but I needn't have said a thing – the terror paling their faces gave me their answer. 'I need you both to be quick and brave – follow me, okay? And keep up!'

'Mother, where are we going?'

'Back the way we came, Billy, and Augustus is not far behind. He'll soon catch up.'

'And where are *they?*' His eyes were so wide when he posed this – full of fear and expecting a Mother's protection.

'I don't know, Billy, but I'm going to do everything I can to keep you safe, okay? And Marcie – are you ready, too?'

But the girl was mute again and wouldn't answer. I reached out to her, encouraged her forward.

'Come on, we have to move. Have to get out here. We haven't time.'

Still, she remained frozen to the spot, petrified by what we could hear – a brutal orchestra reaching crescendo – but couldn't see.

'Come on, love.'

'Come on, Marcie!' Billy cried out, his impatience hurtling past his fear. 'We've no time and I'm not being killed by one of those bloody things!'

And then he was past me, too – running ahead, down those stairs, giving me no choice but to follow.

'Marcie, come on! I can't let Billy go ahead on his own! Please, come on!!'

Finally, the girl shifted, and – as her body began to move – her emotions began to unleash, her silent terror turning into burning tears.

'We'll be fine, we'll get to safety,' I told her, as we hurried along after Billy – down the stairs, back through the huge kitchen and back down into the well of that sprawling house.

As we ran, I tried to work out where the sound was coming from. It was a surround-sound, like the helicopters had been – circling us, wherever we went. In the kitchen, we were given the fright of our lives when one appeared to jump up at us – but it was the other side of glass. The other side of a window.

'They're outside!' Billy exclaimed, recovering from the shock and I wondered exactly what dogs were doing on Monty's land. Recalling the puppy Joe had brought home – the one I'd killed all those years ago – I wondered what exactly our gangster associate had been up to.

'Breeding,' was the only explanation – but why?

I could hear Augustus coming just behind us – *I've got her!* he cried out every ten or so steps, reassuring us he was on his way.

From the kitchen, I encouraged Billy and Marcie to go back through the door that led to the cellar steps.

'Go back down there and then wait by the hatch to the tunnel. I'll just wait for Gus, give him a hand.'

Billy obeyed, though he was reluctant to leave me behind.

'I'm just footsteps way,' I reassured him.

By the time Augustus reached me, he was struggling a little. He had her draped across his arms.

'Heavier than she looks,' he said, an excuse, as his legs struggled to move at a good pace.

'Can you put her down? Will she walk?'

Talking about her as if she wasn't there.

'I can manage,' her voice croaked, coming as if from nowhere. She was starting to look sharper, like whatever had kept her in a stupor was fading. *I don't think it's what's keeping her alive,* Augustus had said of the equipment she'd been wired up to. Had it been keeping her sleepy, keeping her confined? 'Where are we heading?' she asked.

'Down there,' I said, pointing to the open door that revealed the cellar stairs beyond. 'We're leaving by a tunnel…'

'Under the house,' she completed, surprising us both. 'I've seen it,' she finished, a comment we didn't have time or mind to question. And then she made her way to the L-shaped room below us, small steps, but steady enough.

'Come on, Esther, you too – we need to get out of here!' Augustus instructed, urgency back in his voice, now he'd been relieved of his burden. The cruel chorus of barks was intensifying around us. 'They're getting too close for comfort!'

'They're all outside,' I told him, but he shook his head.

'No, some have got inside now. I heard them as we caught you up. So let's get down that hatch, before it gets any worse!'

'Inside? Where the hell have they come from, Gus?'

'I don't think they've come from anywhere, Esther,' he answered, as we made the door and were stepping onto the staircase down. 'I think they've been here all along.'

A crash and sound of glass shattering send a sickening shock through me. The dogs that had been baying at the windows – revealing their killer jaws through the glass, blurring it with their thick saliva – had made sudden progress.

'Quick, Esther!' Augustus shouted, and he shut the door behind us, as I stumbled ahead in the darkness. There was no time to question who had the torch – it wasn't with me – we just had to get to that hole in the cellar floor.

But as we descended deeper into the blackness, I heard frantic scratching at the door above us and then a light broke through again, followed by furious barking and the terrifying sound of animal nails clacking on the stone steps. They were rapidly gaining on us, their closeness nauseating.

'Inside that room – and lock this second door!' Augustus cried and within in seconds we were safe.

At least, I thought we were.

Augustus reassured the children and Otterley – was she a child too? I wasn't sure.

'How are you doing?!' he cried back to me.

'Almost there,' I said, hiding a panic that had crept into my voice, as I tried to secure the door. 'Get them down, okay?! I'll follow as soon as I can!'

And so, as I tried all the keys in my bunch – fumbling in darkness, holding the door with my body, sweating with fear and panic – Augustus set about taking all three of our wards into the well of our city. Back into that wet, narrow network underground.

Did he still have the map?

That was my exact thought when the unthinkable happened.

'Oh Jesus, no!'

As I'd twiddled about, feeling their shapes in my fingers, trying to differentiate between them in the blackness, the keys slipped from my hand. And, as I reached down to find them, feeling with my fingers on the gritty, damp floor, I felt those creatures push harder against the door. The weight of three or four of those mighty canines – that's all it would take.

It's all it did take.

And then they were in that room with us. I instantly felt their teeth on me and hoped in my terrified heart that I'd be enough of a distraction to allow Augustus and the others – including my beloved Billy – to get away unscathed.

As one of them held down my shoulders with his huge, heavy paws and bared his yellow teeth, snarling, I cried out a final instruction to my elderly friend.

'Close the hatch, Gus! Close the bloody hatch!'

The jaw above me cracked open, hissing hot, meaty breath into my face, its saliva dripping down in strings. I turned my head away, unable to look a moment longer into its cold, angry eyes. Wondering why God had intended this end for me – realising that this was the first thought I'd given Him since my nightmare began. After all those years of instinctively turning to my faith, I'd abandoned it without a thought. Without a single look back. Was this my punishment?

I closed my eyes, squeezing them shut, tears cutting through the creased lids. And that's when I felt it – the searing pain in my neck, as it plunged its teeth into my flesh, biting into my lifeline.

And then everything went dark.

16. Augustus

I had no choice – no choice at all. I had to follow her dying words, but I knew the boy would never, ever forgive me.

'Close the hatch, Gus! Close the bloody hatch!'

None would've survived, if I hadn't. It would all have been for nothing. But a young boy, who knows his mother has been left behind to suffer a horrific end, doesn't see it like that.

'No! No, Augustus! NO!!!'

His blood-curdling cry of grief will haunt me forever.

The children were at the bottom of the ladder when – with the heaviest heart – I hauled the hefty hatch back and twisted its rusty wheel lock. But a distraught Billy was instantly back on its rungs – screaming and gripping his way up simultaneously.

'NO! NO! NO! Mother! Mother! MOTHER!'

'Billy, we can't! I'm sorry, boy! But there's no saving her! I'm sorry! I can only save you and the others! I'm sorry, son!'

He'd reached me on the ladder and was trying to overtake me, to get himself back to the top. And I had to be cruel to be kind. I had to do everything to keep him safe – I owed Esther that and so much more.

'Billy! You must do as I tell you! You must go back down!' I continued to shout, knowing he needed a soothing voice – a warm hug and a shoulder to use as a pillow to soak up his grief. But the boy was going to kill us all, if I didn't get him under control. And, unless I got him off that ladder – back down to the ground – that was exactly what was going to happen.

'What are you doing?'

As the final word left his mouth, Billy was on his way back down – falling from the ladder after a firm shove from me. And luckily he landed okay – his pride bruised worse than his flesh, but he was bitter towards me. Unlike his grip on the ladder, his grip on his anger was unyielding.

'I'm sorry, Billy,' I called after him, knowing he had to hear my words, had to know how sorry I was, even if he couldn't, wouldn't accept it.

There was one small mercy we could be grateful for – the thick concrete of the floor above us and the dense metal of the circular hatch meant we were saved from Esther's cries. But, I kept this observation to myself and listened while the boy continued to unleash his heartbreaking anguish upon me.

'I hate you!' Billy cried below, picking himself up. 'You made us come here! So you killed her! I hate you!'

And I wasn't going to argue with the merciless grief of a young boy – he'd know soon enough what the truth was. Who was really the source of his unquantifiable sorrow. He was entitled to it – to his hate, as well. And there was some truth in it, after all. I couldn't deny it.

All I could do was keeping us moving.

Somehow, we all managed that – Marcie, Billy, Otterley and I – we picked ourselves up and moved along the tunnel. Not going back the way we had come, but moving further along. I still had the torch with me, but had been saving its battery. As we were covering unchartered territory again, I used its fading beam to help us find our feet – praying it wasn't long until we found another way out. A place of real safety this time.

But luck didn't go our way at first.

We'd been travelling less than fifteen minutes when the weak light began to flicker and after a bright, sudden burst, accompanied by a *puck* sound, our light was lost for good.

'Is everyone okay?' I asked.

'Yes,' Marcie answered, straightaway.

'I'm okay,' Otterley answered too and I was amazed by her determination and her silent strength. The poor creature had been wrenched from machines and followed us without protest. I was still perplexed by her static physical state – but it wasn't the time or place to question that. But already she seemed stronger, more alert, and this made me question further exactly what all that machinery had been doing to her.

'Billy? Are you okay?' I asked the boy separately, feeling that they were the wrong words for a boy who'd just lost his mother. I feared a retaliation; instead, I got a question.

'What's your plan now then, Augustus?'

His tone was still cold, showing me no love, but at least he was speaking.

'We keep going, Billy. Keep moving, feeling carefully in the dark, until we find another way out. There has to be a way. The man who designed all this – Mr Cadley – that was his idea. An underground labyrinth to use in times of trouble, to lead us all to safety.'

Yet, I didn't believe all that. Not anymore. And as we felt our way along the wet, ancient walls, I wondered just how much of this had actually been Cadley's creation – and how much was already here. Already created for a different purpose in the past, waiting to be rediscovered. I allowed this thought to occupy my mind – keeping out my own grief, helping me stay focused on practical things – as my feet gingerly edged forward.

'Careful as you go. Feel the walls. And just small steps,' I called out every so often, to let them know I was still there, giving them a fraction of the guidance they needed.

We really were utterly in the dark – there wasn't even a shadow of grey in the pitch blackness. And it seemed like hours went by as we crawled along, inch by inch, our eyes dazzled by the oblivion ahead of us.

Then it came.

Like we'd turned a corner – suddenly, there was a small pin of light in the distance.

Its circle grew wider – slowly at first. But the closer we got, the faster we moved – our hunger for its brightness rabid. Billy more so than the rest of us, and he ran ahead of me, running into it before I could stop him. Running without fear or thought – almost a boy again.

And so, he reached it first. Was the first to discover where the light was coming from – where the light would lead us. And when we all joined him, I had all my questions about Cadley's involvement in this underground structure answered for good. Cadley hadn't created this – there was no way. It must have been hidden away, long-forgotten and he'd simply uncovered it, drawn it into his elaborate plans.

'Well I never!' I found myself exclaiming, momentarily caught up in the marvel of what we had found – a break from our grief and our blindness. 'You know what this is?'

Billy shook his head. 'I'm not sure. What is it?'

'It's a station, Billy,' I said, looking at the concrete platform I was stood on, looking over the edge at the track below us. Small circular lights were embedded into the ceiling above us – dull, but bright enough to reveal all the detail. I noted that the walls around us were tiled. 'An underground railway station, Billy. Long abandoned – but.' I nodded at the lights.

'There's power?'

I nodded at him. 'And not just that…'

But the boy was ahead of me again – his hope, his imagination battling successfully against his grief, giving him strength and reason to look ahead. 'There might be trains, too?' he finished, just a hint of his old self coming through.

The image of the train graveyard we'd visited only days ago flashed in mind – when we'd been looking for a place to hide Ronan's remains. Every bright thought was always tinged with a dark one, it seemed.

'There's only one way to find out, Billy' I answered.

With that, we carefully stepped down off the platform – helping Otterley as she struggled a little. And walking in the centre of two sets of railway tracks, we made our way along the disused line…

Asleep

I see him come towards me.

I'm not sure where I am, but he is coming towards me in the river road. Rowing a small boat all by himself.

Even though he has his protective mask on, I recognise him instantly – he's from my class in school. It's Billy Morton.

'Hey, Billy!' I cry out, trying to attract him. 'Hey, Billy!'

But he's distracted by something – something in the water that he's floating towards.

'What is it, Billy?' I ask, but it's like he can't hear or see me.

Like I'm not really there, invisible.

But whatever it is, Billy is frightened!

He rips off his mask and starts screaming! And then all hell breaks loose in the street...

Awake

17. Tilly

I don't know how they created the illusion – I still don't. But I do know it was utterly convincing when it happened. And even though I knew that none of it could be true, there was no shaking the effect it had. No shaking off, even today, the slow cruelty that dawned. The gradual, psychological torture that, inch by inch, crept under my skin and tunneled its way inside my mind…

I reached out for the first door, pulled it open and entered the room behind it. And I was suddenly home, in Uncle Monty's huge mansion. In the hallway upstairs. And there was something ahead of me – a flicker, an image, a person, I think, but I couldn't see. It was all just a little out of reach. But I knew it was important that I caught it up – I had to see it and feel it! So I followed it, running to keep up.

But suddenly there was another door in front of me. In the middle of the hallway. It wasn't normally there, but I didn't question – just reached for it, opened it and dashed through its entrance.

Then I was in the same stretch of hallway again, like a physical echo and what I sought was still just out of reach, just out of sight. I felt my chest tighten with panic.

'I'm here, I'm here,' a voice called out – blurred and faded, a muffled sound I could hear, but also doubted at the same time. 'I'm here, I'm here.'

I was running now, and the hallway turned a corner. Another difference from what I knew – the upper hallway at Uncle Monty's mansion was long and straight, with rooms going off to the left and right. There wasn't a curve there at all – but there was now. So, I must've remembered it incorrectly. I *must* have. Turning the corner, I caught a glimpse – I was certain – of whatever I was chasing.

'Stop, stop!' I cried out, but whoever I was following – a ghost, a shadow – was gone, almost as soon as I thought I'd seen them.

Fear and doubt crawled over my skin. Was I seeing things? And why was this so important? Why did I feel so tense? Why was panic squeezing so tightly at my heart?

I came to another door and went through it without thinking – but beyond it everything was just the same. The long hallway at Uncle Monty's, the curve halfway down that I was certain hadn't been there before, the shadow I couldn't quite see, the doubt that was clutching at my chest – squashing at my lungs now, affecting my breathing.

Then it changed – there was a new door. A hidden door – disguised as a panel in the wall at the end of the hallway. When I went through this, I found a spiral staircase that curled upwards.

More doubt crept in – I'd never seen this at Uncle Monty's before. There was a second floor to his mansion, but it was sealed off, he told me – the whole floor damaged by a storm when the floods came. Yet, here was a secret door and a twisting staircase that led up to it.

Only, it didn't quite.

I could see a light at the top, and I increased my speed, eager to get to the end – to see what was at the very top. But it didn't get me any closer. I picked up my pace, almost tripping over my own feet in my eagerness to reach the light, feeling a warm film of sweat on my skin, my lungs almost wheezing with effort – but it made no difference. No difference at all.

And then the worst things happened.

Two things at once – a realization and an impossibility.

I realised what I was chasing – *who* I was chasing. Her. The woman who'd always been just out of my reach, the woman I had no memory of. And suddenly I felt so very desperate to see her, to get to the top and reach that inaccessible light. So, I called out to her, hoping it would make a difference – hoping that she'd finally stop being a mere shadow.

'Mother! Mother!' I cried, my voice thin and broken, exhausted from all the effort of chasing. 'Mother!'

And that's when the impossible happened. I can't really explain it, even now. It didn't make sense then, and no matter how many times I go over it in my head, it still doesn't make sense. But as I cried out – *Mother! Mother!* – and continued to step upwards, picking up speed with every footstep, I began to descend. Further and further down, like the steps ahead were multiplying and forcing me downwards. And the harder I tried, the faster my feet worked, stumbling up those corkscrew stairs, the faster I descended – the light above me getting smaller and smaller. All the time I cried out for her – for that invisible one, for that doubt – as the light above me inexplicably shrank away. Then I let out one almighty scream – emptying my voice of all noise, squeezing the last of the air out from my gasping lungs – and the tiny speck of light above me went out.

I don't remember a lot of what happened next or exactly how I got back to my prison cell. There are snapshots in my head – like photographs, capturing parts of it. I was plunged into sudden darkness and recall a sense of collapse, as everything I'd seen and felt simply vanished, dissolving mentally and physically all around me. I can see flashes of the preserved laboratory. And I was on those stairs again – the stone stairs – being taken back down below ground, below the dormitory and back into that claustrophobic maze of cells. I remember falling onto the bed in my cell and the woman's voice.

'Tell them your name,' she'd said, almost pleading. 'Tell them who you are, or they'll take you back. And it'll be worse next time. It always is.'

They – she'd said *they,* like it was nothing to do with her.

'Just tell them who you are,' was the last thing I heard before the metal door to my cell was slammed shut and locked.

I'm not sure how long I slept for. Or, before that, how long I was kept in that strange room of illusion, with all those doors. Either could've been days. But I was so exhausted and my traumatized body and mind fell desperately into sleep, quickly drowning in its welcoming, warm sea.

When I eventually woke up, I was still caught up in my dreams and I felt hazy, uncertain. I began to wonder what had really happened in that strange room. What had I really been following? And who was that phantom, just out of my reach – could she really have been my mother?

It couldn't have been true, though – I knew who my mother was, after all. I'd seen photographs of her with Uncle Monty. I had a whole album of her pictures, back at my uncle's mansion. And he'd talked to me about her for hours – reluctantly at first, but eventually he'd been generous with his information. Given me her whole story.

But doubts were worming their way through my thoughts, munching their way into my brain like maggots in an apple. And I began to wonder if this was the true effect of the torture I'd suffered in that strange, empty room – the doubting of everything, an endless sense of uncertainty.

The Chamber of Doors, he'd called it – like it would mean something. The Chamber of Doors – a room of illusion that had broken me, left me weak and wondering, and I couldn't even tell you why or how.

But the longer I was left alone in that cell, the weaker I felt. I flushed hot and cold, although when I touched myself I was neither feverish nor freezing.

It's all in your head, I told myself, but it made no difference – the feeling of panic and paranoia continued.

I felt thirsty and hungry – but I didn't need food or water.

And I kept recalling all my dreams – the people drowning in mud, Billy screaming as he tore his mask off – and they added to my confusion. There was another dream that particularly haunted me – one where I tried to take a mask off my own face, only I couldn't, because it had become part of my face. And the more I struggled to remove it, the sicker I felt. The mere thought of this nightmare left suffocating with nausea – and before I knew it, I was struggling to breathe.

It's only one of your dreams, I reminded myself, trying to focus, trying to calm down. *Only a dream.*

But like with the hot and the cold, the hunger and the thirst, the panic and paranoia, everything seemed out of my control.

I put my face down into the pillow on my bed and tried breathing in and out through the cotton and foam. This helped me settle a little and eventually my lung and brain function fell back to a steady pace.

I'm not sure how long it was before I heard the door unlock and someone come in. I kept my face pushed into the pillow, enjoying the childish comfort I'd found in it. I knew what they'd come for – the question they couldn't help but keep repeating. And it was only seconds before someone was whispering in my ear.

'Who are you?'

They could ask me all they liked, but I wasn't answering. I'd come this far and I was determined it wasn't going to be for nothing. No matter what they did to me, although I hoped they wouldn't put me back in that room of illusions…

We're not the enemy, the woman had claimed. *We're not the bad guys, you must believe me.* But I wasn't so sure any more. It was all too confusing. Maybe Peter had been right – the woman had lied to me, just to win me over. I just didn't know.

'Hey, what's your name?' a voice asked again and I felt irritation rise in me.

Why was my name so important? What was wrong with the one I'd given them? And what would the consequences be if I gave them my real one?

'Hey, we need to get moving. Need to get you out of here,' the voice continued and something made me pay attention – a change in the tone, the instruction out-of-place. I pulled my face from the pillow and turned to a face I recognised – but not one I expected to see there.

Surprised, I went to say her name, but she spoke first.

'I know you,' she said, equally amazed to see a familiar face. 'You're safe now, okay?'

She wasn't much older than me, but there she was being the grown up, coming across as caring and in control.

'We do need to get moving, though. I can get you out of here,' she said, reading my face, trying to assess my state of mind, 'but I don't know how much time we've got. Do you understand?'

I shook my head. No – I didn't understand. Not really. Everything was so confusing; my mind so muddled. The woman had told me I was safe – that we'd all been rescued from imminent disaster. That bringing us here was necessary – at its heart, it was an act of kindness. And yet, out-of-the-blue, here *she* was – the girl in my dreams, the missing girl – and suddenly I was questioning everything all over again.

What had she said in my dreams?

'My name is Elinor and I'm here to rescue you.'

So, I felt two things in my gut, two things almost for certain – it definitely wasn't safe to stay where I was, and my dreams really were coming true.

'Are you coming with me or what?' she asked, staring at me, impatience creeping in, while I was still weighing everything up.

While I was thinking about the dark, scary future that had appeared to me in my sleep.

'Look, we need to get moving. There's no one here at the moment, but they might be on their way back to get you.'

These words were enough focus me.

'What do you mean – on their way back to get me?'

'They've gone,' she answered, her brow creased, as she read the alarm in my eyes. 'Whoever brought you here – they've left. Gone some time, I'd guess.'

'And the others?' I asked, swallowing a lump of dread that had formed in my throat. 'Peter and…' But my voice faded-out.

Elinor shook her head.

In my mind I heard helicopter blades, slicing through the air, whipping it up into a frenzy – the noise that had ended my dream.

'There's no one else here, just you,' she said, holding out a hand. 'And we really need to go. Okay?'

I took a minute to take it all in. Everyone else had gone. I thought of the helicopters. I thought of words the woman had said: *they think you're one of them.* And so they'd left me behind.

'Okay,' I eventually answered, forcing a little strength, managing to control all my fears and uncertainties, 'you had better lead the way….'

18. Jessie

It took us days to reach the wall that Nathaniel had spoken of. We used his speedboat, which carried more fuel and had a faster engine than mine, but still it took days. And it was hidden – behind forests, behind so much I'd never seen before.

As we sailed towards it, Tristan was full of questions for Nathaniel – and Nathaniel continued to give answers where he could.

'So, what did they do – to create this so-called generation of twins? And why?'

'Why? Because they could, Tristan. And because some people still like to think these twisted things constitute progress,' Nathaniel answered, his words blurred a little by the speed at which we moved.

He'd allowed me to take control of the boat – part of an agreement we made before either of us would join him.

'It started with a wonder fertility drug that all mothers took. Free and perfectly safe, so of course every one took it – like it was vitamins. Like it was simply another type of folic acid. Then regular visits to clinics were encouraged for everyone, and what expectant mothers saw as excellent care, was in fact something far more sinister. Sometimes it was a simple injection, a pill on the tongue – other times it was more intrusive. People were put under anesthetic – all in the name of the unborn child – and physical intervention and changes were made. Once twins were confirmed, the doctors – surgeons, scientists, whatever term you think is right for these monsters – once they knew a mother was carrying twins, that's when the manipulation really started. Usually, one embryo was left untouched – and the other altered in some way. But they did some terrible things to some of them, as

I'm sure you've come to expert. Some were made stronger, or given more violent tendencies. Some had their gender altered, but there were worse things. Crazier experiments. The worst…'

Nathaniel stumbled and lost his words – in his face, I read a memory he was returning too. One so painful that he couldn't articulate it into a story. We both let this go – maybe we didn't need to know every detail. And his face told us more than enough.

Yet, there were still cracks in his story. So Tristan continued to push him for details about our generation, about the interventions made, his intense, meticulous questioning showing that he remained unconvinced. But it was a set of questions from Nathaniel himself that ended up casting the biggest doubts.

'And what about your twin, Tristan?' he asked, as we sped along – ahead of us a blurred horizon that suggested land.

'Sorry?'

'What do you know of your twin, Tristan?'

'I don't have a twin.'

'Everyone of your generation had a twin.'

'I'm an only child, Nathaniel, so you're wrong.'

But Nathaniel had shaken his head at this, not swayed by Tristan's cold, defensive tone.

'Everyone. For a whole generation. Part of the experiment. They intervened with every single birth. And so every pregnancy was twins. Altering one, and usually leaving the other to develop naturally, creating a control group that perfectly mirrored the group they'd interfered on.'

'But we don't all have twins, Nathaniel,' Tristan reasserted, an irritation rising in his voice. 'I'd know. As I've said, I was an only child. It was just me and Albert, my father.'

'You just don't all *know* about your twins,' Nathaniel corrected, with what almost sounded like arrogance. I feared Tristan wouldn't let this go. 'That's all. But in this region, for your generation, there wasn't a single pregnancy that wasn't altered, I promise you. I've seen the records. So, you'll have a twin, Tristan – it's just a case of finding out your history. Maybe your sibling didn't make it. Maybe that's why you don't know.'

Tristan simply shook his head in response, not believing this for a second, I knew. And an uncomfortable silence fell between them for a period.

The deeper we travelled into unknown territory, towards this wall Nathaniel spoke of, the more I began to fear that we were veering away from our original intentions. Nathaniel's encyclopedic knowledge of the authorities' dark history was distracting Tristan and me from the key purpose of our trip. And the closer we got to the end – cutting past all the forests, coming to open water that resembled the shots we'd seen in the film he'd left us – the less he seemed concerned with the mission he'd joined.

'You know, Nathaniel – we came in search of people. And answers to questions we already had,' I said to him, in response to another promise that we were *nearly there*.

'I know. I understand, but sticking with me will help you find them. And when we get to the wall, beyond the wall, you'll see the truth – and all your questions will be answered.'

'So you keep saying, but how do we know that? I believe what you've told us – and I can almost say I trust you.' Tristan threw me a look to say he wouldn't take it that far.

'But I'm looking for my brother and my parents, who have more questions to answer than I ever imagined. And there's young Elinor, too – the girl I told you about. We want to know the truth, but the truth about the people we've lost is what's most important to us. That's our priority.'

'Your parents?'

'Yes. The scientists I told you about.' I wondered for a moment if he'd been listening to the information we'd been sharing with him.

'And my father, too,' Tristan added in, and I sensed he too was beginning to question the direction of travel.

'Your father?' There was a curious tone in Nathaniel's voice.

'Yes.'

'Okay. I see. I-.'

Our companion paused, the rest of his words catching on something – a sense of caution.

'What is it, Nathaniel?' Tristan asked, impatience and a small amount of fear in his voice.

'I thought that you'd already found him.'

And then suddenly it was there on our horizon – the shore I'd seen in the video. The same one, it seemed, where my parents had stood proud, a beast at their feet.

'What do you mean?'

I could see what Nathaniel had promised we'd find – in the distance, but within reach. Water and forest in front of it, but soaring in the background. A hundred feet high, maybe more.

'Nathaniel, what do you mean?'

The wall.

We'd reached the wall.

End of Part I

The story continues – Part II available to pre-order here:

http://www.amazon.co.uk/gp/product/B017HZ6IYC

Made in United States
North Haven, CT
03 April 2022